DETROIT PUBLIC LIBRARY

3 5674 00647584 3

DETROIT PUBLIC LIBRARY

BROWSING LIBRARY
5201 Woodward
Detroit, MI 48202

DATE DUE

D1282907

NO MORE GAS

NO MORE GAS

CHARLES NORDHOFF AND
JAMES NORMAN HALL

The Literary Guild of America, Inc.

NEW YORK

NO MORE GAS appeared in the *Saturday Evening Post*
under the title of OUT OF GAS

COPYRIGHT 1939, 1940, BY CHARLES NORDHOFF AND
JAMES NORMAN HALL

ALL RIGHTS RESERVED, INCLUDING THE RIGHT
TO REPRODUCE THIS BOOK OR PORTIONS
THEREOF IN ANY FORM

CL

PRINTED IN THE UNITED STATES OF AMERICA

DETROIT PUBLIC LIBRARY

NO MORE GAS

CHAPTER I

On a cloudy October night, a motorcar with one passenger in the rear seat was proceeding along the road which skirts the coastal lands on the western side of the island of Tahiti. It was well past midnight and the only light on the narrow winding road was that made by the lamps of the car, illuminating with a magical effect the stems of the coconut palms on either side, the tunnels of foliage passed through from time to time, and the scattered houses that emerged from the gloom ahead and vanished into the yet deeper blackness behind. It was evident that the driver knew the road well, every hole and bump and corrugation, but in attempts to avoid the worst, he struck others which seemed fully as bad to his passenger, who was flung from side to side and sometimes bounced high out of his seat. After one particularly atrocious jolt he leaned forward to speak to the driver.

"Have a heart, Manu! *Haeré maru!*"

The man turned his head slightly.

"Kind of rough going along this bit," he called back, cheerily. "The road ain't no better'n when you left, Chester. All they do is chuck a bit of sand in the holes once in a while."

"You du-du-don't need to tell me," his passenger replied. "Take it easy."

"Thought you was in a hurry to get home?"

"I am, but you forget what I got back here."

The driver immediately slowed down. "I wasn't thinking," he said, blankly. "He ain't hurt, is he?"

"Hope not; bu-bu-but another jolt like that last one . . . Stop a minute. I want to have a look."

The car was brought to a halt and the driver got out to join his fare, who had turned a small wooden box on the seat beside him. "Got a *mori pata?*" he asked. Manu nodded, and, lifting the cushion of the front seat, drew out a flash lamp which he handed to the other. Chester switched on the light and the two young men gazed anxiously into the box, enclosed on one side with wooden slats. A cock of brilliant plumage was crouched in a corner of the box. Chester gave a quiet "tuk-tuk-tuk," and the bird sprang to its feet, regarding its owner fiercely, turning its head from side to side. Its reddish eyes gleamed like gems in the lamplight.

Chester gave a sigh of relief, and turned the box gently once more to protect the cock from the draft.

"He's all right," he said. "I was scared for a minute."

"I never saw such a cock," Manu said, in an awe-struck voice. "They ain't nothing on the island can touch him, Chester."

"Wait till you see him in action," the other replied, proudly. "But listen, Manu! If ever you say a word about him . . . !"

"What do you think I am?" the driver said, indignantly. "Don't I come from Vaipopo myself?"

"I just wanted to make sure. You can bet your last franc on him, and all you can borrow besides. But it'd be all off if the Taios found out. What they got now?"

"I've heard they got a fine cock from Raiatea, but they ain't fought him yet, and nobody's seen him."

"They bragging about him?"

"Bragging!"

"Good. Let 'em. We'll clean 'em out if we can keep it dark."

"Don't worry," said Manu. "They'll never hear from me." He took the wheel again. "*Ça y est?*"

"Yes, but go slow the rest of the way."

The driver was now more than careful and they proceeded at not more than fifteen miles an hour. Chester looked out on either side, peering into the darkness more and more eagerly. They had passed through the villages of Faaa and Tarahoi. He'd soon be home now. After a stretch of uninhabited road the first houses of Vaipopo village began to appear and presently the driver slowed down to turn into a grass-grown driveway bordered with untrimmed hibiscus bushes. The moment the turn was made the lights of the car fell full upon a two-story brick house standing some sixty yards back from the road, throwing into pitiless relief, against the background of night, wide ruinous verandas, upstairs and down, a roof of tiles green with age, patched and mended in many places with bits of corrugated iron — every wound and scar which time and hard usage had left upon the ancient dwelling. Manu drew up before the entrance, at a distance of a dozen yards or so, and sounded a shattering blast on his horn. Then he turned in his seat.

"Same old place, Chester. How's it look to you?"

Chester's lips began to move rapidly, but for a moment no sound would come. Then he managed to say: "I bu-bu-bu-been all over the world, but I ain't seen no p-p-p-place that looks so good as this."

The driver sounded his horn again, blast after raucous blast, and presently heads began to appear at open doors and windows, and a murmur of excited voices increased in volume. A moment later a huge man, his thick grey hair standing awry, bare-chested and barelegged, wearing a waistcloth hanging at an angle, came out on the upstairs veranda. He laid his hands gingerly upon the insecure balustrade, his eyes blinking in the strong light.

"*O vai tera?*" he called, sharply.

Manu now stood at the side of the car, but his passenger was still concealed inside.

"Come down and see, Jonas," the driver called back. "You got a visitor. Get the house up."

Dim lights now began to appear, and presently Chester saw his father treading gently as he descended the wide rickety stairway with a kitchen lamp in his hand. This he set on the floor by the entryway and came toward the car. Chester now got out, and next moment Jonas gave a whoop of joy. "Mama!" he shouted. "Nat! Fana! It's Chester!" The returned wanderer was unable to stammer even his father's name as Jonas folded him in a huge embrace. The house was in an immediate uproar. By the time Chester reached the veranda he was met by a seemingly endless stream of brothers, cousins, nephews, nieces, in-laws and out-of-laws, and relatives of yet vaguer connection who poured from the inner recesses of the Tuttle mansion and gathered around him in an ever-widening throng. But of all the meetings, after so long an absence from home, the one affecting him most deeply was that with Mama Ruau, his grandmother. The gentle old lady loved grandchildren and great-grandchildren impartially, but the return of the wanderer, completing the family circle once more, was an event she had long dreamed of and prayed for. After weeping softly for a little, held closely in his arms, she drew back and looked up at him.

"Three years, Chester," she said. "We thought you were never coming home. I don't believe I'd have known you if I'd met you in Papeete."

Chester laughed as he patted her small brown hand. "And what would you be doing in Papeete, Grandma? How would the family get on if you were away from home even for one day?"

"Are you glad to be here?"

"Glad! Grandma, I wu-wu-wu- . . . I been p-p-p- . . . Grandma, if you nu-nu-nu-nu . . ."

She smiled as she laid her fingers over his lips. "There; you needn't try to speak," she said. "I know without your telling me."

Nat Tuttle grinned broadly as he gave his brother a thumping whack between the shoulders. "That used to cure you, Chester," he said. "But I don't know as I'd ever want to see you cured, for good."

"That's what I say," Jonas added. "We've missed that stutter more'n I could tell you, Chester."

"I ain't so bad as I used to be," Chester replied, when he'd found his voice again. "There's plenty of days I don't stutter none at all. But gu-gu-gu-gosh! Coming home again . . . it's mu-mu-mu-made it come back worse than ever."

It was then past one o'clock, but none of the elder Tuttles thought of going to bed again. Numerous small children, after the first excitement was over, fell asleep wherever they chanced to be and were left as they lay, except for some of the tiny ones who were carried into corners and deposited upon mats. Paki, Jonas's brother-in-law, came up from his house on the beach, with his wife, Effie. After a brief stay, Paki stole away again unnoticed, but nobody missed him. He was a Tuttle only by sufferance.

"What's to do first, Jonas?" his cousin, Ropati, asked.

"What I want to know is how Chester got home?" his Aunt Effie said. "There's no steamer in, is there?"

"Now wait, Effie," Jonas replied. "Chester can tell us all that later. Let me get things started, first. Some of you's got to get a pig dressed and hung right away, ready for tomorrow. André, you and Mara better go. Take the big one that's tied under the *mapé* tree in the little gulley off to the right. He'll feed the lot of us. It's too bad, Chester," he added, turning to his son. "The boys didn't have no luck at sea today. There ain't a fish in the house. But we made a good haul the day before."

"Don't talk about fish," Chester replied. "That's all I been eating. Baked pork out of the old *himaa* is what I hanker for. And shrimps, if you got any. Jonas, I ain't tasted a good fresh-water shrimp in all the years I been gone."

"We can give you plenty of them," his father replied. "Pico, take a lantern and go up the river. And don't come back till you got a five-gallon tin full."

"We ain't going to wait till morning before we eat?" Fana asked. "And Chester just come?"

Jonas scratched his head. "I don't see what else we can do. There's nothing on hand to speak of, is there, Tupa?"

The old man shook his head. He was the family cook, and his daughter, Maitu, a woman of thirty, was the willing family slave, who built fires, washed dishes, helped her father, and cared for the small Tuttles when not busy with other tasks.

"I got half a bunch of bananas in the cook shed," Tupa replied. "And a few baked yams. That's all."

Nat gave a snort. "I could eat the lot myself," he said, "and still be hungry. We got to send to town, Jonas."

"At this time of night?"

"I brought a three-gallon demijohn of red wine," Chester put in. "It's out in the car. Maybe we could get along without the food till morning."

"*Eita roa'tu!*" Fana exclaimed. "We got to have a snack tonight to keep us going. And two more demijohns."

"Ru, take the truck and go along in," said Nat.

Ru, a lad of sixteen, was the youngest of Jonas's sons. "Sure I'll go," he replied. "What'll I run her on — river water?"

Nat gave him a blank stare. "That's right," he said. "There ain't no more gas."

"You sure, Ru?" Fana asked.

"You ought to know," Nat said; "using up what little

we had left going all the way to Taravao! And what for?
To see a movie!"

"What of it?" said Fana. "Tamara wanted to, and we
had a good time." He turned to the chauffeur who had
brought Chester home. "Manu, would you mind going
in? Wake up that Chinaman at the east end of the market. He'll get out of bed any time to make a sale."

"*Parau mau!*" the driver replied, heartily. "I'll wake
him; don't worry. What all do you want?"

"We'd better have three more demijohns," Nat suggested. "The whole district will be here tomorrow when
they know Chester's home."

"You're right," said Fana. "And listen, Manu. Get
three dozen pound tins of bully beef, and two gallons
of mustard pickles, and a ten-pound cheese, and two
dozen loaves of bread. And if you can't get the bread,
make it a tin of ship's biscuits, the big kind. And don't
forget plenty of butter. Then . . ."

"Hold on, Fana," his father interrupted. "Who's going to pay for all this?"

"Us, who else?" Fana replied. "We got four hundred
and sixty francs for that last haul of fish."

His father shook his head. "We need part of that for
gas, and I ought to pay the rest to Dr. Blondin."

"Why? I thought you paid him something two weeks
ago," Nat said.

"You know as well as I do, Nat. I had to borrow it
back, and some more besides."

There was silence for a moment. "Jonas is right,
boys," their grandmother said. "We must pay our debt
to Dr. Blondin even if we have to live on clams to
do it."

"Mama!" Effie exclaimed. "And Chester just home? It wouldn't be right! Dr. Blondin would say so himself."

The argument that followed was far from being the first of the kind in the Tuttle household. Mama Ruau found herself a party of one, feebly supported by Jonas, whose resistance melted away by degrees as he listened to the unanswerable arguments of the rest of the family. Chester, who felt himself a little of a stranger after so long an absence, maintained a polite silence, but the other sons well knew whose side he was on. Ropati, their father's cousin, a man of fifty, sat forward in his wheelchair, arguing strongly on the side of the boys.

"It wouldn't be right, Grandma, like Effie says," he urged. "And you don't need to worry at all. The boys can go fishing tomorrow. They're sure to make a big catch and they can take it right on in to market."

Mama Ruau shook her head. "It's tomorrow now," she replied.

"But there's plenty of time," said Nat. "If the bonito's running good it won't take us half an hour to fill the launch."

The old woman sighed. "Well, have it so," she said. "I want Chester welcomed as much as any of you, but we ought to wait till we can do it as we should, on our own money."

This reluctant consent was taken as though offered with the greatest good will. Jonas alone felt uneasy, but with his sanguine nature he readily persuaded himself that the boys were right: they would have fish enough for the Sunday-morning market to pay Dr. Blondin, his ancient and obliging creditor, half the sum he owed him and perhaps more. But when, after a hasty calculation, they had determined the amount needed for food and wine, they found they were sixty francs short. It occurred to no one to suggest cutting down the list of supplies, and they knew how the Tuttle credit stood with the Chinese storekeepers of Papeete.

"You ain't got a bit of change, Chester?" Fana asked, hopefully.

His brother searched his pockets and brought forth a franc and two twenty-five-centime pieces. Small as the amount was, Fana took it.

"That's the lot," Chester said.

"And you been gone three years," Nat replied, with a grin. "You must have worked hard to earn all that."

Chester thumbed his nose at his brother. "I couldn't even pay Manu for bringing me out from town," he added.

"That's all right," the driver replied. "You don't come home every day. Give me what you got, Jonas. I'll make up the balance myself."

"We don't like to ask you, Manu," Jonas replied, apologetically. "But if you'll call it a loan . . ."

"Many's the good feed and good time I've had here that ain't cost me a franc," the driver broke in. "Ought to pay my share for once. What about the things in the car, Chester? Shall I fetch 'em?"

Chester nodded, a smile of anticipation on his face. The driver returned with the demijohn of wine in one hand and a large box, well wrapped in oilcloth, under his arm. He next brought the crate containing the cock, which he set gently down at Chester's feet. Then, with a nod, he started for the door. "I'll be back in an hour, easy," he said. "There's nobody on the road this time of night." A moment later he whirled out of the driveway on his way to town.

The family were now gathered in the living room, a great bare apartment furnished with some homemade benches, a chair or two, and a table for the lamp fashioned of packing cases. Chester stood before the crate smiling mysteriously.

"I bu-bu-bu-brought a present for the whole family," he said. "Now wait, Fana! Get back a little. I'll bring him out." He looked cautiously around the room. "All the kids asleep?" They were. The children lying in the corners and along the walls were again deep in the land of dreams. Chester then stooped to open a little door in the crate. He called softly: "*Té, té, té!*" and the magnificent gamecock stepped out, shaking his ruffled feathers into place. Chester caressed his head.

"Ain't he a beauty? Look how well he knows me."

Fana's mouth dropped open as he stared at the bird. Nat and Ru were speechless, and their father gave a sigh that seemed to rise from the soles of his large bare feet. No dream of a fighting cock could have equaled this reality. He was handsomer, fiercer, more formidable in appearance than the most legendary of Tahiti's cocks.

"Where'd you get him, Chester?" Fana exclaimed.

"Frisco," his brother replied. "They got cocks there that make ours look like pigeons. They're born fighters; they don't do nothing else. Want to see him work? He's

wide awake; a couple of passes won't hurt him. Fetch
me that umbrella."

An umbrella without a handle stood in a corner.
Chester opened it with difficulty, then moved until he
was behind the bird and gave a shrill crow of defiance,
so lifelike that the cock spun about to face him, head
lowered and hackles raised. The umbrella was thrust
at him; he sprang at it twice before Chester could
draw it clear, his spurs leaving long gashes in the fab-
ric. Chester then took him up in his arms and calmed
him by stroking his head. He had hoped to make an
impression on the family and was well rewarded. Nat
was the first to break silence.

"Chester *tané!*" he exclaimed.

Their father's broad face wore an expression of such
beatitude that it seemed to radiate a faint light.

"You couldn't have done better," he said. "We got
a match with Emily Taio next month. Her boys got a
cock I heard was from Raiatea. They'll bet everything
they got on him. Our best bird's just as good, but we
all been worried about that match. We couldn't be
dead sure of taking Emily's money with him. But
now . . ." He gave another deep sigh of happiness, as
though every franc the Taio family might be able to
place on their bird were already in his pocket.

"You know what they call this breed?" Chester
asked, as he carefully placed the cock in the crate again.
" 'Mortgage Lifter.' I don't know what you owe Doc
Blondin, Jonas. Whatever it is, this cock will pay it
for you."

The family now discussed with enthusiasm the com-

ing match with the Taio cock. Fana was an expert
trainer and Chester was the first to acknowledge that
the Mortgage Lifter should be placed in his competent
hands. The bird in its crate was removed to the shed
where the fish truck was kept, and at dawn, before any
of the children were awake, he was to be taken up the
valley, lest one of the youngsters should innocently
give away the secret. There was no need to counsel
any of the grown-ups against this danger.

"Now, boys," their grandmother said, presently, "I've
heard enough about fighting cocks. I want Chester to
tell us how he got home; and why he's been away for
three long years."

"It ain't my fault, Grandma. I been trying to get
back most of the time since I left."

Chester, who was twenty-five, was the second of
Jonas's sons. There had been handed on to him something of his New England great-grandfather's love of
wandering; the other boys were content to remain at
home and had never gone farther from Tahiti than to
some of the adjacent islands. Chester had left Tahiti in
an American yacht that had called at the island to pay
off and send home by steamer an obstreperous and in-
competent crew. The owner then hired five Tahitian
boys to sail his vessel to San Francisco. Arriving there,
Chester had decided to see something more of the
world before returning home, and the family had heard
little from him since, although now and then picture
postcards had been received, with brief messages and
strange-looking stamps, and views of places of which
the Tuttles had never heard.

Now that he had come home, he passed over his wanderings with the briefest possible mention, nor were the family greatly interested in where he had been. A few polite questions were asked, to which he replied in the same perfunctory manner; then the subject was dropped. Like all Tahitians, the Tuttles had little curiosity about the outside world. They knew there were countries called France and England and Canada and the United States and Australia and New Zealand, and others yet more remote; but, with the exception of France, which the children learned about in school, these lands were vague conceptions: places where men were always engaged in war, or foolishly toiling day and night to pile up wealth; places where marine engines came from, and gasoline, flour, tinned beef, and a few other necessities the islands could not provide. Chester had seen these places, all the while longing and trying to find a vessel that would carry him home again. At last he had come. There was no need to say more.

"But what vessel brought you?" his father asked.

"That's something else again," Chester replied. "I didn't come on her all the way home. She was lost."

"Wrecked, you mean?" his Aunt Effie asked.

"We had to abandon her at sea," he replied. "It was three months ago. She was an old barque, the *Charlotte*, been t-t-t-tied up at Vancouver, I don't know how long. There was a company at Vancouver had an idea to patch her up, fill her with lumber and send her to Australia, and sell her, afterward, for whatever she'd bring. I'd worked my passage from Japan to Vancouver, and that's when I heard about her. Maybe I wasn't glad to get a chance to sign on! I knew I could get home from Australia. We stopped at Frisco to take on a lot of gasoline; then we s-s-s-sailed for Sydney."

"And then what?" Ropati asked, after a considerable silence.

"I ain't going to t-t-talk about that," said Chester. "We was well south of the Line when we got in a hurricane. I don't want no more! One was enough."

"But you can tell us what happened, Chester," Hio, Nat's wife, put in.

"We lost the first mate and the cook and one seaman," Chester continued. "When it was over we had the foremast left, and only part of that. We was about two hundred and fifty miles northwest of the Marquesas. The captain was bound to get there if he could. The sails were all gone, but we patched up some old canvas and tried hard for three weeks. But there was a lot of water in the hold and we couldn't make five miles in twenty-four hours. No wind. She might have sunk if it hadn't been for the lumber. But it wasn't so bad on that old tub. We had wonderful weather, after the storm — calm as anything. And any amount of food. Caught a lot of fish, too. *Aita é faufaa:* we couldn't get nowhere. So the captain said we'd take the one boat we had left and go to Nuku Hiva to get a tow. There was eight of us, and it was a f-f-fine big boat. She'd had her stern stove in but we fixed that. Couldn't take much with us, though. I had my sea chest full of presents for everybody, but I had to leave it."

"Chester! What a shame!" Hio exclaimed.

"I couldn't help it, Hio. I had a hard enough time

getting the captain to let me bring the cock. First he said no, but I t-t-told him I'd stay aboard if he wouldn't let me bring my bird. He was an old man, but we all liked him; and when he saw how much I wanted the cock he said all right. So I brought him and one other thing."

"Is that the other thing?" Effie asked, with a nod toward the large oilcloth-covered package.

"Yes."

"What's in it?"

"Nothing so much. I'll show you after a while. . . . We got to Nuku Hiva all right, but there wasn't no vessel there. We had to wait two months, then Donald's schooner came along from here. The captain chartered her right off to go looking for the *Charlotte*. There'd been some dirty weather since we got to the Marquesas and I don't think the captain expected to find her. Anyway, we didn't. We searched two weeks, and Knudson's schooner that c-c-come to Nuku Hiva when the *Tereora* did was out looking too. We didn't see a sign of her. I was glad, then, I hadn't stayed on her like I would have if the captain hadn't let me bring our cock. She must have broke up in the bad weather that came on after we left her."

As Chester finished his story, his grandmother took his hand and held it as though to convince herself that they had him safe.

"Guess you'll stay at home now," his Aunt Effie said. "Why you ever left in the first place is more than I know."

Of a sudden the room, dimly lighted by two small

lamps, was filled with the white radiance from Manu's car, which had just turned into the driveway. "Now then," said Effie. "You men can sit here and talk with Chester while we get supper ready."

The Tuttle cookhouse and dining room shared with the family dwelling the picturesque quality derived from an absence of straight lines and ninety-degree angles. It was in the shape of an L, the shorter line representing the kitchen proper. The table where the food was served was twenty feet long by four wide, supported on several pairs of legs of slightly varying lengths. The result was a series of gentle undulations like the imperceptible roll of the steppes. The roof that sheltered it had once been galvanized, but was now red with rust, and supported on time-defying iron-wood posts. Here the women soon completed the preparations for supper and the men were called in.

It could never be said that there was food and to spare at any meal of the Tuttle family, but on this occasion, with all of the children asleep and with half a dozen of the adults absent, preparing food for the real feast to come, those at table, eighteen in all, were well satisfied with what was set before them. One of the demijohns of wine was broached, and at Jonas's suggestion it was watered to make it last till daylight.

"There'll be everybody here, soon's they know Chester's back," he said. "We must keep the rest of the wine for them." When the remnants of food had been cleared away he leaned back in his chair, glancing benevolently down the long table.

"Now, boys, what about a little music?" he asked.
"Maitu, bring my concertina."

No urging was needed; the Tuttles lived for such
hours as this. There was scarcely a member of the clan
who did not play some instrument, and all could sing
or dance. The latter accomplishments they learned in-
stinctively, acquiring knowledge and skill from babyhood on. The instruments were brought: guitars, uku-
leles, mouth organs, and mandolins, while Ropati had
his nose flute, an ancient Tahitian instrument with four
stops. Jonas's concertina looked like a child's toy in
his hands, but no one was better skilled in drawing
music from it. He settled back more comfortably and
played a few preliminary chords, while the others, with
light touches of the keys, brought their instruments
into perfect tune. Then, with a nod from Jonas, they
fell in together, and of thirty-six bare feet, eighteen
could not have been kept in repose save by some elaborate
attachment of weights and cords. Jonas's right foot
thumped the hard ground rapturously. It was a rol-
licking song, the air French in origin, but so thoroughly
transformed that it was now as native to the island
as the Tuttles themselves. The words were the family's own, in part, though other versions were sung in
other villages. The making of songs is a widely shared
accomplishment on Tahiti; they grow as though by a
natural process, without the people knowing or caring
whence the various contributions come.

Ru, usually the quietest of Jonas's sons, was a different boy the moment music started. The quietness
was still there, but with a drollery imposed upon it that

all the family loved. He was a skilled mimic, and had
in a high degree the Tahitian's gift for improvisation.
This was best displayed in the *paoa,* a type of island
song in which one man does the singing while the others
keep time by slapping the ground or their knees, all
joining in a chanted chorus repeated at frequent intervals.

"Now, Ru," Jonas said, presently, "a *paoa.* We got to
show Chester we're glad he's home."

There was immediate approval of this suggestion.
Effie, who was to be the dancer, rose and tied a strip
of cloth about her hips. Despite her great bulk, when
stirred by music she was as light as a girl in her movements and carried out to perfection in her gestures the
gay or comic spirit of the song.

"Well, Ru?" said Fana, with a preliminary flourish
over the strings of his guitar.

"Give him time," said Jonas. "Ru's got to have a minute to think what he's going to sing. Chester, get your
ears opened up wide. Shouldn't wonder if he's going
to tell you what we think about your being away from
home so long."

Chester grinned, and all waited in keen expectation.
They knew Ru's gift. Once started he was never at a
loss, composing verse after verse as he stood before them,
all in perfect time to the music. A moment later he
got to his feet.

"What's it going to be?" Ropati asked.

The lad smiled. "Why Chester came home without
any money. . . . All right!"

The accompaniment started and the expression on

Ru's face changed at once. He stood before them a perfect imitation of Chester, struggling to speak in a moment of excitement, eyes bulging, lips working. His auditors shouted with delight before a word had been spoken. Then, facing the butt of his song, he began.

His listeners were delighted. Ru imagined himself Chester, explaining to their father why, after an absence of three years, he had come home with only one franc fifty centimes in his pockets; then trying to console the family by describing the wonderful things that might be bought with this wealth. At the end of each verse came the stuttered chorus: —

> *Au-É,* Ch-ch-ch-Chester *'ti é* . . . Heh!
> *Au-É,* Ch-ch-ch-Chester *'ti é* . . . Hah!

which the company repeated after him in great glee, while Effie danced before her world-wandering nephew with gestures and contortions in perfect keeping with the spirit of the song. All of Chester's foibles were brought to the fore, but there was no hint of malice in the song, and as these were shared by the family, the portrayal of them only added to the common enjoyment, in which Chester partook as freely as the rest.

"I wouldn't have thought you could du-du-du-do it so well, Ru," he said, when the song was ended. "Anyway, the rest of you gu-gu-got that f-f-f-franc and a half away from me before I'd been home t-t-t-ten minutes."

Thus far Chester had taken only a listener's part in the entertainment. Jonas regarded him reproachfully. "You used to be a good concertina player, Chester," he said.

Chester had been waiting for this opening.

"I still p-p-p-play a little," he replied.

"Let's hear you, then," said his father, and the concertina was passed to him down the table. Chester fingered it for a moment with intentional awkwardness, while the others waited, abashed and anxious. It was unthinkable that a Tuttle could show such a lack of skill.

"I'm sort of out of practice with the concertina," he said.

"You don't need to tell us," said Fana.

"Now, Fana, there's no call to say that," Jonas said. "Chester wouldn't have much time for music, wandering around the way he's been. He'll be as good as any of you once he gets his hand in again."

"I b-b-b-been playing the accordion lately," Chester explained. "I brought one wu-wu-with me, if you'd like to hear it?"

There were murmurs of polite assent, and Chester, leaving them for a moment, returned with the large box covered with oilcloth. The others waited with interest while he unfastened the cord. In the box was a leather case, and from this he drew forth a superb piano accordion. The astonishment of the family at viewing this instrument was expressed in a common gasp of delight. He adjusted the shoulder straps; then, standing before them, by the side of Ropati's chair, he drew out the instrument and half closed it again, in a couple of minor chords that sent shivers of anticipation racing up and down Jonas's spine.

"What'll I play?" he asked.

"Anything, Chester. Go ahead."

He turned to Fana. "You know the 'Poet and Peasant' overture?" he asked. The only reply was a shamefaced shake of the head. Chester felt that he had repaid his brother for the dig of a moment before. Letting his fingers fly over the keys as a brief preliminary, he then struck into the opening passage, and proceeded with such virtuosity that Pietro himself might have listened in respectful silence. The chorus of applause well repaid him for the innumerable hours spent in acquiring mastery of the instrument.

"*Tapiti! Tapiti!*" they shouted, while Chester stood grinning modestly. He was about to repeat the performance when old Tupa said: "Wait, Chester! I got a harmonica that pitch!" He searched hastily in an empty gasoline case and brought forth his largest harmonica, with a horn attachment. Meanwhile, Ru and Fana had been hastily bringing their instruments into accord. "We won't get it just right at first," Ru said. Chester nodded indulgently and glanced at their father, who shook his head. "I'll have to listen, Chester. That's too fast for me."

The hours flew by like minutes. The family repertoire was an endless one, and after the "Poet and Peasant" had been partially mastered by the others, they went on to music they all knew. At last Jonas, having repeatedly reminded Tupa that it was time for morning coffee, took him by the neck and marched him off to the place where the fire, already lighted by Maitu, threw a clear ruddy light through the half-gloom of approaching day.

CHAPTER II

JONAS TUTTLE's sons loved the sea, and justified their existence, in a practical way, by fishing for the Papeete market. Nat was the oldest, tallest, and most powerful of the boys. He stood six feet three, and weighed well over two hundred pounds. It was Nat who, when a tuna as large as himself had been hooked by one of his brothers, seized the pole from his hands and heaved the fish up to be gaffed. He was expert in every branch of inshore and offshore fishing, and, more than his brothers, had the patient hopefulness necessary to the calling; but on land he was inclined to be lazy. At home he would do what his greater strength required of him but no more. He was not agile-minded like his brother Fana, and it was usually the latter whose guidance he followed, who made the proposals which Nat agreed to, sometimes to his regret, in which case it would be long before Fana was allowed to forget whose was the fault for these impulsive decisions.

Fana was the third of Jonas's sons, the handsomest of the four, and something of a dandy in his love for dress. Ru, the baby of the family, was more like his grandmother than any of the others. He was quiet, intelligent, and dependable, and, like all of his brothers, a lover of gaiety. He was the engineer of the *Zimba,* the family fishing launch, and knew more about the

whims and moods of her twelve-horsepower engine
than the makers of that antiquated piece of machinery.

One afternoon, a few days after Chester's return, his
three brothers were well out to sea in the *Zimba*, which
was proceeding still farther westward at her full six
miles an hour. The engine, a Frisco Standard, had been
on starvation rations for longer than any of them could
remember. The fuel tank, in the bow, had a capacity
of forty gallons, but rarely, even in moments of the
greatest Tuttle prosperity, had the *Zimba* headed seaward with more than fifteen gallons in her tank, and
the usual allowance was less. For all that, engine and
launch were well cared for, according to Tuttle no-
tions. The former never lacked oil, and the launch
herself, although more than thirsty for paint on the top-
sides, was sound below water. None of the few possessions remaining to the Tuttle clan was more valued
than the *Zimba*, and according to Fana's reckoning she
had carried them on offshore fishing expeditions a distance of three times the circumference of the earth.

On the present occasion there was little fuel left
in the tank, which added to a suspense the launch itself
seemed to feel; for not a quarter of a mile ahead was a
fast-moving school of bonito, feeding ravenously upon
the mullet and other small fry they had driven to the
surface; and overhead, moving with them, a cloud of
birds, boobies and noddy terns, were diving repeatedly,
scores at once, indicating to the Tuttle boys the splendid fishing awaiting them within the next five minutes.
Ru was at the wheel; Nat and Fana had taken their
places, side by side, astern. A moment later they had

their poles out, making the pearl-shell lures skitter lightly over the surface of the sunlit water.

"Here they are!" Ru called back. The warning was needless, for already a silvery-blue streak of hunger and vitality had made a lunge at Fana's lure, barely missing it. Fana smiled, taking a firmer grip on his stout bamboo pole. Nat gave an exultant little cry, "*Hé . . . hé-hé-hé!*" as, from the corner of his eye, he caught a glimpse of the fringes of the cloud of birds moving before them. At this moment the engine, after a cough and a sputter, relapsed into silence. The *Zimba* had a character of her own. The Tuttle boys had not fished in her, almost from babyhood, without knowing her moods. As she lost her little momentum she rode the wind-wrinkled swells with an air that said, as plainly as words: "No fault of mine."

Ru steered on as though trying to persuade himself that the launch still had way on her. A few seconds later Nat turned to glance forward with an expression of amazement and indignation upon his face. Fana did the same, then caught the lure swinging toward him, and attached the hook at the butt of the pole, which he slid in with the spare rods made fast along the side of the launch. For a moment no one spoke; Fana struck the low rail with his fist.

"The bitch!" he exclaimed. "She meant to do it! That's the second time this week!"

"And whose fault is it?" Nat asked. "Not *Zimba's*. One more gallon of gas would have filled her with fish. I advised it, didn't I? Who talked me down? Who couldn't go one afternoon without cigarettes?"

Fana was silent.

"One more gallon," Nat went on, accusingly. "Eight francs' worth. It would have been enough and to spare. But no; you was bound to have the smokes!"

"*Mamu!*" Fana replied. "Where's the good of talking of it now? And the gas would have cost ten francs, bought of Ah Sin."

"We could have done with half a gallon," Nat went on, as he gazed sullenly after the receding birds. "Look to the feed pipe, Ru. Maybe it's choked."

Ru went forward, unscrewed the deck plate, and thrust down his measuring stick. He drew it forth as dry as the blistered planking of the deck itself.

"There's one good thing," said Fana, after a moment of silence. "Emily's boat's not out today."

Emily Taio was the owner of the rival fishing boat from the village of Tarahoi, and it was a matter of pride with the Tuttles to excel Emily's sons in every form of activity from fishing to cockfighting.

Nat shook his head. "We've not seen 'em, but they may be out." He took a last pull at his cigarette before tossing the butt over the side. "Get sail on her. There's breeze enough to take us home."

Forward of the deckhouse was a mast used in these common emergencies. Fana unfurled a sail that looked as ancient as the launch itself. Nat stretched out on the deckhouse with the sheet in his hand. Ru took the wheel once more, and the launch, gathering way imperceptibly, crept toward the distant land.

The Tuttle clan, insofar as their heritage of American blood was concerned, was not an ancient family, as families go in Polynesia. The first of that name in Tahiti history was a New Englander, Nathaniel Tuttle, who in the year 1853 had arrived at Papeete in a ship's boat with a dozen other survivors from the wreck of the *Orazimba*, a Yankee clipper bound from Boston to Canton, via Cape Horn and Valparaiso. The *Orazimba* had been lost amongst the Low Islands to the eastward, and during the long wait at Tahiti, Nathaniel Tuttle, second mate of the vessel, had decided to return home no more. He was then in his twenty-fifth year. He married two years later, his Tahitian wife bringing him, as her dowry, the valley of Vaipopo, on the west coast of the island. For the next twenty-five years Nathaniel followed his family calling, first as skipper, later as owner of various island schooners. When he retired he had two sons approaching manhood and a comfortable fortune which he resolved to invest in a home for the Tuttle descendants yet to come.

This house, erected in 1878, was for years thereafter one of the show places of Tahiti. There had gone into it the rugged character, the solid enduring qualities, of old Nathaniel himself. Its massive beams were of the heartwood of Douglas fir, with ceilings and floors of the same material. The walls were of brick and the tiles for the roof had been brought from Valparaiso in one of his schooners. It was a two-story mansion with wide verandas on all sides, upstairs and down. The twelve spacious rooms were far too many for the Tuttles of the oncoming generation, but Nathaniel was providing for the grandchildren and great-grandchildren to come, all to be endowed with the energy, the thrift, the foresight of the founder of the family fortunes. When the mansion was complete to the last detail, Tuttle spent five of the happiest years of his life acquiring furniture that should be worthy of it: wardrobes, beds, sofas, tables and chairs, of mahogany and black walnut, mirrors for the *salon,* and masterpieces of the pictorial art of the sixties and seventies which one could never tire of admiring, or of not admiring, as the case might be.

His wife, born Manaura à Tipaihu Tuavara, the sharer in all this splendor, was neither awed nor bewildered by it. She had provided the land upon which the house was built, and the rich little valley enclosing it, with its coconut palms, breadfruit, orange, and mango trees. More deeply than her husband she understood the importance of land, the true source of wealth. Secretly, perhaps, she felt that her own contribution to the family fortunes exceeded Nathaniel's; that it would remain for their descendants when the house and its contents had long since vanished. Nevertheless, she took great pride in the possessions provided for her, so far exceeding those of any of her kindred.

Her husband had not long to enjoy his retirement. He died in his sixty-first year, owing no man a penny, at peace with the world and himself, leaving to his sons his knowledge and love of the sea and two schooners, the source of his own prosperity and, as he hoped and believed, to be the continuing source of theirs. He was laid to rest in the family burying ground where two of his children who had died in infancy were already sleeping.

It would be difficult to set a date, thereafter, when the Tuttle fortunes began to decline. Had there been

another reënforcing tributary of New England blood
in the second generation, these allied strains might have
held their own for a considerable time against the
encroachments of the Polynesian strain; but both of
Nathaniel's sons married island women as their father
had done. For all that, there was an unmistakable Tuttle
stamp upon the family, even in later years. After their
mother's death a division of property was made, the
elder son, Ethan Tuttle, receiving the home place, and
his brother the two schooners, with which he sailed to
Rarotonga, in the Cook Islands, to establish himself
there. From that time on the only connection between
the two branches was an occasional exchange of letters
which became increasingly rare as the years passed. The
Tahiti family waxed in numbers as their material fortunes waned. Carefree, improvident, they lived with
gusto from day to day; tomorrow's needs could be met
when they came; nevertheless, they clung to their land.
By the time that Jonas Tuttle, Ethan's oldest son, had
grown to manhood, the Tahiti clan, occupying the old
house at Vaipopo, counting the near and remote connections who now lived there, had grown to large proportions. Ethan had died long since, though his wife,
a gentle old lady now in her seventies, still lived at
Vaipopo, greatly loved by her children, grandchildren,
and great-grandchildren. Mama Ruau — Grandma —
they called her.

As for the old house, little remained of its splendor
of the eighteen-eighties. One upstairs chamber alone,
Nathaniel's bedroom, had been kept, thanks to Mama
Ruau, as it was in those early days. However pressing

the family's needs she would allow nothing in this room to be sold or loaned or mortgaged. Elsewhere, the house looked as though a series of hurricanes had passed over and through it, and so they had, in fact: hurricanes of gaiety and good cheer to provide which the magnificent furniture had gone, piece by piece, until the rooms, both upstairs and down, were all but empty. In the living room there remained one decayed horsehair sofa and a mirror in a tarnished oval frame which still had virtue enough to reflect the bare wall, with its scaling plaster, and a segment of the floor on the opposite side of the room. But the Tuttles were skilled at makeshifts. They made benches, tables, shelves, and the like, from old packing cases and odds and ends of lumber; and as these were built for use and not for show, they had the fitness use gave them.

Jonas was now head of the family. He was a huge man of fifty-five, dark-eyed, dark-skinned, a thorough Tahitian and yet an unmistakable Tuttle. Certain family characteristics continued to emerge in each generation. The high Tuttle nose appeared and reappeared, although there had been imposed upon it a fleshiness that had not been there originally. Jonas Tuttle had such a nose. He had his grandfather's ample frame as well, but the great girth of belly had been built on, so to speak. Large as it was, it seemed to belong there, and this rotundity had nothing soft about it. It was a solid belly which Jonas carried with ease, and it was only when one saw removed the length of four-inch belt enclosing it that one realized the full extent of that middle circumference. His voice was in odd contrast to his size:

a soft tenor, clear, persuasive, and ingratiating. When he laughed, which was often indeed, it rose yet higher, in a steep incline, till it was lost to hearing; but the belly and shoulders continued to shake and the brown eyes all but vanished in rolls of fat.

He was a widower, and, as chief of the clan, he ruled it with what might be called a rod of soft iron. He could be imposed upon easily enough; he could be flattered, persuaded, cajoled, but there were points beyond which his good nature could neither be led nor driven. His generosity and kindness of heart were such that he had gathered under his roof various landless connections of the family whose relationship was so remote that no one could have defined it with certainty. The attitude toward him of his four sons was that of affectionate familiarity. Everyone, even his grandchildren, called him "Jonas," but they knew who was head of the family. In times of stress, sons and grandsons, all the connections by blood or marriage, sheltered behind this ample guardian of their fortunes.

The original Tuttle, although he had learned to speak the native language well, had allowed nothing but English to be used in the family circle. But after his death the sons had followed the line of least resistance, and by the time the third generation appeared there had developed a curious language for family use, based upon the native tongue, but with elements of both French and English mixed generously with it. But when occasion demanded it they could speak French or English almost as readily as their native Tahitian.

The clan was known throughout the islands as

Jonas-ma, or Tuttle-ma, the *ma* being a most convenient suffix which might well be adopted for use in other tongues. It signifies "and associates," "and retainers," or, as one might say, "and all the others," so that when people spoke of Tuttle-ma, they could thus briefly refer to Jonas and the entire army of Tuttles whom he held together at Vaipopo in a closely knit clanship, the pride and boast of every member of it.

Jonas was anxiously awaiting the return of the launch. Thus far the bonito season had been a poor one, but it might well be that the boys had run into a fine school somewhere in the Moorea Channel and were now homeward bound, the *Zimba* loaded to the gunwales. Supposing they had caught no more than seventy. Save fifteen for family consumption — this would leave them fifty-five to be sold in the Papeete market, and they would bring six francs each at this time of year. They would have three hundred and thirty francs in cash. Not bad, not bad at all for six hours of fishing in such a poor season. Jonas leaned back in his deck chair on the rickety veranda as he closed his eyes and dreamed of this good fortune, coming at a time when it was urgently needed. He had the happy faculty of wish fulfillment in his daydreams, so that whatever good he saw in his mind's eye became in a moment solid, actual, there to be handled and partaken of.

He now dreamed the launch inshore, with the engine slowed down as Ru steered across the lagoon for the boat shed near Paki's house. He heard Fana's exultant shout, signifying an excellent catch, and a moment later

he saw the boys carefully transferring the fish to the
landing. Out they came and out they came, not a round
number, of course — they rarely were. There would be
seventy-three, perhaps, or seventy-nine, or as many as
eighty-one. It would be a great load for the surrey. A
pity the truck wasn't running. The fish would have to
go to market in the surrey, but with three or four hundred francs in cash they could buy what was necessary
to repair the truck. That's what they would do with
the money: not a five-centime piece for any other purchase until the truck was running again. No matter
what the boys might say.

He was roused from his reverie by one of the children, a pretty child of ten who came running up from
the beach.

"They're coming, Jonas!" she called. "They're in the
pass now!"

Jonas nodded as he rose ponderously from his chair.
The foot-polished boards of the veranda gave under his
weight, and one plank flew up as he trod upon it absent-
mindedly. He shifted it back in place, muttering to
himself as he did so. How many times had he reminded
André and Pico and Mara, each of them in turn, to
nail a piece of joist under that board? He'd have to
speak about it again.

He halted as he was about to descend the steps. The
sun had vanished behind clouds that had appeared from
nowhere and gathered around the shoulders of the
mountains. There would be a heavy shower in a moment or two. He turned to the little girl at his side.

"Get the tins and basins, Nana," he said.

He waited while the child hippety-hopped through the hallway which divided the lower floor. She returned with a dishpan filled with tins and bowls of nicked enamelware. These she distributed at various points over the wide veranda. A moment later the clouds released their burdens in solid sheets, and the old house streamed like Noah's Ark at the beginning of the flood. Water spouted at a score of holes in the rusty eavestroughs. The two-story veranda, which extended beyond the body of the house, had originally been roofed with tiles, but many of these were now missing and others broken. In a heavy downpour, the water, leaking to the upper floor, dripped and trickled through to the lower one. Nana, with the skill of frequent experience, had placed the tins and basins where they should be, although one or two had to be shifted slightly to catch the dribbles from above. Jonas nodded approvingly as the child made these adjustments.

"That's right, Nana. Mustn't let the floor get mucky. Stay here and watch your tins. I'll go along to the beach."

"I want to go too," the child replied. "I want to see the boys come in."

"No, you wait. Skip upstairs now with your other tins. It won't last, this shower. You can be at the boat shed by the time the boys are."

The child pouted for a moment, but the mood quickly passed. Wrinkling up her nose, she thrust out her tongue at Jonas; then, with a merry laugh, she ran to do his bidding.

Opposite the Tuttle house, on the farther side of the

road, was an area of land, half a dozen acres in extent, with coconut palms scattered over it, and *purau* and *tamanu* trees shading the long gentle slope of beach. Here Paki, Jonas's brother-in-law, had his house. It was a three-room frame dwelling with a veranda on two sides, nicely painted and kept in excellent repair. It stood on the border of the lagoon, not far from where the Tuttle boat shed rested on its half-rotten piles.

The rain slackened as Jonas reached the beach; he could see the launch, a quarter of a mile distant, moving slowly across the lagoon. The boys were rowing her in; they'd run out of gas again, that was sure. Jonas regarded the boat more narrowly. She was high out of the water; there could have been no good take of fish. For all that, there might be fifty or so in the cockpit. But his hopes faded as the launch drew near. Fana stood in the bow, with a boat hook in his hand.

"How many?" his father called.

Fana shrugged his shoulders. "*Aita hoé,*" he replied.

A throng of Tuttles, large and small, had gathered by this time. When the boat was tied up, Nat, Fana, and Ru waded glumly across the shallows to the beach. Paki came to the door of his house and stood looking on.

"Where's the fish?" he called. "There was flocks of birds offshore. I could see 'em from here."

"Oh, you could?" said Fana. "You saw more than we did, then."

"You hear him?" said Nat, turning to his father. "Fana wants you to think it was bad luck. We could have foundered the *Zimba* if we'd had another gallon

of gas. Never saw a bigger school. We was right at the
edge when the engine quit."

"I gave you nine francs," said Jonas. "Didn't
you . . ."

"No, we didn't," Fana broke in. "I'll take the blame;
Nat's aching to put it on me. We bought smokes with
the money." He drew forth his packet and offered it
to his father. "Have one, Jonas?"

The elder man shook his head. "You boys got no
sense," he said, in a voice of mild vexation. "You never
will have."

Fana grinned. "What d'you expect, with the father
we got?" he replied. "Oh, Paki! I'll have supper with
you and Effie tonight if you want me to."

His Aunt Effie laughed good-naturedly. "All right.
Come the three of you. You can do with a meal, I
guess, from the look of things."

Jonas's sister was a feminine counterpart of himself.
She was full of gaiety, though this mood could change
to one of sudden, tempestuous anger. She had the Tahitian zest for good living, and the Tahitian woman's
indifference as to what love of food did to her figure.
Paki, her husband, was a spidery-legged, gnomelike man
of fifty, from the island of Anaa, in the Low Archipelago. Three men of his size would scarcely have
equaled his wife in bulk. Like most of his countrymen
from the Low Islands where life is hard, and food, other
than coconuts and fish, scarce indeed, he was as close
and thrifty as his wife's people were open-handed in all
their ways. He listened sourly to Effie's offer of hospitality.

"They'll have no supper with us," he said. "There's enough for ourselves and no more."

"*Taata paari!*" Nat replied, contemptuously. "Keep your supper! I want none of it. You'd give us the third of a tin of beef to share amongst the lot!"

Effie turned fiercely upon her husband. "You lizard!" she cried. "You Low Island bonefish! It's so you'd treat my nephews, is it? Whose land are you living on? Ours! Whose fish, when there are any, go into that wizened little belly? Ours! Where would *you* be if it wasn't for the Tuttles — if it wasn't for me? On Anaa, with the rest of your stingy people, eating clams and shark meat!"

The others looked on in gleeful silence as Paki sidled away, crab-fashion, followed by his mountain of a wife. These clashes between High Island Aunt Effie and Low Island Paki were common enough. They all knew Paki's worth, and none better than his wife. He more than paid his way in the family. He was a mechanical genius; he could make any piece of mechanism work, and his services were in constant demand throughout Vaipopo village. He repaired watches, sewing machines, phonographs, anything that ran by wheels or cogs. It was Paki who kept the *Zimba's* engine in order, and that of the Ford truck, bought years ago at second hand; and he had passed on to Ru, his favorite nephew, something of his own skill. But while the Tuttles admired and respected him, it could hardly be said that they liked him, and they enjoyed seeing Effie put him in his place. But Paki, small as he was, had a firmness of character that his wife stormed against in vain. He was, however,

willing to make small concessions which Effie accepted
as complete victories, and in this case he agreed that Ru
should come with them for the evening meal. He had
meant, from the first, that Ru should come. The other
boys were to take potluck with the rest of the family.

Potluck it was on this particular evening. Tupa had
been hard put to it to provide food for so many hungry mouths. But he was skilled at improvisation, and
when the others thronged into the dining shed, two five-
gallon tins filled with stew were steaming and burrum-
bling over a fire of coconut husks. Adults, youths, maid-
ens, and small children slid into place haphazardly on
the benches ranged on either side of the long table; there
was no order of precedence except that Jonas sat at the
head, with his mother at the opposite end where the
smaller children usually assembled. When Maitu was
ready to serve the food it was discovered that most of
the bowls and basins were missing. Jonas remembered
that they had been used as rain catchers during the
shower, and some of the children were sent to fetch
them. At last the stew was ladled out and distributed,
the children waiting with impatience till all had been
served.

Grace before meat had been the invariable custom in
the household of old Nathaniel Tuttle. This was carried
on by his sons, although their father's long invocation
had been gradually abridged until it amounted to no
more than "Make-us-truly-thankful-Amen." In the
third generation there had been a further curtailment.
When the last bowl was filled and on the table, Jonas
glanced down the board, half-hidden in clouds of lamp-

lit steam; then he closed his eyes, dropped his chin on his chest, and a second later raised it again. This was the signal for falling-to and was eagerly obeyed.

The family ate in noisy silence for a moment or two; then André, an indeterminate Tuttle-ma connection, spoke.

"What's to do tomorrow, Jonas?"

With his tin spoon, the head of the family was searching his basin without relish for whatever solid food it contained. When he had consumed the last morsel, he left the broth to cool.

"Ask the boys," he replied, with an air of injured dignity. "Ask Fana. He knew how to spend his father's last nine francs: in tobacco smoke. He'll tell you how we're to go on now."

"Sure I will," said Fana. "Go see Doc Blondin. What if I did buy the smokes? How much farther could the *Zimba* have run on a gallon of gas? We'll need plenty if we're going to follow the bonito this time of year."

"Another gallon would have loaded the *Zimba* to-day," Nat said. "I'll have that known. We was right at the edge of the school."

"You've had it known a dozen times," said Fana. "Give it a rest. Will you see the Doc, Jonas?"

Jonas's mother looked appealingly down the table toward her son.

"No, Jonas," she said. "Let none of the boys persuade you to do that again. How are you ever to pay Dr. Blondin what we already owe?"

"With fish, Grandma. How else?" said Nat. "We came near enough this afternoon to making the biggest haul

of the year. There was thousands in that school. We'd
have had twelve hundred francs' worth in another five
minutes. I had that money good as spent when the
engine died."

"And so it would have been by tomorrow morning,
if you'd caught the fish," his grandmother replied. "Dr.
Blondin would have seen none of it."

"Now, Mama, give us time," Jonas said. "Dr. Blondin knows how it is with us, with so many mouths to
feed. He's in no hurry for his money."

"Has he told you that?" his mother asked.

"Well, no, not exactly, but I can see he ain't. *Éaha
nei!* He's doctor for most of the people in Papeete and
the villages on both sides. He can't spend half the money
he makes."

"So he may as well give it to us; that's what you and
the boys think."

"Don't f-f-forget about the Mortgage Lifter,
Grandma," Chester said. "We'll make enough out of
him to p-p-pay the Doc three times over before the
year's out."

"Well, will you see him, Jonas?" Fana asked once
more. "Eighty francs is what we need. That'll buy us
ten gallons."

Jonas sighed. "Yes, looks like I'll have to. But this
is the last time, Mama. I'll almost promise you that."

Tupa, who was leaning against one of the ironwood
posts, gave a dry chuckle.

"What's so funny, Tupa?" Nat asked.

"I was thinking you might call on Paki," he replied.

CHAPTER III

ON the following morning, Jonas, ready for his journey to town, was waiting on the front veranda for Riki, one of his grandsons, who had gone to hitch Nellie to the surrey. Jonas wore a wide-brimmed pandanus hat, a white coat, frayed a little along the lapels and around the collar, but spotlessly clean, and a pair of blue dungarees. His feet were bare, not only for comfort's sake, but because he had never been able to find a pair of shoes large enough to enclose them.

He rose and went slowly down the steps as Riki appeared from behind the house with the horse and surrey.

"There's a buckle come off the bridle," the lad announced, "but I got it fixed all right."

His grandfather regarded the repairs gravely. "Good a job as I could have done myself, Riki," he said. The springs of the surrey flattened as he climbed aboard and took the reins. "You know that loose plank on the porch?" he added. "I want you to tell André or Pico or one of the boys to nail a piece of joist under it." With a nod to his grandson, Jonas then drove down to the road and urged the little mare into a four-mile trot.

For all the times he had made the journey to Papeete, Jonas never tired of it, and he liked best going in the surrey, and alone. The truck got him there too soon. In the surrey, he could count upon three hours before

he would round the hairpin turn at Hotuarea, just outside the town. During this time his mind was at peace.
Family cares and responsibilities were left behind, and
the vexatious errands that awaited him in Papeete need
not be thought about till the town was reached. There
were stretches of road dappled with sun and shadow
where no houses were. Jonas loved these, and the mare
too, it seemed, for she would slow down to a walk,
whereupon Jonas would fall into a deep reverie when
time seemed to stand still for him, and the surface of
consciousness would be faintly stirred by influences as
gentle as the catspaws that spread fanwise over the
surface of the lagoons.

He roused himself presently; he was approaching the
first houses of Tarahoi village. It was a pretty little place
of two hundred inhabitants, the dwellings, like those of
Vaipopo, scattered along a mile of road, some on the
lagoon beach, others inland, on the mountain side of
the road. A few moments later Jonas came to Emily
Taio's fine plantation where cattle grazed on the lush
grass that made a shadow-dappled carpet beneath the
rows of well-spaced coconut palms. He sighed as he
glanced about him, at Emily's neat fences, her nicely
painted copra sheds, at the dwelling house where everything was in such meticulous order and such perfect
repair. Well, well! Emily was a good manager; no doubt
of that. She seemed always to get on; whatever she did
turned to her advantage. But most of all Jonas envied
her the *Hina*, the new fishing launch in which Emily's
boys contended with the *Zimba*. A pity the Tuttles
couldn't have such a boat. His boys were worth a dozen

of Emily's. Given plenty of gas and a launch as good
as hers, they could earn more in a month than the Taios
could in a year.

Leaning forward, elbows on his knees, the reins held
loosely in his hands, Jonas gazed complacently before
him, as though he had not a care in the world. Out of
the corner of his eye he had seen Emily coming down
the pathway to the road, but he pretended not to have
seen her.

"Jonas!" she called.

He turned his head slowly and drew up his horse.

"Ah, Emily."

"*Haere oé hia?*"

"To Papeete."

Neither spoke again for a moment. Emily gave him
a shrewd glance.

"I didn't hear the boys going by to market last night.
They caught nothing?"

Jonas regarded her gravely. "Next to nothing," he
replied. "Four tuna and fifty-one bonito. But they got
in late from sea. We sold the fish in the village, what
we didn't keep for ourselves. How did your boys make
out?"

"Well enough for such an off season," Emily replied.
"Our catch sold for five hundred and ninety-two
francs."

"Ah," Jonas remarked, drily. "Nat told me they
didn't see the *Hina* yesterday. Where was your boys
fishing?"

Emily smiled with an air of mystery. "Tell Nat to
ask Moa and see if he can find out."

Rivalry between Jonas's sons and Emily's sons was keen, and it was a matter of principle, with the heads of the two families, to boast, with or without reason, of their catches and the money received from them. Each knew that the other could and would check statements made, but it was impossible for them to speak truth in these matters.

"Why didn't your boys take their fish to town in the *Zimba?*" Emily asked.

Jonas sighed. "No gas. They didn't have enough even to come home on."

"You're a foolish man, Jonas," said Emily. "You should keep a supply on hand. That's what I do."

"*Éahahoia!*" Jonas exclaimed. "It's well enough for you to boast. If you had a family as big as mine . . . The boys have their cock in training by now, perhaps?" he asked, innocently.

Emily hesitated. "Our bird is in poor condition," she said, with the air of making a forced admission. "At present he could hardly match the poorest of your cocks."

Jonas raised his eyelids slowly, as though all the strength in his great body had been gathered for the effort, gave Emily a hasty glance, and dropped them again.

"I'm glad you spoke, Emily," he said. "Our best cock's been going light these two weeks past. Fana can't find what's wrong with him. We'd better call the match off."

"I wouldn't say that," Emily replied. "There's nearly

a month to go as we've arranged it. That's time enough to get our birds in shape."

"Perhaps," said Jonas. "Shall we let the date stand, then?"

"My sons are willing. Of course, if yours wish to back out . . ."

Jonas grunted. "You know better than to think it," he said. "But we expect to take all the money you can put up. Fana won't run the risk of losing for us with a poor-conditioned bird."

"I've heard your cock is from Tubuai?"

"People seem to know more about our birds than we do ourselves," Jonas replied. "I'd be pleased to see your new one, if he's hereabout."

"Moa keeps him on the plateau, beyond the valley," Emily replied.

"He's a Raiatea cock?"

Emily laughed. "I would have kept that a secret, Jonas, but there's no hiding anything on Tahiti. Maybe he is, and if he's fit for the match we'll back him gladly against your Tubuai wonder."

"So be it, then," said Jonas, as he took up the reins. "*Parahi*, Emily. I want to get to town before the heat of the day."

As the horse jogged slowly on, Jonas's meditations were pleasant ones. The rumor the boys had spread about as to the origin of the new cock to be pitted against the Taios' had reached Emily's ears as they had foreseen. Let them think the bird was from Tubuai; there would be a grand surprise on the day of the match. Jonas had no doubt as to the result. No island-bred bird could stand up against the Mortgage Lifter. They would clean Emily out. This happy prospect gave Jonas matter for thought all the way into town.

It was ten by the cathedral clock when he hitched his tired little mare in the market place. Business for the day was pretty well over, and the townspeople had settled down to quiet enjoyment of the long sunny hours to come. Jonas walked slowly along the waterfront and seated himself on a bench in a shady spot near the *Bureau du Poste*. A score of copra schooners and Low Island cutters were moored along the sea wall, lying motionless in the midmorning calm, their sails, hoisted for drying, hanging limp from the gaffs. A fine schooner-yacht, with the name *Yankee* in gold lettering on her stern, was lying near by, looking self-conscious and superior in that humble workaday company. Her decks were immaculate and her brasswork shone with a dazzling brilliance in the morning sunlight. Jonas leaned forward as he read the name of her home port: MARBLEHEAD.

Wasn't it from Marblehead that his grandfather had come? Yes, so it was; he remembered, now. Like enough there were Tuttles still living there: *fetii*, relatives of his of whom he had never heard. His grandfather must have had brothers and sisters in America. A strange thing it would be if some of their descendants were on this very ship, moored within twenty paces of him. He had a mind to go on board and make inquiries, but instead of this he dreamed himself doing it. He felt the varnished gangplank giving under his weight as he stepped aboard; then, in the easy gracious manner that came as second nature to him, he imagined himself speaking to the well-dressed *popaa*, the owner, no doubt, lounging in a deck chair under the awning.

During the next hour Jonas lived through one of those delightful fairy tales he so loved to invent, and, having invented, for the moment believed. Jonas Tuttle of Tahiti met Jonas Tuttle of Marblehead. But the Nathaniel Tuttle who had come to Tahiti so long ago had never kept in touch with his New England relatives, with the result that the Marblehead branch were in complete ignorance of where he had gone, after the wreck of the *Orazimba*, and how he had fared in later life. The owner of the *Yankee*, as astonished as he was delighted at this chance meeting with his namesake and relative, had gone with him to Vaipopo where the Tuttles had combed land and sea for food for such a feast as only Tuttle-ma knew how to prepare. But for all the abundance spread before him, Jonas Tuttle of Marblehead could see how matters stood with his island relatives. A bachelor, possessed of a fortune so great that the income alone was far beyond his power to spend, he had, with increasing warmth and earnestness, pressed Jonas Tuttle of Vaipopo to grant him the privilege and pleasure of restoring the family fortunes to what they had been in former days. Jonas, firm, at first, in refusing the generous offer, had at last consented, and never would he forget the smile of pleasure that had greeted his announcement. His distant cousin clasped his hand warmly. "Carte blanche, Jonas," he said, laughingly. "I insist upon that. You're to give me perfect freedom to go as far as I like. And first of all, before we restore your grandfather's dwelling, I want to see a new fishing launch on the beach there, under a boat shed that shall be worthy of her. The family of whom you spoke, in that other village — what's their name again?"

"Taio," Jonas of Tahiti had replied. "But . . ."

"No, no! No 'buts,' Jonas!" his relative exclaimed, gleefully. "Leave everything to me. As soon as it can be designed and built, your boys are to have a fishing launch that will make the Taios' boat look like an abandoned dory. And another thing: I want to put a substantial 500-gallon storage tank convenient to the boathouse. For gasoline, you know."

The cathedral clock struck the half-hour. Jonas roused himself with an effort, surprised to find that it was the half after eleven. The deck chair under the *Yankee's* awning was now empty. Its occupant must have gone to lunch, on shore, perhaps, at the Diadème or the Blue Lagoon Hotel. And Dr. Blondin would be at lunch now, and then it would be the siesta hour. He could not, with decency, call to see him before two. What of his own midday meal? Not a franc did he have; not a fifty-centime piece. He would be obliged to strain his credit once more, at one of the poorer Chinese restaurants. With a discouraged sigh he considered the possibilities; then, rising ponderously, he set out in quest of the most promising one.

Dr. Blondin, his face slightly flushed from his midday nap, went to his bathroom for the refreshment of a shower. His afternoon office hours were from two-thirty to four-thirty; then he would have his calls to make. He knew the patients he would find in his waiting room: a native with yaws, a Chinese mother with a child or two to be dosed for worms, a filaria case — all the usual complaints. And, more than certain, some young fool of a tourist who had entered to his hurt into the larger island freedom along the Papeete waterfront.

Getting into fresh garments, Dr. Blondin slipped on his white apron and was just coming from his dressing room when the house bell tinkled. Coming through the hallway, he found Jonas Tuttle standing at the entrance to the veranda.

"Well, Jonas?" he said.

"Good afternoon, Doctor. I just happened to be in town today, so I thought I'd call in for a few minutes."

There was a ghost of a smile in Dr. Blondin's eyes. "What's the trouble? Someone ill in the family?"

"We're never sick; you know that, Doctor," Jonas replied, gently. "It's not time for your office hour?"

Blondin glanced at his watch. "In twenty minutes," he replied. He motioned to a chair. Jonas lowered himself into it carefully and placed his hat on the floor beside him.

"Didn't see the boys at the market this morning," the doctor remarked. "No luck yesterday?"

Jonas shook his head. "They came as near as anything to the biggest bonito catch in years," he said. "Nat tells me they had three thousand francs' worth as good as in the boat. They was right at the edge of the school and had just put out the rods." He broke off with a deep sigh.

"And then, what?"

"The engine died on 'em. No more gas."

"Whose fault was that?"

"Nobody's. It was just hard luck."

"Hmmmm . . . Well, better luck next time."

"That's what I say," Jonas replied. "I don't mind telling you this, Doctor, as long as you don't pass it on to Emily Taio's boys: for all it's an off season for bonito, my boys has seen big schools running down the far side of the Moorea Channel. And when you see 'em there at this time of year, you can count on 'em being there for a good two weeks afterward. I don't know why it's so, but it *is* so."

"Good. I'll say nothing, of course. I wish the boys all the luck in the world."

Jonas raised his eyelids in a characteristic manner, glanced mournfully at the doctor, and then gazed at the floor between his bare feet.

"Little good it'll do to know where they are," he said. "It's all of fifteen miles from our place . . . And gas eight francs a gallon," he added, after a long pause.

Dr. Blondin made no reply for some time; then he leaned forward in his chair.

"See here, Jonas! I'm going to give you a straight-from-the-shoulder talk. You Tuttles need it. Your boys are the best fishermen on the island. Everyone knows that. There's no reason on earth why you shouldn't be one of the most prosperous families on all Tahiti. There's not a richer little valley opening on the Broom Road than yours, and yet . . ."

"You forget the mouths I've got to feed, Doctor," Jonas put in.

"And *you* forget that you are the most wasteful, lackadaisical, improvident lot on the whole of Tahiti, bar none!" the doctor replied. "What the devil do you do with all the money you earn, from fishing alone? Where does it go?"

"Many's the time I ask myself the same question," Jonas replied, in a puzzled voice. "It goes — that's all I know about it."

"Well, it's not all that *I* know about it, Jonas! It goes for good cheer at Tuttle-ma's. It goes to entertain every Tom, Dick, and Harry who takes a fancy for stopping at Vaipopo for a week, or a month — as long as the food and wine hold out."

"You wouldn't have us be mean, Doctor?" Jonas replied, reproachfully.

"Yes. Until you can be hospitable at your own expense, not mine. *I'm* the one who pays for the entertainment at the Tuttle homestead — did you ever stop to consider that? *I'm* the one . . ."

"No, Doctor," Jonas broke in, earnestly. "I've never spent one franc of the money you've loaned me for anything but gasoline and repairs for the *Zimba* and . . ."

"Yes, yes, yes! Granted. And your own money goes for the entertainment; for the demijohns of wine; for the bets on Vaipopo cocks that seldom win. . . ."

"We've won four out of five matches this year," said Jonas.

"Then all the bets must have been on the one you

didn't win," the doctor replied. "Jonas, do you know how much money you owe me?"

"I couldn't say, offhand, but I've got it all down, at home."

"I'll tell you, then." Drawing a notebook from his pocket, Dr. Blondin glanced through the pages. "Seventeen thousand, nine hundred and sixty francs," he announced.

"There'd have been four thousand francs knocked off that as sure as anything if the boys hadn't run out of gas yesterday," Jonas replied, sadly. "Maybe five."

"No there wouldn't, Jonas. I know you Tuttles. There would have been another celebration at Vaipopo, with all your hangers-on for miles around taking part at your expense — at my expense. And a day or two later I'd have seen you just where I see you now, explaining very plausibly how it all happened, in spite of your earnest efforts to prevent it."

Jonas was silent. He sat gazing mournfully at his sturdy bare toes, as though every one of the ten were a son, or a cousin, or a fifth cousin, who should have been here in his place, listening to these just reproaches.

"Isn't it true?" the doctor insisted.

"We ain't had a party at our house in I don't know when," Jonas said, lamely. "If you'd seen our supper last night, Doctor, you wouldn't think we was living so high. Stew made of leftovers, and barely enough to go round."

Blondin smiled. "You'll get no sympathy from me on that account," he said. "I've yet to see a Tuttle that looked undernourished."

"My boys are a handful, that's the plain truth," said Jonas. "They won't listen to me. If they wasn't such wonderful musicians . . . I guess it's that as much as anything brings so many outsiders to our place."

"You're no novice, yourself, when it comes to playing the concertina," the doctor replied. "But music and good times should be the ornament, not the business of life."

"We only play evenings, mostly."

"Nonsense! Tell that to someone who doesn't know you as I do. See here, Jonas! What do you mean to do?"

Jonas ran his fingers through his thick black hair.

"Well, tomorrow we was aiming to fish again while the bonito's running like they are in the Moorea Channel. But . . ."

"I'm not speaking of that," said the doctor. "I want to know when you mean to begin payments on your debt of seventeen thousand, nine hundred and sixty francs." He paused. "That debt has been piling up, little by little, for the past five years. What you have paid has been more than offset by what you have continued to borrow. I've not charged you one penny of interest, Jonas, and I don't mean to now. But, by the Lord! For your own sake I'm going to insist that you begin to whittle down this debt!"

Jonas's face brightened. "That's what I came in to speak about, Doctor. I was figuring that, if we paid you two hundred francs a week, we could soon clear the whole thing off. Like enough, some weeks we could pay more. If we was to make a good haul like the one the boys just missed yesterday when the gas give out, there'd be six or seven thousand francs off all at once. And with bonito running the way they are now, we might get twisted round so's we could pay every penny by the end of this month. Shouldn't wonder if that's just what'll happen," he went on, eagerly. "The boys told me they never saw a bigger school than the one they lost on account of no gas. A good half-mile across, Nat said, and thousands of birds over it. All we need is to have luck like that for a week and . . ."

"Wait a minute, Jonas. I'm not asking you to cancel it in a week, or a month, or six months, or even in a year. I'll be entirely satisfied with what you suggest: two hundred francs to be paid every Sunday-morning market. I *do* want you to pay that sum. You can, easily. But will you?"

"That's what I was saying, Doctor. That's why I come to see you. Just as soon as we get twisted round . . ."

"You're twisted round enough, already. I want you to get *un*twisted. Very well, then; it's settled. And mind you! No excuses, barring hurricanes, pestilences, and other acts of God."

"You won't hear any, Doctor. You could count on having the first payment this coming Sunday if . . ." He hesitated, was about to resume, but remained silent. Dr. Blondin knew that he was suffering, but he regarded his visitor coolly, waiting for him to proceed. Jonas raised his eyes for a hasty glance; then he sighed, and groped for the hat on the floor beside him.

"Well, I guess I better be going," he said.

The doctor relented.

"I want you to have a fair start, Jonas, now that we have this matter arranged. But remember! It's the last loan you'll get from me. How much gas does the *Zimba* need for a week's fishing?"

Jonas's face lighted up. "That depends, Doctor. When there's a good breeze and no birds up, the boys sail the launch. It's when they see the birds they start the engine. Of course, if there's no wind . . . But ten gallons a day is a fair average."

"Good. That's sixty gallons for the six days."

The doctor went to his desk. Jonas waited until he returned with the bank notes. "There's four hundred and eighty francs to be added to the debt."

Jonas beamed. "It won't be added long," he said. "More'n likely I'll be in here day after tomorrow with . . ."

"All right, all right. Hope so. It's time for my office hour. Good luck to you."

Half an hour later, with six ten-gallon cases of gasoline in the back of the surrey, Jonas started on the homeward journey.

CHAPTER IV

THE afternoon was dead calm, with a long glassy swell rolling in from the southeast. The sun was slanting toward the neighboring island of Moorea as the *Zimba* moved out through the Vaipopo Passage at her cruising speed of five knots. At each explosion of her slow-turning, heavy-duty engine, the launch gave a slight bound, like a tired horse touched with a whip, seemed to hesitate, and then repeated the motion.

Ru stood at the wheel, shading his eyes from time to time as he stared ahead, eager to be first to sight the birds. They would look no larger than a swarm of gnats, low on the horizon. He had a lively imagination, and at times was almost convinced that the flecks swimming across his eyeballs were the birds themselves; then he would rub his eyes and gaze ahead once more at the vacant heaving glitter that met the skyline. His three brothers lounged in the cockpit behind him.

"That's what he told me," Chester was saying — "beef with a little red p-p-pepper chopped up in it, and every night stale bread soaked in milk."

"Don't worry, he's getting it," Fana replied. "For grain I give him a mixture of corn and unhulled rice, and he has his oysters every other day. You saw him work out last night."

"You've du-du-du-done wonders with him, Fana," Chester admitted. "That long voyage, cooped up the way he was, was awful hard on him."

"What'd he weigh, last time?" Nat asked.

"I got him down to two kilos, eight hundred. There ain't fat enough on him to grease a watch. If we have some luck out here — get some money to bet with . . . We got to!"

"If we du-du-don't, we must save him, Fana. We could put that cock of Ru's into this next match. When the old Mortgage Lifter comes on we want to be sure there's some real money for him to lift."

Nat rose for a glance around the horizon. "Don't look too good," he said. "What we need is a little northeast breeze to ripple the swell."

"We'll find 'em yet," Fana replied, hopefully. "It's too early for the birds to work."

Nat turned to the helmsman. "Keep her right on the west end of Moorea, Ru. I'm going to take a snooze." He lay down on the soft bed of fronds spread over the floor of the cockpit to prevent the bruising of fish as they struck the deck, and a moment later was snoring loudly.

"What do you reckon Emily'll bet on this match?" Chester asked.

"Plenty," Fana replied. "The whole family's crazy about their Raiatea cock. But if we can make four or five good hauls, with fish dear like they are now, we can cover as much as they'll put up. And *then!*" He grinned, exultantly. "I'm waiting for that day, Chester."

They fell silent as the *Zimba* chugged steadily west-

ward over the calm, empty, gently heaving sea. They
were now far offshore and the subtle change made itself
felt that marks the lapsing of early into mid-afternoon.
Fana sang softly to himself. Nat slept on, but an hour
later he turned on his back, rubbed his eyes, stretched,
and stood up. He glanced carelessly around the skyline.

"There's the Taio boys," he announced.

The keenness of Nat's sight was proverbial in the
Tuttle family, but Ru felt vexed that he had not been
able to make the announcement for once. When the
two launches, miles apart, rose simultaneously to the
swell, all could make out the *Hina* headed toward her
rival boat.

"No fish up to the north," Nat said. "They got nothing, that's sure." He glanced around once more, then
touched Ru's shoulder. "Head off, southwest."

"What do you see?" Chester asked, getting to his feet
again.

Nat gave a nod to the south. "They're working on
fish."

The others now perceived, about a mile distant, a
pair of white terns, barely discernible as they dipped and
circled in a manner that was unmistakable. Nat took the
wheel. Ru crouched under the hatch, performing the
difficult feat of getting a few extra revolutions out of
the engine. He touched the ancient make-and-break
ignition system, twiddled something on the carburetor.
The sound of the exhaust grew sharper and Nat nodded
with satisfaction as the *Zimba* increased her speed by
half a knot. He was staring fixedly at the birds and at
the sea beneath them. He turned his head quickly.

"Take the wheel, Ru! Tuna, boys! They're on mullet. There's a million of 'em!"

No further speech was needed. Automatically, the Tuttles cleared for action. The dozen or more bonito rods were stacked on the forward deck and made fast where they could come to no harm. Fana brought aft a pair of stout bamboos, equipped with lines ending in lures of heavy pearl shell with thick barbless hooks of bronze. Chester seized two gaffs, handed back by Ru, and hooked one on either side of the stern. Nat was making a bundle of coconut fronds, lashing the butts together. All was in readiness well before they reached the fish.

"Look! The Taios have spotted 'em now!" said Fana. "Go on, *Zimba*! Let us down this time and we'll scuttle you!"

"Don't worry," Nat said, quietly. "We'll beat 'em to it, easy."

Close ahead, half an acre of calm sea was churned and lashed white by the feeding tuna. They had herded into a compact mass a great school of young mullet, and were gobbling down the little fish with insatiable ferocity. The tuna were in hundreds; their prey, frantic with fear and excitement, and without so much as a floating coconut husk beneath which to take refuge, in tens of thousands. Only the two small white birds circled above them. Chester seized Fana's arm. His lips were moving fast, but no word would come.

"You don't need to say it, Chester. I know: there's the money for the Mortgage Lifter."

His brother nodded. "He nu-nu-knew we needed it

for him. That b-b-bird brings us luck even out here."

"All ready!" Nat warned.

Ru steered the launch straight into the midst of the welter, where the clear blue sea was stained with blood and bits of flesh. "*Tapéa!*" Nat yelled. His brother closed the throttle and pulled out the clutch. Nat flung his bundle of palm fronds over the stern, making it fast to a cleat at the end of a couple of fathoms of line. As the *Zimba* lost way, the small fry on all sides made a frenzied rush for the boat and the shelter of the floating fronds. Tuna snapped at them, leaping clear of the water and flinging spray over the Tuttle boys.

"All right," Nat ordered, over his shoulder. "Slow, now, and make the wheel fast."

Ru pushed in the clutch without opening the throttle, and the boat moved slowly forward. He sprang aft to his station where he stood stooped, one hand braced on his knee and the other holding one of the gaffs in readiness. Chester, at his side, was in the same position, where their shoulders would act as fulcrums for the heavy rods held by their brothers close behind. The lures were flung out.

Chester yelled as a fifty-pound tuna nearly jerked the rod from Fana's hands. The thick bamboo bent as Fana bore down on it. After a brief struggle the fish's head was levered to the surface; Chester's gaff shot out and the tuna slid over the transom to land on deck with a muffled thump and drumming of his tail. Nat was fast to a fish that required all his strength to bring alongside, where Ru gaffed and drew him on board with a single swift movement.

"*Hé, hé!*" he shouted. "Forty francs!"

"And another forty," Chester yelled, forgetting to stammer as he gaffed a second fish.

The boat moved over the glassy sea at a bare three knots, followed, almost surrounded, by the tuna, darting at the mullet which had taken shelter along the keel, or beneath the fronds towing a few yards astern. The Tuttle boys labored mightily; sweat streamed into their eyes, and they were spattered with showers of blood flung aloft by the drumming tails. "Thump! Thump! Thump!" the fish came in, and the lures were flung back to be seized without an instant's pause.

The work was so furious that none of them observed the *Hina* until she turned and slowed down, to steer a parallel course, fifty yards distant. To have come closer to share in the fishing, under the present circumstances, would have been a gross breach of etiquette, but their yells as each big fish came on board were as exultant as those of their lucky rivals. The Taios were good sportsmen, like all Polynesians, and their pleasure in the scene was scarcely less keen because they were compelled to be spectators. Half an hour passed; then, in the mysterious manner of their kind and as if at a preconcerted signal, the tuna sounded and were gone. Nat wiped his face with the bloodstained sleeve of his shirt. Fana dropped on a locker and sat leaning forward, breathing heavily. The Taio boys, observing that the fishing was over, steered the *Hina* alongside. The *Zimba* was now deeply laden. The Taios regarded her enviously.

"That's once you beat us to it," Moa Taio called.

"Once?" Fana replied, derisively. "You got a bad memory, Moa."

"How many?"

"We ain't got room to count 'em," Nat said, rope bucket in hand.

Chester and Ru were giving the *coup de grâce* with short clubs of ironwood to the fish which still slapped and drummed with their tails. Nat threw bucket after bucket of sea water over the catch, then drenched his brothers, who gave him a bath in turn. Balancing himself on the rail, Nat leaped into the Taios' launch, almost capsizing the *Zimba* as he leaped across. He shook hands ceremoniously with all on board — Emily's three sons and two neighbors who fished with them.

"We need a bit of help, Moa," Nat said. "You mind taking our fish to market and selling 'em for us? I see you got plenty of room."

There were only four small bonito lying in the *Hina's* cockpit. Moa smiled shamefacedly, observing Nat's glance at their catch.

"You had all the luck there was going today," he said. "Sure, Nat, if it'll oblige you. What is it? Small bill owing?"

The request was not an unusual one. For all the rivalry among the crews of the different fishing boats, in matters that concerned their relations with the world ashore, all stood together as members of a guild. The hawk-eyed creditor, a constant menace at the Sunday-morning market, must be avoided, if possible.

"Yes, in a way," said Nat. "We don't want Jonas to know about this catch. He's got a debt he thinks he ought to pay. We want the money for the cockfight."

"We won't say no to that," Moa said, with a grin. "You ought to get around three thousand francs for what you got there. It's as good as ours, already."

"Keep on thinking so till Sunday week," said Nat. "That's all we ask. Well, shall we load?"

The Taios dropped a couple of old tires as fenders, and the launches were made fast, side by side. The tuna were then transferred to the larger boat, handled carefully to prevent bruising. They tallied seventy-six, most of them between forty and fifty pounds.

"Which of you's going in with us?" Moa asked, when the transfer was completed.

"I am," said Chester, as he leaped across. Nat returned to the *Zimba*, the lines were cast off, and the two boats drifted apart.

"Remember, Moa," Nat called back. "The Tuttles had no luck today."

Moa nodded and waved his hand. His brother, Tihoti, at the helm, pushed in the *Hina's* clutch and spun the wheel, opening the throttle as he did so. Her bow rose as she gathered speed, sweeping round in a half circle to head for Papeete, twenty miles distant. The throttle was then pulled to the end of its ratchet, and the *Hina* responded with a full twelve knots. Chester knew that this showing-off was done for his benefit. The Taios had bought the *Hina* during his absence from Tahiti, and this was his first time aboard. He was bound to make his acknowledgments.

"Not b-b-b-bad, Moa," he said. "She's got twice the *Zimba's* speed. With a bu-bu-bu-boat like this you ought to get all the fish. But twelve knots didn't seem to do much good t-t-today, did it?"

"Crow while you got a chance," Moa replied. "You don't often have it. Slow down, Tihoti," he called to his brother. "All I say, Chester, is take good care of what you get for these tuna. Don't go spending it for something foolish before the fight. We need that money."

"Call it three thousand francs — will you cover it?"

All of the *Hina's* men had gathered to listen to this conversation and to be near Chester, whom they had known from boyhood. Tihoti glanced back.

"Cover it? Is that what you said?"

"That's ju-ju-just what I said."

"All that and as much more as Tuttle-ma can scrape together."

"That's okay with us," Chester replied. "But we don't want to break you Taios. I'd kind of hate to see Emily get excited and bet money you might need. I'm telling you: your cock ain't got a chance."

The Taio contingent laughed louder and longer than before. They exchanged knowing glances, and Moa rejoined: "We been hoping you'd think so. Keep right on. We ain't worried."

"Tell me that when you've seen our bird," said Chester.

"Emily don't want to see him. None of us don't. We're willing to put up before they're shown."

"That'll suit us," said Chester.

Throttled well down, the *Hina* ploughed her way smoothly through the calm sea. The sun had disappeared behind the mountains of Moorea, sending up streamers of light that pierced the thin vapors clustered about the peaks. To the eastward, shadows were deepening in the gorges of Tahiti and flowing down over the coastal lands. Chester lolled back against the rail, enjoying this golden half-hour before the coming of dusk. His glance traveled slowly up the valleys and across the high plateaus.

"Pretty, ain't it?" he observed, with a nod toward the land. "No place like Tahiti, and I've seen 'em all."

The scene struck Moa as commonplace enough, but he nodded agreement. He drew a large clasp knife from his pocket and whetted it pensively on the sole of his bare foot.

"Well, Chester, time we was cleaning them fish."

The launch was slowed down once more, so that they could finish their task at sea. Dusk faded to night, and the lights of the little town ahead twinkled along the waterfront. It was past eight when the guiding lights fell into line and the *Hina* turned to enter the passage. A little crowd of Saturday-night strollers gathered as she approached the sea wall where half a dozen fishing launches were already moored. The Taio boat was the last in that night.

"What luck, Moa?"

"A few tuna."

"Where'd you get 'em?"

"Off Tiarei," said Moa, alluding to a region thirty miles from where the catch was made. There was a laugh from several fishermen lounging on the sea wall.

"Sure you did," one replied. "We're just back from Tiarei ourselves. You was right there with us, wasn't you?"

They looked down at the launch as she was made fast for the night.

"A *few,* did you say!"

"And all tuna! Moa, you been shot with luck today! We all came home empty."

"You got all there is. Don't let 'em jew you down at market. They'll fetch fifty francs apiece if you hold out."

"We ain't going to give 'em away," Moa replied.

"Chester, what you doing in the *Hina?*" a third man asked. "You ain't fishing for Emily?"

"Thought I'd go out with 'em for one day and bu-bu-bu-bring 'em a little luck. The Taios need it."

Tihoti, who was helping tie the fish in pairs, gave him a jab with his elbow for this ungrateful thrust. "We'd have caught twice as many if we hadn't had a Tuttle along," he said.

The first lot were now slung on a stout oar, a load of well over four hundred pounds. Moving at a quick shuffling gait, Moa and Farani Taio carried the fish to the market place, where they would hang, guarded by a policeman, until half-past five in the morning. Chinese shopkeepers, standing in their doorways, glanced at the fish keenly, estimating the price in advance. Citizens with their wives and children, out for after-dinner strolls, stood by to let the fishermen pass, but although Moa's face wore the expression of a man to whom the carriage of his fish to market was no more than the conclusion of a long day's work, he missed no murmured comment, no glance of interest.

Chester and the others, on board the launch, were enjoying the same agreeable publicity. When most of the launches had come home empty, the fishermen of a lucky one by no means regretted that the townspeople should know of their catch in advance. Men strolled down from the brightly lighted veranda of the Bougainville Club in the hope of a bargain on the waterfront. One of them turned a flashlight on the *Hina's* deck and surprised exclamations went up from the crowd.

"Selling any tonight, boys?"

"No, not till market time."

"Thirty-five francs for your smallest one."

"Sold!" said Tihoti Taio, with a grin. He picked up a three-inch mullet cut out of the belly of one of the tuna and offered it to the customer, a *fonctionnaire* who immediately drew back and disappeared in the darkness, followed by the laughter of the crowd.

When the last load had been carried to the market and the launch cleaned, Moa turned to Chester.

"You'll stop the night with us?" he asked.

"Raita's still in town?"

"Sure. Where else would she be? Come along. She'll be glad to see you, Chester. The rest of the boys will eat at Marcellin's."

They went up a narrow side street, dimly lighted, and Moa pulled open a whitewashed gate, leading Chester into his town establishment. Like many of the fishermen, he had a wife at home, in the country, and another in Papeete. The fact that his married wife, who lived with Emily at Tarahoi, had borne him no children justified, in his mother's eyes, the large family he had reared with Raita. Though well aware of one another's lineage, age, appearance, and possessions in the way of clothing, jewelry, and the like, Moa's two spouses took good care not to meet. It was otherwise with the children, who often visited their grandmother at Tarahoi, where they were looked upon as members of the Taio clan in the best of standing.

The handsome young woman whom they met on the veranda welcomed Chester warmly.

"Chester *tané!*" she exclaimed. "*Ua hoi mai oé?*"

"Here I am," he replied. "Raita, you look younger than ever."

"And you're as big a liar as ever," she replied, laughing. "Where's your *popaa* wife? We thought sure you'd bring one back with you."

"One! That was the trouble, Raita: there wasn't room on the bu-bu-bu-boat, so I thought I'd better leave 'em all behind. How many children now?"

"Three more since you left."

"*Éahahoia!* You and Nat don't lose no time."

"We're trying to keep up with the Tuttles. What do you boys want for supper?"

"Anything you got, Raita," said Moa. "Whatever it is, it will be a feast to Chester, after what he's used to at home. I brought some tuna livers. Send one of the kids out for a couple of bottles of wine."

Hearing their father's voice, the children swarmed out from the back of the house, pulling their father down on the steps, where they climbed all over him.

"You know the way to the bathroom, Chester," he said. "There's clean clothes in the *armoire*. Help yourself. And remember, I'm waiting. Don't stay all night under that shower."

It was still dark when the bell announced the opening of the market, but the Sunday-morning crowd was already awaiting the signal to stream in, under the electric lights. Moving slowly around the fish department, with the air of a casual spectator, Chester made a hasty appraisal of the display of fish. Scarce and dear, he thought. A few bonito hung on the racks, and a scattering of small fish netted inside the reefs. The tuna made the only showing of the lot. The crowd passed slowly before them, an occasional voice asking Moa the price.

"Sixty francs," he announced, each time.

"Robber!" shouted a fat old lady. "I'll starve before I pay that!"

The thought of Madame Le Grange starving brought a laugh from the crowd. No one thought of buying, for another half hour, at least. The citizens of Papeete were shrewd buyers, and on each Sunday morning they played the same waiting game. They knew that the fishermen hated the business of selling and longed to dispose of their catches and enjoy their well-earned rest in the carefree atmosphere of Cornelius's bar, or at some other waterfront establishment. The fishermen knew that they knew it, and tried to appear as casual and unhurried as possible. Housewives, later on, returning home with the day's marketing, would exchange shouted inquiries with their neighbors, and she who had bought a tuna, a bonito, or a string of small fish for half a franc less than her neighbors had paid would bask in a warm glow of satisfaction for the rest of the day.

Forcing his way gently through the crowd, greeting an old friend here and there, Chester reached the tables where strings of *pahua*, or Tridacna clams, were laid out for sale. The odor of these molluscs is the richest, fishiest, of all marine smells. Chester inhaled it deep into his lungs. Even more than the perfume of the Tahitian gardenias in a wreath about the neck of a girl near by, it brought him the full, soul-satisfying realization that he was at home.

The people were beginning to buy at last, and when certain that the tuna would fetch an average of forty-five francs he left the market and returned to Raita's house for morning coffee. He found Emily Taio there, having early breakfast with her extralegal daughter-in-law.

"Well, Chester, the *Zimba* didn't do so bad yesterday," she remarked. He nodded and took his place at the table while Raita poured him a bowl of hot coffee and set before him sausage, bread and butter, and a pitcher of coconut cream.

"The boys told you?" he asked, as he ladled tablespoonfuls of sugar into his coffee. "We don't want Jonas to know. This money's for the cockfight."

"Suits me," said Emily; "but I won't promise not to tell your father."

"You'll spoil everything if you do," Chester said, earnestly.

"Bosh! He's as sure of winning as the rest of you. The money's ours whether I tell him or not."

"You ain't got a chance with our cock. I'm warning you. But if you think you have, you better not tell Jonas about this money. He says we got to pay Doc Blondin whatever we make this week. We won't have nothing to bet if he does."

Moa now came in and dumped on the table the contents of a cloth bag he carried. "All sold," he announced. They smoothed out the crumpled five- and twenty-franc notes and made little piles of the coins. Moa counted it over twice.

"Three thousand, four hundred and twenty francs. Not bad, Chester."

"*Manuia roa!*" Chester said, warmly. "We're sure obliged to you, Moa. Take five hundred for helping us out. It's only fair."

"No he won't," said Emily. "We'll have it all a week from Sunday anyway."

Moa swept the bills and coins back into the bag and tied it up with a bit of twine. "Take care of that, now! You're going home with us. Mother's right: can't have you spending any of *our* money around town."

"Tell you what, Chester," Emily said. "Leave the money with me. Then you'll be sure not to spend it."

"Good idea, Emily," Chester replied, handing her the bag. "And you wu-wu-wu-won't tell Jonas?"

Emily smiled. "I won't say that, but one thing I'll

promise: every franc of this money will be lost on your Tubuai wonder."

"That's good enough for me," Chester said. "All I say is what I told Moa: keep on thinking it till the fight comes off."

The Taio truck with the other boys in it drew up at the door. Emily rose briskly. "All ready?" Having embraced Raita and all of her grandchildren, she led the way to the street.

"I'll be in again on Wednesday, Raita," she called back. "Have the children ready. I want them to come out and spend a week."

"All right, Mother. Thanks for the taro."

Raita stood waving her hand till the car turned the corner.

CHAPTER V

ON a Friday morning, ten days before the date set for the cockfight, Paki was hastily preparing to leave on his semiannual, 300-mile voyage to Anaa, in the Low Archipelago. He was the owner of valuable lands on that coral island where his copra was cut twice a year, by a relative who worked on half-shares. On these occasions, Paki, who knew almost to a kilo the amount to expect if there had been no thieving, took passage by schooner or cutter to be present when the copra was sacked and weighed. Word had come that morning that the *Vaité*, one of A. B. Donald's schooners, would be sailing at noon, direct to Anaa, and Paki was bound to seize this opportunity for so economical a voyage. Often he was compelled to sail on vessels that called at a dozen other islands before touching at Anaa, and as passage money was paid by the day, these roundabout voyages were expensive. Jonas was to take him to town in the truck, and Effie was now getting his things together. She had assembled the clothing he would need and was making a neat stack of it which she tied up in a *pareu* cloth.

"There. Your *otaa* is ready," she said.

"I'll be gone two weeks, maybe three," said Paki, after a moment of reflection. "You got eleven tins of beef and nine salmon, four kilos of sugar, two tins of butter, and plenty of tea and coffee. I told Ah Sin to leave a loaf of bread morning and evening. Take care of the sugar. Don't you give none to Jonas-ma."

Effie's face flushed. "I'll do what I please. Here's Jonas giving you a ride to town and you talk like that!"

"I paid for the gasoline."

"Was there ever such a miser!" his wife said, witheringly. "And where's the money for me? Do you expect me to live three weeks without a franc?"

"What you want it for? You got everything you need."

Effie stood with her hands on her hips, looking at him in so contemptuous a manner that Paki was unable to meet her glance. "Well," he said, grudgingly. He reached in his pocket and drew forth a twenty-franc note which he handed to his wife. She threw it on the floor, taking care, however, to cover it with her bare foot.

"Twenty francs! That's all, is it? And I wash your clothes, cook your food, slave for you from morning to night! Why did I ever marry such a penny-squeezer? I had a hundred chances and I picked you and still live with you! But one of these days, you undersized *oura*, you'll find yourself without a wife! There's nobody else would have you and don't you forget it!"

Effie was working herself into one of her real tantrums. She endured Paki well enough except on such occasions as this when she saw his more thrifty nature at its worst. For all her anger, she did not forget to stoop, pick up the twenty-franc note, and thrust it into the bosom of her dress. Paki took this opportunity to glide into the house. On the lagoon-side veranda, close to his workbench, stood a small safe, salvaged from the wreck of a sailing vessel, which he had bought years ago. Glancing warily over his shoulder, he twirled the combination, hastily pulled open the door, and stripped from a large roll of bills on the shelf inside a sum sufficient for the most economical of voyages to Anaa and back. He had just pocketed the money when Effie appeared. She came on with a rush; Paki had barely time to close the heavy door of the safe and give the combination a swift whirl, his expression of alarm changing to a triumphant grin. In a fury of disappointment, Effie made an open-handed swing at his head, but Paki ducked it, seized his bundle, and made a run for the road, where Jonas was awaiting him in the truck. His wife waddled desperately after him but was forced to halt when halfway to the road.

"Don't take him, Jonas!" she screamed. "Don't you dare take him! He's left me no money! . . . Jonas . . . !"

Rage and shortness of breath deprived her of further speech. Jonas was used to these outbursts. "All right, Effie, all right," he called as he thrust in the clutch. Paki was already in the seat beside him. He waved his hand with another malicious grin, and a moment later the car was far down the road.

It was midafternoon when Jonas, on his homeward journey, brought the truck to a halt before Emily Taio's gate, at Tarahoi. Several of her grandchildren, small sons and daughters of Tihoti and Farani, were playing near the house.

"Grandma here?" Jonas asked.

A little girl shook her head. "She's up the valley."

"Go fetch her, one of you."

He mounted the steps slowly and sank down with a comfortable sigh in one of Emily's wickerwork chairs, glancing around the broad veranda with a kind of sad enviousness. Everything was in its place here, neat and well-kept. The floor had been newly painted, there were fresh chintz curtains at the doorways, and ferns and flowering plants hung from the eaves in moss-lined baskets. Jonas puffed out his cheeks and let the air escape from them slowly. A vestigial instinct, inherited from old Nathaniel Tuttle, stirred him faintly, imparting to his thought a momentary somberness. Emily's earnings were, certainly, no greater than his own, nor was Tarahoi Valley bigger or richer than Vaipopo. How was the difference in family fortunes to be explained? Luck — that must be it, for the most part. The Tuttles were born unlucky. They never seemed to get ahead, no matter how hard they tried. His reflections were broken in upon by Emily's brisk voice.

"Well, Jonas: *mea maitai anei outou?*"

Jonas rose to take her hand. "All fine with us," he replied. He lowered himself into his chair once more, every withe of the wickerwork seeming to cry out as it felt his weight. "You got a neat place here, Emily."

"There's work enough to keep it so."

"How do you manage? You ain't got the houseful we have, but you've a tidy lot of grandchildren."

"I keep them outside. There's all the valley for them

to play in. They know better than to mess things up in the house."

Jonas nodded. "That'll be it, I guess. We can't seem to manage it at our place. They're everywhere, inside and out."

Emily smiled. "And why shouldn't they be, with a grandfather like yourself? You're too easy-going, Jonas. It's the children that do the managing with you."

"Shouldn't wonder. Well, they're happy; that's the main thing."

"So are mine, but they know they can't boss their grandmother. . . . Didn't I see you going by with Paki early this morning?"

"Aye. He's off to Anaa to get his copra."

"What do his lands there bring him?"

"Around sixteen tons."

"Effie don't have much good of that, does she?"

Jonas chuckled. "Paki's awful close. Can't help it, I guess, being a Tuamotu man. He left her twenty francs to get on with while he's away. . . . That was a good haul of tuna your boys made Saturday."

Emily nodded. "Better than three thousand francs' worth."

"We been unlucky the last couple of weeks. The way things are, looks to me like we'll have to call off the cockfight for Sunday."

"Oh, Jonas! Getting scared, are you?"

"Scared! You know better'n that. Your cock's licked already. But we got nothing to bet."

Emily waited for him to proceed.

"There's one thing we might do, Emily, if you're so set on having the match Sunday . . ."

"We should, Jonas. We announced it, didn't we? Everybody from Papeete to Taravao is planning to come."

"I know. We oughtn't to disappoint 'em. . . . What I was thinking was this: our vanilla crop's coming on fine; it'll be the biggest we ever had from the look of things. The auctions come in March; that ain't far off. Now if you'd loan me a thousand francs to back our cock, you could come to the vanilla auction and collect right there."

"O Jonas *rahi!*" Emily's smile broadened and she laughed aloud. "You got a cheek! Asking me to lend you money to win more from me with!"

"To win? Thought you fancied your Raiatea cock?"

"So we do. . . . Well, you can have it. I'll make it two thousand if you like. It'll all come back on Sunday, and you'll still owe it to me."

"I ought to warn you," Jonas said. "We got a wonderful cock, and he's in A-1 condition now."

Emily shrugged her shoulders. "Much obliged. I'm still willing to lend you the money. You'll take two thousand?"

He nodded. Emily went into the house, returned with writing materials, and seated herself at a table to compose a document in which J. Tuttle, Agriculturist, acknowledged receipt of two thousand francs from Madame E. Taio, agreeing to repay this sum, with interest, after the public sale of his vanilla. She handed the paper to Jonas. He read it slowly, affixed his signature, and returned it to Emily, who folded and placed the note in her purse.

When the little business ceremony was completed, a girl appeared from the back of the house with two tall rum punches on a tray. The glasses were frosted with cold and a generous amount of cracked ice tinkled within them.

"You live well here, Emily."

"You're speaking of the ice? Why shouldn't I have it? It's not dear. I have forty kilos sent out twice a week. Well, Jonas! *Manuia taua!* To the winning cock!"

"You're drinking to ours," Jonas replied, gravely. "That reminds me," he added, as he set down his glass. "The boys was saying you'd rather not have us show the birds till the bets are made."

"I did suggest it," Emily replied, in an offhand manner. "We're both so sure of winning, I thought it might add to the fun if the bets were placed first."

Jonas's heart leaped with pleasure, but he gave no outward sign. As a usual thing the birds were shown first, and what he feared was that the mere sight of the Mortgage Lifter would frighten away all possible takers of Tuttle money.

"That'll suit us," he replied, in a manner as casual as Emily's had been. "Since you suggest it, we might do it this way for once."

Emily studied her guest as he sipped his drink. She knew Jonas better than he knew himself, and her liking for him equaled her understanding of his nature. She felt a little guilty, thinking how she had abetted his sons in concealing the facts about the tuna catch. But she had made them no promises, and she now decided that it was her duty to tell their father the truth. She had little doubt as to what Jonas would decide to do with the money, but it was only right that the decision should be his. He would then have no cause to reproach her at some later time.

"There's something I must tell you, Jonas. It was your boys who caught the tuna on Saturday. They didn't want you to know."

Jonas straightened up in his chair. "*Éahahoia!* And why not?"

"They wanted to keep the money to bet on your cock, and they were afraid you would use it for something else."

"Who's got it?"

"The tuna sold for three thousand, four hundred and twenty francs. They gave me the money to keep for them till Sunday."

Jonas shook his head. "My boys are a handful," he remarked, sadly. "A fine trick to play on their father!"

Emily left the room and returned with the money, which she placed in his hands. "There it is," she said. "You can tell them I've told you or not, as you please. I made them no promises."

Jonas stowed the cloth bag in a side pocket. He then drained his glass and took up his hat.

"Glad you did, Emily. But I won't say nothing to them. Not now, anyway."

"Don't blame them too much. Their intentions were good, Jonas. They're as sure as you are about winning. As I said, there's three thousand, four hundred and twenty francs in that bag. They wanted to give you a big surprise. They all expected to hand over to you just twice that amount, after the match."

And with this parting word for Jonas to ponder over on his way home, Emily bade farewell to her visitor.

Jonas felt that no time was needed in coming to a decision. He was shocked, put out, by what the boys had done. It was the first time anything like this had happened. There was nothing dishonest about it; he had to admit that. On Sunday they meant to give him just twice what they'd got for the tuna. But it couldn't be that way. No. Tomorrow morning, the first thing, he'd go into town again. He had Emily's two thousand francs to bet with. He would add a thousand of the tuna money to that. The rest was going to Dr. Blondin. He saw himself walking into the doctor's office and laying two thousand, four hundred and twenty francs on his desk. "We've had some luck, Doctor," he heard himself saying. "And Monday morning, around this time, I'll be in here with six thousand more. You can count on it."

But by the time Jonas turned into the drive at Vaipopo, he had decided that the odd four hundred and twenty francs might as well be added to the cock-fight money. Two thousand was a good round number. That's what he would take to the doctor.

He ran the truck into the shed. Ru came out to meet him, unscrewed the cap from the gas tank, and thrust in the measuring stick. He held it up: the end was barely wet.

"You'd have been stuck if you'd had another hundred yards to go," he said.

"It's all right, long's I didn't have. Where's the rest of the boys?"

"*I uta*," said Ru, with a nod up the valley.

"Who's got Nellie?" Nellie was the Tuttle horse.

"Grandma went to Paca this afternoon, to see the minister's wife. André drove her up in the surrey."

"Tell André, when he comes back, not to turn Nellie loose. I got to go to Papeete again, first thing tomorrow, and I want to go in the surrey. I don't get a morsel of pleasure driving the truck. I'm never sure I'm going to get all the way. Had to stop three times coming home."

"What's wrong?" Ru asked.

"I guess it's the carburetor. Have a look at it, Ru."

"I will, in the morning. Fana's working out the cocks this afternoon. I want to see 'em."

"You're not going to see 'em," Jonas replied, firmly. "You'll stay right here and fix that engine. Why didn't you boys go fishing? The Taios are out."

"Nat said it was no use. He had a look offshore. No birds up."

"He fancies himself, Nat does," Jonas remarked, with a touch of heat. "I saw any amount of birds as I was coming home. And not a mile past the reef."

"Jonas, can't I go up to see the workout? I know what's wrong with the engine. Won't take me half an hour to fix it."

"Then you get right busy at it," his father replied, and left him.

Ten minutes' walk up the valley was a glade near the vanilla plantation, bordered on one side by Vaipopo River, flowing quietly beneath *mapé* and *burau* trees, after its swift descent from the higher lands beyond. Coops for the various cocks were scattered about this secluded spot. The training table, well padded and about five feet long, stood under an open shed by the river-bank. Jonas found Nat, Chester, and Fana at this place. The two older brothers were watching critically while Fana walked the Mortgage Lifter back and forth, one hand under his breast, the other pressing lightly down on his back. This exercise, designed to strengthen the muscles of the legs, was continued for some little time. Fana then took the cock by the legs and tilted him backward over the edge of the table, forcing him to flap his wings.

Presently he let the bird rest, stroking him gently.

"How's he look to you, Jonas?" he asked.

His father reached across to feel the bird's hard breast muscles, observing with satisfaction how close the plum-age lay, the fierce brightness of his eye, the redness of trimmed comb and wattles.

"You got him in fine shape," he replied. "There's no man on Tahiti can beat you training, Fana. I'm bound to say that. Let him buckle a time or two when he's rested. Try him with that *tipapé* cock of Ru's."

Chester fetched a fine silver-spangled cock, the best of the Tuttles' native birds. Padded-leather muffs, like tiny boxing gloves, were made fast over the spurs of both cocks. After a moment of billing the antagonists were released.

They crouched, heads lowered, hackles raised; then like a flash the Mortgage Lifter attacked. Once, twice, three times, they met in mid-air, breast to breast. Fana sprang for his bird, but before he could seize his legs, the imported cock had leaped at the other once more and pecked out one of his eyes as they were disengaged. Chester gave a cry of dismay and snatched up the wounded bird.

"I never saw his beat," Jonas said, solemnly. "Too bad about Ru's cock."

"It don't matter so much," Chester replied. "We won't need him, now we gu-gu-got the Mortgage Lifter. What you feeding him tonight, Fana?"

"A little corn and a couple of oysters. And this is his day for cheese. Wish we had a million francs to bet on him."

Their father was thinking the same thing. His indignation toward the boys, for hiding the tuna money, gradually vanished. After all, their purpose had been to give him a double pleasure when the time came to confess. Nevertheless, Blondin was to receive a thousand francs just as soon as he could get to town in the morning. For the doctor's own sake it would be wrong to pay him more at this time. There was no doubt of it. Not a cock on all Tahiti could stay five minutes with the Mortgage Lifter.

"Put him away, Fana, and come along down soon's you've fed him. Supper's about ready."

The following morning, after his early coffee, Jonas seated himself in his deck chair on the back veranda.

He had his mail-order catalogue on his lap and had just settled himself for half an hour's enjoyment when André came round from the front of the house.

"All ready, Jonas, any time you are," he said.

"What's that?"

"Ru said you was going to town this morning. The surrey's out in front."

"Oh. . . . I meant to tell you, André. Guess I won't be going after all. Not this morning, anyway. Maybe tomorrow. I'll let you know."

CHAPTER VI

It was half-past eleven when Jonas and his family came home from church. He walked first, with Mama Ruau, followed by Ropati in his wheelchair, then the others in indiscriminate fashion, the babies in arms, the small children kicking up the dust with their bare feet, all of them seemingly determined, despite their elders, to soil their Sabbath clothes thoroughly before they reached home. The church was little more than a quarter of a mile beyond the Tuttle house, so that the family, Ropati excepted, always walked to service unless some special occasion demanded the service of the truck or the surrey. Ropati had been crippled for life in a fall from a coconut palm when he was ten years old; nevertheless, he was among the gayest and most useful members of the household. To their lighter hours he contributed his splendid bass voice, for singing, and his skill with the nose flute. In addition to these accomplishments, he was an expert net maker and repairer. He was as useful to the family as any of the boys. His wheelchair was one of Paki's mechanical masterpieces, supported on a pair of motorcycle wheels, and propelled by a lever which turned the axle through a connecting rod. Two small front wheels steered the vehicle.

Jonas was a sincerely devout man, in the Tuttle

fashion. As an indication of the position he occupied in the affairs of his village and district, it may be said that, while he had never been made an elder of his church, he was, nevertheless, looked upon as such: an elder without portfolio. And although he had never been elected chief of the district, there was no man in it who was listened to in local matters with greater attention and interest. This position suited him; he had the rewards and none of the responsibilities of office. Had he been an elder of the church, chief, or even subchief of the district, he would have been compelled to assume an irksome dignity unsuited to him. Occupying no public position, he had greater influence with his friends and neighbors than those who did, with the added advantage that he was free to be himself. None of those who saw him trudging home from church at the head of his clan thought it at all unseemly that, later in the day, they would see him again at the cockpit in Vaipopo Valley. He was at home in either place, and belonged to both.

Sunday dinner, usually a long-drawn-out affair with the Tuttles, was quickly dispatched on this occasion. No man loved his food more than Jonas, but even he ate hastily and absent-mindedly. All of the family, his mother excepted, were in the same state of subdued, deeply stirred expectancy. Mama Ruau was no lover of cocks in their capacity as fighters. Egg-fertilizing cocks were among the most valuable possessions a family could have, but these others, treasured so highly by the men of her family, were worse than useless. They knew her feeling about them, but she had long since said all that could be said against Sunday matches or any other matches. Their infatuation with the sport was incurable. She could do nothing more except to insist that cocks and cockfighting should not be discussed in her presence. Effie was as bad as the men, which was Mama Ruau's one grievance against her only daughter.

It was generally known that the match to be held on this Sunday afternoon would be something out of the ordinary. Spectators began arriving, on foot and in vehicles, while the Tuttles were still at their noonday meal. Several chartered trucks, converted into coaches for the occasion, had already arrived from Papeete. They were crowded to capacity, their passengers, in holiday mood, singing as they came. Chinamen, appearing mysteriously from nowhere, set up their booths where watermelon, ice cream, cakes, and other refreshments could be had. Ah Sin, the Vaipopo bread baker, was there with a wagon of his own. While he entirely disapproved of the Tuttle love for cockfighting which kept the family continually in his debt for bread, he felt it all the more a reason why he should turn such occasions to account; and often he made more at these Sunday matches than a full week of breadmaking and distributing would produce.

Emily and her oldest son, Moa, were the first of the Taios to appear. They had come before the rest of their family to settle the preliminaries. Chairs and benches were brought to a shady spot, where Jonas refreshed his rivals with the cool liquor of freshly plucked green coconuts. It was an unwritten law on the island that there should be no drinking at a cockfight, and

Jonas was as particular as Emily herself in observing the law, even to a point beyond what the spirit of it required.

When they had discussed other matters for some little time, Emily turned to her host.

"We agreed, Jonas," she said, "that the bets for this fight should be placed before we show the birds."

Jonas nodded. "It was your own suggestion, Emily. I agreed, as you say, and I'll stick to it."

"Very well. How much money do you wish to place on your cock?"

Jonas leaned back, gazing into the checkered shade of the mango tree above them. "We got a pretty good cock," he said, presently. "I warned you about that, Emily."

"*Maururu*. Well?"

"We got five thousand four hundred francs says he's a better cock than the Taios have or ever will have."

"Good. I'll cover it," Emily replied, quietly. "Cornelius, will you hold the stakes?"

Cornelius, the proprietor of the Bon Ton Bar, in Papeete, and a great follower of the sport, readily agreed to act. Emily took out a purse of finely woven pandanus leaf, and counted out the larger part of the sum in crisp five-hundred-franc notes. The Tuttle stake, of various denominations from five- to one-hundred-franc bills, took longer to count, but at last all was checked and placed in the barman's custody.

"You seem pleased with your bird, Jonas," said Emily.

"So we are," said Jonas.

"Pleased enough to bet something more on him? I'll cover anything you want to put up."

A murmur of astonishment went through the crowd that had gathered around the principals in this affair. Five thousand francs on a side was an extraordinary wager for island folk, even for such wealthy ones as Emily Taio. That she was willing to risk more, to the farthest limit of Tuttle-ma's capacity to bet, caused a stir. But all knew the somewhat tarnished quality of the Tuttle fortunes, and a moment of reflection convinced the spectators that Emily was, probably, safe enough in making this proposal. It was a mere gesture on her part, a way of showing off before her less wealthy neighbors.

Jonas gazed at his bare toes. What a pity, he thought. Here was the chance of a lifetime and he couldn't take it. Moa Taio spoke up.

"How about your accordion, Chester? Willing to risk it?"

Chester was so eager to accept that not a word would come. He looked appealingly at his father, who turned at once to Moa.

"What'll you put up against the accordion?"

Emily spoke for her son as Jonas had for his. "It's secondhand, of course," she said. "However, as Moa wants it, I'll stake three thousand francs against it."

Chester now found his voice.

"Th-th-th-three thousand?" he exclaimed. "I pu-pu-pu-paid two hundred and s-s-s-sixty-eight dollars for it in Frisco. That's better than eight th-th-thousand francs."

After a prolonged discussion, Emily agreed to raise the bet to four thousand, which was accepted. Then Effie took a sudden resolution, surprised that she had not thought of it before.

"You've still got money to bet, Emily?" she asked.

"As long as there's something worth having to put up against it."

"*Mea maitai!* You know my furniture. There's my brass bed, my wardrobe, my new bicycle, my Wilcox sewing machine. I'll bet the lot if you'll cover them for what they're worth."

A gasp went up from the spectators. This was to be a historic match and no mistake. Nat gave his aunt an enthusiastic slap in the middle of her broad back, and Jonas beamed approval. Effie's possessions were carefully appraised, and Emily pushed across the table to Cornelius a stack of bills from a seemingly inexhaustible supply.

No sooner had this latest wager been covered than a distant rhythmic booming was heard, far down the road, growing more and more distinct. It was the other Taios announcing their approach from Tarahoi with bass drums and bamboo drums. Effie, immediately stirred by the sound, sprang to her feet, facing Emily with her hands on her hips, her eyes challenging and scornful. She began to dance in time to the far-off drumming. Emily leaped from the bench to accept the challenge. She was no longer the dignified woman of business. With her head thrown back and her eyes shining, she danced her defiance in a way that brought cheers from the delighted audience. This was what they liked:

good friends and good sportsmen on both sides, and their women dancing confusion to their opponents. The Taio truck turned into the drive and came to a halt, discharging a noisy band of men, women, and children, almost as numerous as the Tuttles. Tihoti Taio remained on guard beside a mysterious coop which was covered with a red cloth. Jonas stepped forward to greet the folk from Tarahoi.

The Vaipopo cockpit, where most of the important matches on the west coast of Tahiti were held, was on the Tuttle land, across the river and about two hundred yards from the house. A dense thicket concealed it from the road. Tuttles and Taios, in a mingled noisy throng, now took the short cut across the stream. An unusual number of devotees were already gathered in the hidden clearing. Some held cocks for the preliminaries which the crowd was inspecting while they waited. The cockpit itself was a circular space about twenty feet in diameter, floored with sand well packed, and enclosed by a low fence. The railing surmounting it offered good elbow rests for the spectators. There were a number of benches for participants and the more notable visitors.

Jonas and Emily strolled about, shaking hands and exchanging greetings with their friends. Announcement was made that the Tuttle and Taio cocks would not be shown until after the other matches were over. Ropati drove his wheelchair along the path at a smart clip, and a place was made for him next to the barrier. Jonas and Emily took their customary ringside seats, and the spectators, a crowd of between two and three hundred, gathered closely around. A preliminary match was being made, cautiously, and with true Tahitian disregard for time. The trainers, two young stevedores from town, subjected one another's birds to a scrutiny as deliberate as it was minute. The fight agreed upon, the betting began, each bettor privileged to examine the birds as long and thoroughly as he desired. At last the owners stepped over the barrier, billed the birds for a moment, and released them on the sand.

Match after match was fought to a decision while the shadows of the coconut palms lengthened farther and farther to the east. There came a pause in the proceedings. The last of the preliminaries was over. All eyes turned to the heads of the Tuttle and Taio clans. Emily smiled brightly as she regarded her rival.

"Time we were showing them, Jonas."

"Suits me," said Jonas.

He sat, relaxed and easy, his hands clasped around his belly. He signaled Fana with a slight lifting and lowering of the eyebrows. Moa and Fana moved off briskly to fetch the two champions. Craning their necks and whispering amongst themselves, the spectators waited impatiently. Fana was the first to return. The crowd gathered around Jonas till they formed a ring three-deep. Emily waited complaisantly, with an air of indifference. At a sign from his father, Fana removed the covering of the little coop and permitted the Mortgage Lifter to step out. The cock shook himself, glanced about with fierce bright eyes as if in search of an antagonist, and crowed. A collective exclamation of wonder and delight rose from the spectators.

"*É aha ra!*"

Emily's smile faded as she stared at the bird. She turned to face the man at her side.

"Tubuai?" she exclaimed, accusingly. "That cock's from none of our islands! I know better! He's from Sydney!"

Jonas shook his head. "Frisco," he corrected, gently.

A louder murmur of interest rippled through the crowd. "Frisco! From California! *No te fenua popaa mai!*"

Fana took the Mortgage Lifter under his arm as Moa approached with the Taio warrior. Jonas moved slightly for a better view. His broad face wore an expression of interest more courteous and perfunctory than real. Squatting in the center of the ring, Moa opened the tiny coop he carried, and the Taio cock stepped into view. A second long-drawn "*É aha ra!*" went up from the spectators.

The bird was of about the same weight as the Tuttle cock, but of a different type: standing more upright, heavier in the leg, and with a look of cruelty about eyes and beak. He crowed. The Mortgage Lifter replied, struggling in Fana's grasp. Jonas's hands left his belly and gripped the bench; his eyes seemed to protrude slightly as he stared at Emily's bird. His jaw fell, but for a moment the evidence of such duplicity left him speechless.

"You can't fool me, Emily," he said, indignantly. "That ain't no Raiatea cock! Where'd you get him?"

"From Australia, Jonas," Emily replied. "I've had him these three months past."

The eyes of the two owners met. Jonas's great body shook with a soundless chuckle.

"Well, Emily, you thought of it first. Guess neither one of us is as smart as we thought we was."

"You'd like to back out now," Emily replied. "But it's too late."

"Me? Back out?" Jonas gave a snort. "That bird ain't got a chance with ours!"

The two trainers were circulating among the prospective bettors, permitting the birds to be examined and appraised. Emily looked thoughtful. The expression of Jonas's face did not betray the inner qualms and doubts stirred by the sight of the Taio cock. No match for the Mortgage Lifter, of course, but still . . . the fight wouldn't be quite the sure thing the Tuttles had counted on. There was a look of cold ferocity about the Australian cock that Jonas didn't like. Listening without appearing to listen, he was a little depressed to learn that the betting slightly favored the Taio bird, but the Tuttle morale received a great boost when Cornelius, an excellent judge of cocks, after much study, backed the Mortgage Lifter to the sum of three thousand francs. It stiffened yet more when Fana bet his guitar against Farani Taio's. Stirred into last-minute action, old Tupa bet all three of his mouth organs. Then voices were hushed and the trainers stepped over the barrier to bill the cocks. Jonas leaned forward, every faculty concentrated upon the birds. Emily, a tight-lipped smile on her face, sat motionless, chin in hand. The people pressed shoulder to shoulder around the barrier, and the trees above their heads were filled with boys, perched on every limb that would bear them. A long "Ah-h-h" went up as the champions were released.

Fitted for battle by generations of skilled selective breeding, the two cocks eyed each other warily, crouching beak to beak with hackles raised. The Taio bird attacked. They buckled in mid-air. They crouched, bloody and panting, only to leap together once more, to contend with a skill and pertinacity that brought low-voiced exclamations from the crowd. The battle was prolonged and evenly matched. Jonas seemed scarcely to breathe as he watched, clasping and unclasping his hands. Emily's small bare foot tapped the ground noiselessly. A shout went up as the Australian bird, half-blinded, retreated totteringly from his foe. They squatted, regaining their strength, pecking at the sand beside them. As the Australian bird rose, the Mortgage Lifter made for him at a trot, but in a last weak buckle, Emily's cock drove his spur into a vital part.

"*Aué tatou é!*" Jonas exclaimed, in a voice of anguish.

The Mortgage Lifter fell on his side, struggled gamely to regain his feet, and went down for good. Fana and Moa sprang over the barrier, and Emily leaped to her feet with a shout of triumph.

Scarcely able to realize the full extent of his misfortune, Jonas sat staring at his feet, drawing in and expelling his breath in long inaudible sighs. The Mortgage Lifter, declared by experts to be invincible, was dead, and the Tuttle fortunes, so bright in prospect, had fallen with dizzy speed to an all-time low.

Jonas rose heavily. "Come over to the house, Emily."

The sun was near to setting and the spectators were straggling homeward in small gesticulating groups. As he walked across the brook, Jonas had a glimpse of his sister Effie on the way to her house on the beach. Her carriage, her gait, her whole general appearance of collapse, brought home yet more clearly to Jonas the nature of the disaster that had overtaken Tuttle-ma.

Tuttles and Taios assembled in the outdoor dining room. A stranger, seeing the two families at that moment, and for the first time, could have separated the members of one from the other without chance of a mistake. Jonas sank upon a bench. Virtue seemed to be oozing out of him, but not to be lost in the wide air. It was being sucked into Emily's substantial frame as fast as it escaped from that of Jonas.

"Well, Emily," he admitted. "You've cleaned us out this time."

Cornelius smiled wryly as he handed the winner her gains. "It ain't often I'm wrong in judging cocks," he said. "There's my three thousand to go along with Jonas's lot. I ain't complaining. It was worth it, to see such a fight as that."

Emily opened her capacious handbag and stowed her winnings neatly inside.

"Live and learn, Cornelius," she replied, briskly. "I'll be on hand, Jonas, when your vanilla's sold." She turned to her sons. "Get your instruments, boys; then we'll go down and pick up Effie's things."

Chester handed over his piano accordion.

"You got to give me lessons, Chester," said Moa, as he took the instrument.

"Lessons?" said Chester. "Nu-nu-not me! You can learn to p-p-play it yourself."

The Taios climbed aboard their truck. Jonas followed them down the drive and stood watching while the vehicle was backed up to Effie's veranda. The brass bed, polished to a dazzling splendor by Paki's hands, was taken apart and placed on the truck, followed by the wardrobe with its mirror of plate glass and the sewing machine. Farani Taio's wife took the bicycle to ride it home. Effie came down the steps of her sacked house and joined her brother by the mango tree.

In silence they watched the Taio truck return to the Broom Road and head toward Tarahoi. Moa was fingering the piano accordion with the hands of a novice, drawing from it sounds no more discordant than Chester's thoughts. The Taio drums struck up. Emily, who stood near the tailboard, gave a shrill whoop of triumph, grinned at Jonas and his sister, placed her arms akimbo, and began to dance. This was more than Effie could bear. She did a smart about-turn to present her back to the Taios; then, leaning over, she flipped her skirts in a gesture of contempt and defiance that brought a shout of delight from the triumphant Taios.

Jonas turned his head slowly. Tupa was approaching from the other side of the road.

"Tea's ready," he announced, glumly. . . . "But they ain't no sugar for it."

CHAPTER VII

DR. BLONDIN, returning home from an evening call, found the attorney, Maître Dorme, awaiting him on the veranda. Dorme, an old friend of the doctor, glanced up as he heard his step and laid aside the magazine he had been looking through while he waited.

"Finished for the evening?" he asked.

The doctor smiled wearily. "Expectant mothers granting it," he said. "I'll be with you in a moment."

He returned presently in his faded smoking jacket and the beret he wore of an evening to protect his bald head from the coolness of the night breeze that came down the Mission Valley after set of sun. The doctor was a thick-set man of fifty-six whose clear grey eyes gave evidence of the brightly burning flame of life within. The son of a doctor who had come to Tahiti as a young man, Blondin had gone to France for his education and had returned to take over his father's practice. He had never had time to marry and lived alone in his shabby little house on a side street leading away from the waterfront. The house was kept by an old native woman, Maria, both cook and housemaid, his servant for nearly thirty years.

Dorme and the doctor had met when the two were studying in Paris, and it was the latter who had persuaded his friend, a dozen years later, to come to Tahiti and establish a law practice there. The attorney was a tall, stoop-shouldered, cadaverous man. Poor health and long experience in his profession had given him a somewhat jaundiced attitude toward mankind. The one close friendship of his life was that with Dr. Blondin, whom he loved and respected, although his attitude toward him was designed to conceal his deeper feelings.

Maria entered with a tray which she set on a small table at the doctor's side.

"You'll have a whiskey?" Blondin asked.

"If you insist. Half an inch — no more! And plain water, if you please. . . . What kind of a day have you had?"

"The usual kind. Delivered a fine child half an hour ago, the third since morning."

"Native, I suppose?"

"Yes. The race is increasing, Dorme. They're doing much better than hold their own in these days; on Tahiti, at least."

The attorney grunted. "You say that as though you approved of it."

"Approve? To be sure I do. My father believed that this branch of the Polynesian race was doomed to go the way of the Marquesans, but some mysterious law of Nature seems to have been at work here. They're on the up track again."

"The up track to what?" Dorme asked. "The overpopulation that Wallis and Cook and Bougainville found here a century and a half ago? To the infanticide practiced then to keep their numbers within bounds?"

"They've a long way to go before danger of that is

again reached," the doctor replied. "My hope is that
the Government at home means to reserve the Marquesas
for the overflow, when the time comes, from other groups
in French Polynesia. No more enlightened policy could
be adopted."

"Hmmmm!"

Blondin set down his glass. "Just what is the significance of that comment?" he asked.

"I was looking into the future," the attorney replied.
"I was thinking of such islands as Hiva Oa, Nuku Hiva,
Fatu Hiva, peopled with increasing tribes of . . . of
. . . well, your Tuttles, let us say, for one clan. Strikes
me there are enough and to spare here without scattering
them through all Oceania."

"Enough? You're wrong there," the doctor replied,
heartily. "There will never be enough Tuttles in the
world."

The attorney gave an exasperated snort. "You tell me
that!" he exclaimed. "Of all the worthless families . . . !" He broke off, as though at a loss to estimate, properly, the vast extent of Tuttle worthlessness.

"And yet, you sit at table, three times a week, I'll
venture to say, with baked fish, broiled fish, curried fish,
most of it of the Tuttle boys' providing," the doctor
replied. "It's a kind of worthlessness, if you must call
it that, which we Europeans could not well dispense
with."

"Of *your* providing, if the truth were known," said
Dorme.

"Nonsense!"

"Blondin, tell me this. It's none of my business, of

course. I merely ask as a matter of curiosity; I should like to know the full extent of your imbecility. How much do they owe you now?"

The doctor laughed. "A tidy sum, I admit."

"I know, but how tidy? Twenty thousand francs?"

"No, no," the doctor replied, with a deprecatory wave of the hand. "Seventeen thousand and some odd."

"Not one franc of which you will ever see again," Dorme said, warmly.

"Oh yes I will. As a matter of fact, Jonas and I have an agreement now. He's to repay me at the rate of two hundred francs a week."

"And when was this agreement made?"

"Three weeks ago, or thereabout."

"Since which time, no doubt, he has been right on the mark with the promised payments?" Maître Dorme leaned forward in his chair, enjoying his friend's discomfiture. "None of the money was squandered, I suppose, on the cockfight which took place last Sunday? Don't tell me you haven't heard of it; the whole island's been talking of little else all week."

Blondin nodded. "Yes, I knew of it. But there's this to be said: if the Tuttles had won, Jonas would have been in to see me before the day was over, the winnings in his pocket. I know him well enough to believe that."

"To believe it? To hope it, you mean, and with small ground even for hope. And now they're cleaned out, worse than they've ever been. You've not seen Jonas, of course?"

The doctor shook his head.

"And you won't see him, that's certain, unless he has the brazenness to come in for another touch."

Blondin smiled. "Don't call it that. I always feel guilty, after one of Jonas's visits, when I've doled out to him fifty or a hundred francs, knowing with what gusto he could spend ten times the sum, whatever it might be. It warms my heart to know that there are such people in the world, with a capacity for day-to-day enjoyment of life that puts the rest of us to shame."

"Enjoyment? Precisely: at other people's expense."

"You don't know the Tuttles as I do. Many a generous act have they performed . . ."

"Once more, precisely: at other people's expense."

Dr. Blondin threw out his hands, as much as to say: "I can see it's useless to argue the matter. You wouldn't understand."

The attorney rose from his chair, took a turn up and down the room, his hands behind his back, and seated himself once more.

"Blondin, I'm going to ask a favor. Will you grant it? You can, easily."

"In whose behalf?"

"The Tuttles'. I want you to take a mortgage on their land."

"A mortgage! Good God . . . !"

"Wait! Let me finish. I know what you'd say: land is the Tahitian's most sacred possession. Natives without it have lost their reason for living, and the rest of it. I know all that as well as you do; better, perhaps, being an attorney. But it's high time, after more than a century and a half of contact with Europeans, that some of them were learning the sanctity of a money obligation. And there's no family on all Tahiti in greater need of the lesson than your precious Tuttles. You've demoralized them with your easy-going ways in this matter. Can't you see that? Why should they care how the money they earn slips through their hands? There's always Doc Blondin to call on when a pinch comes. And they will come, more and more often, unless I can persuade you to take a firm stand against them. It isn't as though they couldn't pay their debts. Many a time I've seen them take in five hundred, a thousand, two or three thousand francs with a single catch of fish, sold at the market."

"But remember the size of the family," Blondin replied. "What with . . ."

"I've no doubt of that being Jonas's stock argument," the attorney interrupted; "but it will no more hold water than his pockets will hold money. And what of yourself, my friend? What of the X-ray machine you have dreamed of so long? It's absurd, your having to send your patients to the hospital for examinations which might a great deal better take place in your own surgery. You yourself have told me that you could buy a machine for thirty thousand francs that would serve your needs admirably. Then why not have it? I don't know what you lack of the sum, but I'll make a guess that, if the Tuttle debt were canceled, the X-ray would be ordered by the next mail. Isn't it true?"

The doctor nodded. "Yes, I'm short around fifteen thousand francs of the purchase price. But my dear fellow! A mortgage . . . !"

"For their own good," his friend urged. "I want you to put the fear of the Lord into their hearts, and the fear of the Law. I'm not asking you to foreclose, if it should come to the point. I know you too well to expect that you'd ever consent. But I want the Tuttles to believe that you will — sincerely believe it. You'll never see a five-centime piece of your money unless you take my advice."

"How could it be done?" the doctor asked.

"I know how the title stands; I've just been looking it up at the notary's. Eight years ago, Jonas's mother deeded the land to her two surviving children, Jonas and Effie. I suppose that she wanted to be free from responsibility with respect to it."

"I knew that," Blondin said. "There will be no need, then, for the mother to know of the mortgage? I wouldn't for the world trouble that gentle-hearted old lady. As a matter of fact, I doubt if she has any idea of the extent of Jonas's borrowings."

"The mother can be kept in complete ignorance of the transaction," said Dorme. "Effie will have to sign with Jonas, of course. I've no doubt that both of them will be only too glad to keep the matter secret. Well?"

The doctor reflected for some little time. "I'll do it," he said, at last. "I must, for their own sakes, as you say."

"Good," his friend replied, in a relieved voice. "You won't retract? You'll place the matter in my hands? Let me go ahead with it at once?"

"You have my promise. What do you propose?"

"That we both go to Vaipopo tomorrow, if you can spare an hour or two. We needn't be gone longer than that. I'll have the papers made out, ready for them to sign." Mâitre Dorme smiled. "And then," he said, "if Jonas fails to live up to the terms of the mortgage, I'll give him the fright of his life." He rose and took up his hat. "I mean to see that you have your X-ray, my friend. You shall, too, if you don't interfere."

The Tuttle place was all but deserted the following afternoon. As there was no food in the house and no gas for the *Zimba*, the boys had gone fishing in canoes, off the barrier reef, a mile distant across the lagoon. Other members of the family were variously employed: some in the depths of the valley, weeding the taro beds, under Mama Ruau's supervision; some in gathering *mapé* nuts for feeding the pigs. Others had been absent since dawn, on a search for oranges and mountain plantains which grew wild in the upland valleys, miles distant from the coast. Only Jonas and his cousin, Ropati, were in the house, Ropati in his wheelchair on the front veranda, where he was busy mending a casting net, Jonas stretched out in his deck chair on the back veranda, turning through the pages of an old mail-order catalogue.

The catalogue provided Jonas with a never-failing source of pleasure in his leisure hours. Wetting his huge splay thumb, he would turn the pages slowly, examining the illustrations of automobile tires with their beautiful treads, farm implements, musical instruments, household furniture, engines, paint for dwellings and outbuildings — the thousand and one desirable articles which he dreamed himself ordering and enjoying. He saw the family mansion completely refurnished, in all its former splendor, with magnificent beds, wardrobes, mirrors, cabinets, dining tables with chairs, sideboards, and china closets to match. Often he would so lose himself in his dream as to provide himself with paper torn from one of his grandchildren's school exercise books; then, with a stub pencil, he would compose a letter beginning: —

MONTGOMERY-WARD & COMPANY,
CHICAGO.

DEAR SIR:

I enclose a draft for $4982.54, for which please send me . . .

and then would follow a long tabulation of wanted articles ranging from windmills to mouth organs.

He was in the midst of such a dream on the present occasion when he was awakened by Ropati, who came through the hallway from the front veranda at such a speed that his wheelchair caromed from one of the veranda posts, turned on its side, and spilled the occupant out at his cousin's feet.

Jonas glanced up from the catalogue, a beatific smile still on his face; then, taking in the situation, he quickly righted the chair and set Ropati in it once more.

"What's this?" he said. "You ain't been . . ."

"Jonas! Doc Blondin's coming!" Ropati exclaimed.

Jonas gazed blankly at him. "Not here?"

"Yes! He's stopped on the road a minute to talk to someone, but the car's headed for the house! Dorme's with him!"

Jonas continued to stare at his cousin. He had no doubt as to the reason for the doctor's visit: he would have heard all the details of the cockfight before this. There was no one on all Tahiti he would rather not see at that moment. The fact that the lawyer was with him was ominous. There was not a moment to spare if he were to avoid a meeting.

"I'm going upstairs," he said, and off he went, mounting the back staircase in desperate haste.

"Jonas! Wait!" Ropati wailed, in a guarded voice. "It ain't my place to see 'em!"

His cousin turned at the top of the stairs. "There ain't no time," he replied. "Tell 'em I'm sick. I can't see nobody." And with that he vanished.

He ducked into the boys' room, which was closest to the stairway, pulling off his shirt as he entered. There were no beds in the room; all the boys slept on mats on the floor. As usual in the daytime the mats were rolled, the pillows and coverlets folded inside, and stacked neatly against the wall. Seizing one of the mats, Jonas spread it quickly, shook out the coverlet, and lay down, with his head turned from the doorway. Not till then did he remember that the last excuse in the world he should have asked Ropati to offer Dr. Blondin for his nonappearance was that of illness. But there was no time now for further instructions. He heard the car halt at the front steps, and the slamming of doors as the visitors got down.

Gathering his courage, after repeated rappings coming from the front of the house, Ropati wheeled himself through the hallway.

"Oh, there you are, Ropati," the doctor said, heartily. "Isn't this rather unusual? Where's all the family?"

"Most of 'em's up the valley, Doctor. They've gone for *fei*."

"Jonas here?"

"Well, no, not exactly. That is, he *was* here, but I don't know just where he's got to."

"Having a siesta, perhaps?" the doctor suggested.

"He ain't been feeling well these few days," Ropati added.

"All the more reason why I should see him, then. I'll just step up to his room. Perhaps he's there."

Ropati racked his brain for a plausible reason for Jonas's being at a distance, but before he could find one the visitors had already mounted the front staircase leading from the living room. Having brought most of the younger Tuttles into the world, Dr. Blondin was familiar with every room in the house, but this was Dorme's first visit and he looked about him with interest. Doors stood open along the veranda and he had glimpses of large high-ceilinged rooms almost bare of furniture but scrupulously clean, with rolled sleeping mats along the walls. He laid a hand on his friend's arm.

"*Quelle maison!*" he said, in a low voice. "Like an army barrack. There's nothing left in the way of furniture?"

Blondin smiled. "Sheer luxury. Needless encumbrances. Bartered long since for the necessities of life."

Jonas's room was at the end of the veranda. The doctor rapped briskly, and, receiving no response, stepped in.

It was a spacious chamber, like the others, with walls

of discolored plaster enclosing nothing except the customary mats and one large camphorwood chest, darkened with age, that stood in a corner.

"Hmmm. Not here," the doctor remarked. He paused to reflect for a moment, then turned to his friend. "Your first visit to the Tuttle place?"

The attorney nodded.

"In that case, I'm going to take the liberty of showing you one room that remains as it was in the old days. Jonas wouldn't mind. It's the bedchamber of the original Nathaniel Tuttle. Thanks to Jonas's mother, it's not been gutted like the rest of the house."

They proceeded along the north veranda to the opposite corner of the house. The door of this room was closed but unlocked. The two men stepped in. A dim light filtered through the shuttered windows, and when his eyes had become accustomed to the gloom, the attorney noted the massive bed of black walnut, the *armoire à glace,* built on the same generous proportions. An old-fashioned *secrétaire* stood between two of the windows, and against the opposite wall was a table with a marble top, supported by legs richly carved, with gilded ornamentation long since dulled with age. A sofa had an elaborately crocheted doily over the headrest of faded green plush. On the walls hung several paintings of rural landscapes: "An Autumn Evening," "Sunday on the Farm," and the like. The one Maître Dorme examined with the greatest interest was a portrait of Nathaniel Tuttle himself.

"It was painted in the eighties, during his last visit to San Francisco," the doctor explained. "So I've been told by Jonas's mother. What do you think of the founder of the family? Plenty of character in that face, eh?"

The attorney nodded, without speaking, still gazing at the big-framed patriarch whose full beard still seemed to be crackling with vitality, and who seemed to be keeping resolute watch upon these few remaining possessions, collected with such care.

"What's become of it all?" Dorme asked.

"The Tuttle character? It's still here. I've caught glimpses of it now and again. But remember that all those sleeping mats we've seen belong to the third, fourth, and fifth generations, and additions from the maternal side of the family. Polynesia has conquered New England. Nature knew what was best, granted that the family were to remain here. 'Dilute the Tuttle blood,' she said, and did."

"You imply," his friend remarked, "that all Tahitian blood is like that which has conquered the Tuttle strain. I haven't found it so."

"You misunderstand me," said Blondin. "Polynesians vary in character as much as people of other races, but you will admit that taking thought for the morrow is not among their common qualities. It's a curious thing: Jonas's mother, who hasn't a drop of white blood in her veins, is more European in this respect than any of her children or grandchildren. The family would be among the most prosperous on the island if she could have her way."

Dorme smiled faintly. "I'm glad to hear you admit that Jonas could do with a bit more of that quality of thriftiness. Where will he be, I wonder? I shan't let you leave the place till we have this matter settled."

They returned slowly along the rear veranda and were about to descend when they caught a glimpse of a huge form, enveloped in a coverlet, lying on the floor of the room next to the staircase. The two men exchanged glances.

"Oh, Jonas," Blondin called.

No response. The massive shoulders rose and fell with an almost too perfect regularity.

Entering the room, the doctor moved softly around the sleeper until he could see his face, hidden to the eyes by the coverlet. He waited in silence, and presently the eyes opened warily, to be immediately closed again. The doctor stooped and laid the coverlet gently back from Jonas's shoulders, whereupon the sick man gave a groan. Opening his eyes once more, he gazed at the doctor with an air of patient suffering.

"Doctor?" he said, weakly, as though not quite realizing that he was there.

"Well, Jonas! What's this? First time I've ever known you to be ill. Been eating something you shouldn't have?"

Jonas shook his head feebly.

"You've got no fever. Where do you feel badly?"

"I don't know exactly. It's kind of all over me, Doctor."

"How long have you been like this?"

"Sunday night. I ain't slept hardly any since . . . not till this afternoon."

"I see." Blondin paused. "Couldn't have been too much cockfight?"

Jonas gazed mournfully at the coverlet. "You heard about it?" he then asked.

"Something. A bad day for the Tuttles, I understand. I should think you might *all* be sick."

The patient raised his eyelids and dropped them again. "I was coming to see you, Doctor, but I thought I'd better wait till I got twisted round and feeling better. Our losing the match kind of took the heart out of me."

"I can understand that. Emily Taio seems happy enough."

A flicker of returning vitality seemed to show itself in Jonas's eyes. With an effort he rose to a sitting position and bolstered himself up, with his pillow behind him against the wall.

"That's what I was wanting to see you about," he said. "We made the match because we wanted to pay off our loan so bad. If we'd won we could almost have wiped it off all at once. I was sure as anything I'd be going into town last Monday with better'n ten thousand francs in my pocket."

The doctor smiled, somewhat grimly.

"If you had won, the moment you reached town you'd have forgotten the way to my house."

"No, Doctor! Don't you think it! I'd have gone, sure as I'm sitting here!"

"Well, I'm afraid there's little need to discuss what you might have done. The question is, what do you mean to do *now*? I've really lost patience with the lot of you, Jonas. Your intentions are good, perhaps, but you never carry them out. Every time you run short

of money you come to me, and that's the last I see of
you till you need more."

"But it ain't going to be, Doctor. It'll be paid, every
franc, before the year's out. We expect to be net fishing any day now, and once the *aturé* begin to run . . ."

"All right, all right," Blondin interrupted. "You
needn't go into that. I've no doubt about the fish being
caught. What I do doubt is that I'll see any of the
money from the sale of them."

Jonas was about to interrupt, but the doctor held
up his hand. He felt guilty at speaking to Jonas in this
blunt manner, in the presence of a third party, but
having given Dorme his promise he was bound to proceed.

"Wait, Jonas. I want no more verbal promises. You've
tried my patience too far. I'm going to insist, now, on
fulfillment of some of the promises you've made in the
past. That's why I brought Maître Dorme with me
today. Dorme, you do the talking from now on."

"You will understand, Jonas," the attorney began,
"that this debt of yours is in a most irregular status
at present. You have been adding to it from year to
year, and the few payments made have always fallen
short of the amounts you have continued to borrow.
The doctor insists that no interest shall be asked of
you, a more than generous concession, in my opinion;
one which few men in his case would be willing to
grant, to say nothing of offering it freely. All the
more reason why you should feel under the deepest
obligation to liquidate the principal at the earliest possible moment."

"That's what I've always said, Monsieur Dorme. The doctor knows that. I won't have a minute's peace till we've paid every cent we owe him."

"Precisely. Meanwhile, I'm sure you will agree that it is to your interest as well as the doctor's to have this obligation secured in legal form, and its payment provided for within a definite period of time. The best means will be for the doctor to take a mortgage on your land."

If the attorney expected Jonas to demur at this suggestion, he was agreeably disappointed.

"That's just the way it ought to be, Monsieur Dorme. Don't know why I didn't think of it myself, except I was always expecting I'd get it cleared off any day."

"Good," said Dorme. "I was sure you would agree; therefore, I've brought the papers with me, ready for signature. You know, of course, the amount of your obligation. The sum is now eighteen thousand, four hundred and forty francs."

"We can pay that off easy," said Jonas. "What I was thinking would be the best way, Doctor, was to pay it all at once when our vanilla crop comes in. You remember when you was here in July, when Nat's wife had her last baby? The children was marrying the flowers then, and I told you how good things looked. The vanilla's beaned out wonderful, and with the price up the way it is, I shouldn't wonder if we got twenty thousand francs from our crop this year. Maybe any amount more."

"So the doctor himself thought," said Dorme. "It's in March, is it not, that the vanilla is ready for picking?"

"You know that as well as I do, Monsieur Dorme."

"Precisely: in three months' time. Very good. I will now read the terms of the mortgage, and if you agree to them we can get this matter settled at once."

The attorney then proceeded, Jonas listening with an air of profound relief and pleasure, as though the document whose terms were being revealed were a will drawn in his favor. In view of the family's recent losses to Emily Taio, the weekly payments Jonas had promised to make had been reduced from two hundred to one hundred and twenty-five francs, to be paid, as formerly agreed, after each Sunday-morning market. In March, when the vanilla auctions were over, the balance was to be paid in a lump sum.

"That's all right with me, Monsieur Dorme," Jonas said, when the attorney had finished. "If you got a pen handy I'll sign right off."

"Your sister, Effie, will have to sign with you," the attorney remarked.

"I'll send down for her." Throwing back the coverlet, Jonas got to his feet with surprising agility. Then, remembering that he was supposed to be ill, he said: "I'm feeling a lot better already, Doctor. Shouldn't wonder if it *was* the cockfight made me feel so miserable. I didn't see how I was going to tell you about that."

The house shook under his tread as he walked across the veranda. Several children were playing below. "Tané," he called. "Run down to Aunt Effie's house and tell her I want her. Right away!"

"And we must have a witness," Dorme continued.

"Is there anyone here who could serve? Your cousin, Ropati, of course, would not do."

"I don't want him to know, anyway," said Jonas. "There's no need to tell the rest of the family about this."

"So I think, Jonas," said Blondin. "We'll say nothing."

"Tupa's around somewhere. He can't read French, so he won't know what he's signing."

Returning to the railing, he called for the old cook, who appeared a moment later.

"He's not related to you?" the attorney asked. "Can't have a witness who belongs to the family."

Jonas scratched his head. "I'll have to think a minute. There's so many of us around here, it's hard to remember who's in the family and who ain't. And Tupa's been with us so long . . ."

After a brief conversation with Tupa, in the native tongue, he turned again to the attorney.

"No, he ain't a Tuttle. I remember, now: he was raised up from a baby by my mother's cousin's uncle and his wife, but he wasn't any kin to 'em. He was a feeding child. And when *they* died . . ."

"Tupa will do very well," the attorney said. "Have you a table here?"

Jonas looked hopefully around the bare room, as though there might have been a small table somewhere about, overlooked until that moment. "There's one in the spare room," he said. "You wait here, Tupa. I'll tell you when I want you."

He led the way along the veranda to the chamber kept sacred by Mama Ruau to the memory of her hus-

band's father. Jonas halted to throw back the shutters
of one window, forgetting the precariousness of their
hold to the frame on either side. Both shutters swayed
back unevenly, and one fell with a clatter to the floor,
the screws of the hinges drawing with them tiny rivu-
lets of wood dust. With an apologetic glance for the
lawyer's benefit, Jonas stooped to stand the shutter
against the wall before he opened the door and followed his guests into the room. They waited, convers-
ing in desultory fashion, until Effie appeared, when the
attorney explained to her the nature of the present
business. Jonas turned to his sister with a slight shrug
of the shoulders.

"If it's all right with you, Effie?" he said. "It's only
till the vanilla auctions."

"Of course it's all right," said Effie. "You're head
of the family. Where is it you want me to sign, Monsieur Dorme?"

Tupa was called in. A shaft of afternoon sunlight
fell full upon the portrait of Nathaniel Tuttle the First.
The portrait hung over the marble-topped table where
Jonas, Effie, and Tupa affixed their signatures, and by
some trick of the wavering light, the old gentleman's
beard seemed to be quivering with rage at this last in-
dignity offered him by the present chief of Tuttle-ma.
Jonas didn't notice this. He was thinking of Tupa and
of the need, on his account, for some plausible explana-
tion of this legal business. Therefore, he smiled as he
handed the pen back to the lawyer.

"There — that's done, Monsieur Dorme. I'm glad we
got it settled about the vanilla."

CHAPTER VIII

WITH no money for gas, the Tuttle boys enjoyed a breathing spell which was literally that for the eldest of the sons. Shortly after having his morning coffee Nat would retire, with a mat and pillow, to a shady spot on one of the upstairs verandas, stretch out at ease, and fall asleep, breathing deeply and noisily, for all the household activity that went on around him. Fana and Chester fished from canoes along the reef, and Ru spent much of his time in overhauling the *Zimba's* engine, against the day when, by some stroke of fortune, they could resume offshore fishing. The rest of the family went about their usual tasks. The children made their daily search for eggs; André and Pico looked after the pigs, the women gathered on the riverbank for the never-ended task of washing clothes, and the brisk thumping of their wooden mallets accentuated the stillness of the morning hours. Every member of the family, Nat excepted, had his or her work to do, while Tupa and Maitu were busy in the cook shed from dawn till dark, preparing the food which the others brought in. For all the resources, — shellfish from the reef, shrimps from the river, combined with Nature's bounty from the rich soil, — with so many to be fed, demand kept daily pace with supply and sometimes exceeded it.

Jonas was, therefore, more than content when Nat, having all but slept the clock round for a week, asked one morning: "Net in good shape, Jonas?"

"Ropati's finished going over it," his father replied. "We got it all piled, ready for paying out. I was thinking it was about time you was going up."

Jonas made the suggestion with some deference, for Nat enjoyed the reputation of being the greatest fisherman along twenty miles of coastline. It was to his knowledge, and to an instinct transcending knowledge, that Tuttle-ma owed the greater part of their fortunes at sea. He knew precisely where to go, and when, for the various kinds of fish that approached the land, and never had he been caught unaware when the *oraré* or *aturé* began to run. Jonas knew that the *aturé* were due at any time now, but he trusted Nat's instinct. He would know the day when a lookout should be kept and the village warned to be in readiness.

The Vaipopo net, five hundred meters long and four fathoms in depth, was owned by the Tuttles, although two other families had small shares in it. No event of the year was looked forward to with more eagerness than the day when the *aturé* came in. The hauling of the net required the help of most of the village and there was never any lack of assistants.

The beach opposite the Faafano Pass, where the net was kept, was nearly a mile south of the Tuttle place. Nat strolled along the road, enjoying the excitement caused by his coming, for all knew what the conch shell slung over his shoulder signified. Nat Tuttle was going on watch for the *aturé*. Small boys, eager to be noticed by him, gathered in his train, while their elders greeted him from afar or came down to the road to inquire whether or no they would dare to risk undertaking other work on that day.

"I was planning to haul my copra to town this afternoon, Nat," one of his neighbors remarked. "You think it's safe? I wouldn't want to miss the netting."

"You better ask the *aturé*," Nat replied. "They won't wait for nobody. All I can tell you is I'm going on watch."

And so he watched throughout the day. Perched among the fronds of a tall coconut palm opposite the pass, he gazed seaward while groups of natives lounged in the shade beneath. But it was not until the following morning that he blew a mighty blast on his conch shell. Fana, there beside him at the moment, and who prided himself on his keen sight, turned to his brother incredulously. "Sure you ain't made a mistake?" he asked. "I don't see a sign of 'em."

"You wouldn't," said Nat. "They're on the way right enough, but whether they'll come in or not . . ." He broke off, and putting his horn to his lips once more blew a second blast heard from one end of the village to the other, the deep vibrant note echoing and reëchoing among the distant hills. And now all up and down the road which skirted the valley mouths and serpentined around the promontories faint jubilant cries were heard, and the villagers came thronging from either direction. A group of children with drums of

bamboo which they beat with small sticks marched
along, chanting: —

> *Oraré, oraré,*
> *E pae pené te tui!*

scattering to either side as the Tuttle truck, Jonas at the
wheel, clattered up on two gallons of borrowed gas,
at its full thirty miles per hour, all but smothered
beneath the Tuttles who clung to it; and far in the
distance Ropati could be seen approaching in his wheelchair at a speed seldom equaled in that kind of convey-
ance. At the netting, Jonas was leader of the activities
on the ground, while Nat directed operations from
his perch in the coconut palm.

"Where away, Nat?" his father called.

Nat peered down through the fronds that hid him
from view.

"Just beyond the pass," he shouted. "Get ready! No
time to lose!"

The announcement caused a stir, for it often happened that the fish were long in coming into the lagoon,
the school moving along the reef and away to seaward
again before consenting to stream in through the pass.
Men, women, and children were hastening to the spot
from either end of the village; a babble of talk mingled
with exultant cries rose in the morning air, and Jonas's
voice could be heard above the clamor, giving his orders.

The net, carefully piled, was already in place on the
platform of the largest canoe in the village. Jonas stood
forward to direct the paying-out. The canoe was moved
slowly into deeper water, while sixty fathoms of stout

rope, attached to a bridle at one end of the net, was held by a group of men standing in the shallows, ready to draw in when the time should come.

"Right!" Nat shouted. . . . "Now left! . . . More left! . . . Straight ahead! . . . Wait! Stand by!"

All were silent now as the canoe moved farther and farther offshore, following Nat's directions. Other canoes, with three or four occupants in each, followed, taking stations one by one as the net was paid out in an ever-widening curve. The large canoe was now well out, the men in it dependent upon Jonas for direction. He scanned the water intently. "Steady," he would say. "Wait, wait! There's more coming! . . . Now . . . Easy, easy!"

Ru, in one of the small canoes, peered into the sun-streaked water with an exclamation of wonder. The lagoon floor with its scattered clumps of coral was not more than twenty feet below, and the sandy bottom was all but hidden by the flashing silvery bodies of the fish, darting this way and that as the canoes advanced.

"Millions of 'em!"

"*Mamu!*" his father ordered. "We ain't got 'em yet. Paddle, you others! Put your backs into it."

They moved on, across the passage, and turned slowly toward the beach once more, until the last fathom of the great net was safely out. The rope was then carried ashore to be grasped by the men waiting to receive it.

Erect on now empty platform, Jonas resembled some old Polynesian god of the sea, just risen from the deep. His naked body streamed with sweat as he stood looking toward the palm where Nat was still perched.

"How is it, Nat?"

"Never better," came the reply. "All but a few inside."

With a joyous whoop Jonas dove from the canoe and came up to lend his strength to those drawing slowly in at this end. Far offshore, scattered in a semicircle just beyond the net, were the canoes that had followed. Most of their occupants were now in the water, diving from time to time to free the bottom of the net from rocks and lumps of coral as it was drawn with infinite care toward the beach. The forty or fifty meters of open water along the drawing ropes were guarded by swarms of naked children, weaving patterns of brown legs, arms, and bodies against the white floor of the lagoon as they swam this way and that to keep the fish well within the belly of the net. Jonas stood waist-deep, pulling steadily, pausing at moments to shout instructions to the crew opposite. And slowly, slowly, the net came in.

On this same morning, at the same hour, Paki, Effie's husband, was trudging homeward from Papeete, where he had arrived from the Low Islands shortly after dawn. His voyage to Anaa had been a profitable one; his coconut lands there had yielded him nearly ten tons of copra for the six months just past. Having sacked and weighed his crop, he had returned with it by the schooner that had carried him out. The morning round-the-island bus had left Papeete before he had completed the sale of his copra, and although he had been tempted to hire a car, he could not bring himself to spend forty francs so needlessly. He decided to walk home. In an envelope, secured in his shirt pocket by safety pins, was the money he had received for his copra: eleven thousand, one hundred and twelve francs, fifty centimes.

Paki had heard, in town, of the cockfight which had taken place at Vaipopo during his absence, and how the Tuttle bird had lost. He had not paused for details, but it cheered him to think of the pleasure he would have, dragging them out of Jonas, later. Was there ever a bigger fool than Jonas? And that Fana, who knew it all, of course, and was going to win thousands of francs from Emily Taio's boys! Well, they'd had another lesson, and much good it would do them! Ru was the only one worth his salt, and even he was as crazy over cockfighting as the rest. As for Effie . . . Paki smiled to himself, thinking how wise he had been to leave no money in her hands. She would have lost every penny of it.

The sun was three hours high as he approached Emily Taio's place. Paki felt a reluctant admiration for Emily. On one side of her nature she was exactly like Jonas-ma, loving big feasts and cockfights as much as they did. But there was a streak of saving common sense in her character. Paki knew where that came from — her paternal grandfather was a Tuamotu man. It was only her Low Island blood that kept her from being as thriftless and happy-go-lucky as the Tuttles themselves. That strain pushed Emily on in spite of herself; and she had her grandfather's secret influence to thank for her well-kept plantation, her fat cattle, all the solid

material possessions that made life worth while. Paki
shook his head in exasperation as he contrasted the
Tuttle and the Taio fortunes. There was no excuse for
Jonas-ma. They were better fishermen than the Taios
and earned more than they did, but every franc was
squandered as soon as earned. And, which exasperated
him particularly, they seemed to think that was all
money was for.

Paki halted at a shrill hail and saw Emily approaching from her copra sheds. "What's all this?" he thought,
for there had never been much cordiality between himself and the Taios. Something gone wrong with the
Hina's engine, like as not. It was only on such occasions, when they needed his help, that they seemed
aware of his existence. He waited till Emily came up
on the other side of the fence.

"Home again, Paki," she observed. "And you've
walked all the way out from Papeete?"

"Why not? The road belongs to all of us."

"*Parau mau,*" Emily replied, graciously. "You're a
man of sense, Paki. I've always said it. What news from
Anaa?"

"Better than news hereabout, from what I can learn.
Tuamotu folk go to church of a Sabbath. You'll find
none fighting cocks in the afternoon."

Emily regarded him closely, but with an air of
carelessness.

"You've heard of the match, then?" She laughed
lightly. "Where's the harm in it? And we can't all
win, Paki."

Paki gave a contemptuous grunt. "It's nothing to me

who wins or loses. You got none of *my* money. I made
sure of that before I left."

Emily laughed again, more gaily than before. "I
know," she said. "You're a shrewd one, Paki. Is Effie
expecting you?"

"How should I know? What do you want, Emily?
Something wrong with the *Hina's* engine?"

Emily shook her head, the same happy smile on her
face.

"I'll be getting on, then," and, with a curt nod,
he proceeded on his way.

"Give my love to Effie," she called after him.

Paki trudged on, mumbling to himself as he walked:
"What's she want, I wonder? . . . There's something
in the wind, mark my words! She didn't stop me just
to pass the time of day. . . . It was like she was crow-
ing over me as well as Jonas-ma. . . . She's bound to
crow, give her any reason; and being married to Effie,
she lumps me in with the rest of the family. . . .
What I think is, she feels it because she can't never get
the best of me. She's put out because she got nothing
of mine at the cockfight. . . . Aye, that'll be it,
maybe."

Paki arrived hot and weary at Vaipopo, but taking
a somewhat disgruntled satisfaction at thought of the
forty francs saved by walking. There were no people
about the houses at the northern end of the village and
the Tuttle place had the same deserted aspect. The
fronds of the palms hung motionless against the midday sky, and the mango trees made pools of deep shade,
grateful to the eyes after the glare from the road and

lagoon. Turning toward the beach and his own house, he saw Tupa's daughter, Maitu, sitting under a tree, keeping watch over half-a-dozen small children who were splashing in the shallows of the lagoon. She glanced around, and, seeing who it was, turned quickly away as though frightened at sight of him.

"Where's Effie?" he asked.

There was no reply. Taking up the hem of her dress, Maitu twisted it nervously in her hands.

"You ain't deaf, are you? Where's Effie and the rest of 'em?"

"They're up at the net," said Maitu.

"Thought that was it. The *aturé's* come in, have they?"

Maitu was a patient, good-natured, inarticulate girl, loved and imposed upon by children and adults alike. The thought of what Paki would soon discover, — his half-empty house, the splendid brass bed gone, the wardrobe with its shining mirror gone, sewing machine gone, bicycle gone, — and no one but herself here to explain what had happened, was too much for her to confront. Her lips began to quiver and she burst into tears.

"Now what's all this?" Paki asked, in an exasperated voice.

"You mu-mu-mu-mustn't bu-bu-blame her too much, Paki," Maitu blurted out.

"What's wrong with you? Mustn't blame who?"

"It wasn't her f-f-f-fault. They was all sure our cock was going to win, and . . ."

Paki took her by the shoulders, shaking her roughly.

"What's all this?" he repeated. "Who you talking about? Effie?"

Maitu nodded, covering her face with her hands.

"She lost all your f-f-f-furniture, and the bicycle too."

Paki drew in his breath sharply. After a wild incredulous glance at Maitu he ran along the beach to his house.

Opposite the Faafano Passage, the net was still coming in, inch by inch. Great as the excitement had been during the encircling of the fish, it was doubled now that all realized the richness of the haul. Those nearest the net were still waist-deep in the water, and all maintained a steady concentrated pull, electrified by the ceaseless hard tremor that ran from the net, bulging with innumerable struggling *aturé,* along the ropes and into their bodies.

The upper slope of the beach beneath the trees was thronged with older people looking on at this most interesting of village events. Every family would share in the catch, for although the Tuttles, owners of the net, would receive the money for the great surplus to be sold in town, all the helpers would have their abundant rewards in fish, divided according to the numbers in each family. Vaipopo village knew the generosity of Tuttle-ma. There was nothing mean in their dealing with their neighbors.

The half-circle of canoes was drawing in. Chester was in one of these, with Fana and their Aunt Effie in the water alongside, diving repeatedly to free the bottom of the net from obstructions on the lagoon floor. Effie was in her element here; she was an excellent swimmer and could remain at this work for hours without weariness, taking such rest as she needed by the canoe, her hand resting on the gunwale. Her hair was plaited in two tight braids to keep it out of her eyes, and she wore a pair of water goggles which gave her an owlish appearance, as though she were a fat, middle-aged mermaid with a taste for literature.

Coming up from a dive, she took breath for a moment with her broad back against the straining net, treading water as she beamed at Chester, whose eyes gloated at sight of the rich spoil there before them.

"Won't the Taios be sick wh-wh-when they know about this catch!" he said. "The f-f-f-first thing I'm going to do with my share is buy back my accordion."

"*Éahahoia!*" said Fana. "What do you think your share's coming to?"

"I'll add mine to Chester's if none of the rest of you will," said Effie. "We need the accordion most."

"He can have mine too, far as that goes," Fana replied. "But what about your own things, Effie?"

"I'll make Paki buy me some more," she replied. "He's rich enough, the old skinflint!"

Fana grinned. "When'll he be coming home? I want to be on hand when he walks into your house."

"But *you* better not be, Effie," Chester said.

Their aunt gave a scornful laugh. "You think I'm afraid of that shrimp? If he wants trouble I'll give him enough! I'll put him down and sit on him till he cools off."

"Below, it's caught again," Fana warned, and down they went to free the net from a mass of dead coral.

On the beach, Jonas was everywhere at once, shouting instructions to those offshore, pausing to direct the men at the ropes. He had long since cast aside his shirt and trousers and wore only a piece of faded *pareu* cloth twisted around his great solid belly. His water goggles, attached by an elastic band, were pushing up on his forehead, holding aloft a shock of hair like a banner, a flag of triumph. He halted where Ropati was sitting in his wheelchair, Mama Ruau beside him.

"Well, Mama, what do you think now?" he asked. "We got a lucky day at last."

She gave him an anxious glance.

"It will be wonderful if we get them in," she said. "I wish the next half-hour was over. Will the net hold?"

"I spent two weeks going over it," said Ropati. "There wasn't a mesh looked weak that I didn't mend. But it won't last another season, Jonas."

"It don't need to as long as it holds for this one. Mama, didn't I tell you it was foolish worrying about Dr. Blondin's money? We can pay the whole debt off with what's out there."

"And you will? You promise me that?"

"Every penny; just as quick as we sell the fish."

"What do you reckon it'll bring?" Ropati asked.

"This catch?" Jonas paused, a rapt smile on his face as he gazed at the busy scene before them. "If there's one fish in that net there's twenty thousand francs' worth. When we get 'em in, shouldn't wonder if we find there's half as many again."

Nat and Tupa, the Tuttle cook, stood side by side at one of the ropes. There was not space for a pair of hands on either line that was not occupied. This haul would be something phenomenal. Never before, in Nat's memory, had they needed so many helpers.

"Steady," he called. "Slow and easy does it, but keep her coming in."

Tupa let go for a moment to spit on his hands. "Sacred name of Ruahatu!" he exclaimed. "There never was such a day!"

"*Mamu!*" Nat said, savagely. "Want to spoil our luck, you splay-footed idiot?"

To utter, in that tone of voice, the name of Ruahatu, one of the ancient patron saints of island fishermen, was to invite disaster, and Tupa was heaped with abuse by others on the line.

And whether or not it was Ruahatu's doing, disaster came not five minutes later. Cries of dismay were heard from those beyond the net, and at the same moment the men on the lines felt them go slack in their hands. They stared at one another, not daring to believe; then a vast communal sigh, streaked through with feminine wails, rose in the air and floated slowly seaward, after the escaping fish. The net had burst midway, in so great a rent that there was no stopping the torrent of *aturé* that streamed through it to safety. Frantic efforts were made to close the gap while the men on the lines drew in the net with desperate haste; but when at last it lay in the shallows, not more than

a dozen small fish were seen struggling in the meshes.
Jonas took one of them up between thumb and forefinger, regarding it with an air of reproach and deep
chagrin, as though this particular fish had been the
miscreant, responsible for the escape of all the others.
Fana, who was wading ashore, burst out laughing at
the sight.

"That our share, Jonas?" he asked. "Tupa'll have a
hard time making it go round for the lot of us."

"*Maamaa!*" Nat exclaimed, bitterly. "It's Tupa we've
got to thank for this! Where is he?"

But the cook was nowhere to be seen. He had stolen
away in the midst of the excitement and was well on
the road toward home.

After the first keen edge of disappointment had been
dulled, the crowd began to arrange the net, talking
and laughing good-naturedly, realizing that the joke was
on them. But Jonas needed more time to adjust himself, after the happy dreams of a few moments before.
He sat, chin in hands, speaking to no one, gazing
seaward as though believing that he might yet, somehow, wish all those myriads of *aturé* back into the net.
He was aroused by a murmur of excited voices, and
Chester seized his arm.

"L-l-l-look who's coming, Jonas! Now we'll see some
fun! Wh-wh-where's Effie?"

Striding toward them from the road with an air of
unmistakable determination came Paki, approaching
in a thundercloud all but visible to the lookers-on. Effie's losses at the cockfight were known to everyone, and
Paki's return had been awaited with increasing delight

and suspense. As he approached, the crowd parted to give him easy access to the beach, where Effie, still unaware of his presence, was standing in the shallows among the scattered groups who were piling the net. Paki ran down the long slope, his little eyes darting fiery glances to right and left as he sought his wife. They saw one another at the same instant. Paki halted within a dozen yards of her, folded his arms, and gazed at her as though, by a process of will, he could blast her where she stood.

"Where's my brass bed?" he shouted. "Where's my *armoire* and bicycle and sewing machine? What have you done with 'em, you mountain of fat?"

Effie assumed a defiant attitude. So long had she been accustomed to ruling Paki, to shouting him down, that she had no doubt as to the victor in the contest at hand. And she was never in better form than when she had an audience to witness her triumphs.

"*Yours*, you land crab? *Your* sewing machine? *Yours*, is it? Since when, tell me that? It's at Emily Taio's house, if you want to know. What good was it to me? What did I have to sew on it when you give me a new dress once in five years? Go to Emily and ask her to stitch those ugly lips together and spare yourself the cost of eating for the rest of your life! Think of the money you'll save, you bald-headed penny-squeezer! You can put it all in that iron safe you're so proud of; that you hope to carry off with you when you die! And a good riddance it would be if . . ."

Paki darted to one side and seized a dead branch of a *burau* tree that lay, bleached white, on the beach. He made a rush at his wife, who stood waist-deep in water. She ducked to receive the blow on her shoulders, and the stick, a rotten one, broke at the impact.

There was something in the determination and impetuousness of this attack that was new to Effie's experience. Rarely, in twenty years of married life, had Paki raised his hand against her.

"You'd beat me, would you, you rat-eaten coconut!" she shouted with a shrill laugh. She shot sea water at him and ducked to receive another blow. The stick again broke, close to Paki's hand. The crowd gave a shout of delight, in which the voices of the Tuttle boys were loudest. Their sympathies were really with Paki, but they liked to see Aunt Effie holding her own. But she didn't hold it for long. Paki darted away in search of another stick, but found none that would serve. The laughter of the crowd and the taunts of his wife aroused him to the highest pitch of anger. Rushing back, he gave a spring from the border of the beach. Effie turned in time to receive him on her shoulders. With a heave she threw him off and plunged into deeper water. She was a strong swimmer, but Paki would have been no Low Island man had he not been better at this game than his wife. She was not more than thirty yards out when he caught her. Putting his hands on her shoulders, with a dextrous leap he was astride her back. They rolled over and over in the water, but Effie couldn't shake him off. Out of sight both went, and when they broke surface Paki was still in his former place. They submerged once more, for a longer time, and when they reappeared Effie spouted like a grampus, treading water desperately, regretting, now that it was too late, that she had given her husband so great an advantage.

"You had enough?" he asked.

In the struggle that followed the water was lashed to foam, but at the next emergence Effie's eyes were staring wildly. She gasped for breath, but Paki, who had been a diver for pearls in his younger days, was as fresh as ever.

"Let me go!" she choked. "You're drowning me! . . . Paki . . . !"

"You give in?"

She nodded, unable to speak, coughing and spitting out sea water. Paki released her and she swam feebly to the beach; but once her feet touched bottom she seemed to regain a shadow of her old defiance. But Paki gave her no time to recover. Seizing a paddle from one of the canoes, he gave her a resounding thwack with the flat of it on the most ample part of her anatomy. "Get home!" he cried. Effie, after one amazed and frightened glance, obeyed without a word, Paki marching after her with the paddle over his shoulder.

Jonas, who had been looking on this while with an air of annoyance and reproach, broke into one of his hearty laughs, belly shaking and shoulders heaving.

"I never thought to see it," he said. "I never did! . . . Nat, don't tell me that's our Effie going down the road!"

CHAPTER IX

FEBRUARY was the height of the bonito season, but Jonas was in a mood of rare depression one Sunday morning as he stood on the beach awaiting the *Zimba's* return from market. The sky had been filled with sea birds the day before; no doubt the boys had made a big catch, but the market would be glutted with bonito. The price would be next to nothing; however, the boys might have earned enough to buy a few kilos of fresh beef, some rice and potatoes and, maybe, a demijohn of wine. Jonas clung to that hope, for there was practically nothing to eat at home.

His disappointment was bitter when the boys returned with the news that bonito had sold two for a franc.

"No use fishing these days," said Fana, glumly. "Might as well give 'em away."

"Buy any gas?" their father asked.

"Two tins. We was top boat, and that's all it gets us."

"Any news around town?"

"The *Tagua's* in from Rarotonga," said Nat. "Got a letter for you, Jonas. Handwriting looks like it's from that cousin of yours. What's his name — Makitua."

He handed his father a crumpled envelope, bearing a Cook Islands stamp. Letters were rarely received in the Tuttle family, and Jonas examined this one with interest before opening it. He began to read, holding the paper at arm's length. Seeing her brother with a letter, Effie came out to learn its contents.

"They're coming to visit us," Jonas announced.

"Who's coming?"

"Our relatives from Rarotonga."

"They are? *Parau mau?*" Fana asked, eagerly. "Now we'll have some fun!"

All of the boys were delighted at the news. None of them, not even Jonas himself, had ever seen their relatives from the Cook Islands. Their coming would be a break in the monotony of life at Vaipopo, for, in Polynesia, a visit from relatives, more particularly those coming from a distance, was an event calling for the most generous display of hospitality. What made the present prospect the more interesting was that Makitua's daughter, Hester, had just been married to a young Rarotongan of ancient family. The visit would be in the nature of a wedding present to the young couple, who would be accompanied by the bride's parents, and Enoch, another of Jonas's cousins of about his age.

"You don't seem glad, Jonas," Effie remarked. "You ought to be, this first time our relatives have ever come here."

"I'm glad enough," said Jonas, "but . . . I don't see how we're going to manage. We ought to give 'em a real welcome, and the way we're fixed now . . ."

Mama Ruau shared her son's anxiety, when he brought her the news. Their relatives would arrive on the next north-bound mail boat, due in little more than a week.

"What can we do?" she asked, anxiously. "I don't see how we're to get the money to entertain them as we should."

"That's what worries me, Mama. There's only one way I know."

"And what's that?"

Jonas hesitated. "It's the vanilla crop. Ah Sin told me a day or two ago that he'd buy it on the vine, if I wanted to sell it that way. He'll give eighteen thousand francs for it. He knows it'll bring more at the auctions, but that's what he'll give now. I hate to do it, but it seems like we'll have to, with our relatives coming."

"And what of Dr. Blondin?"

"He'll just have to wait a little," Jonas replied. "Suppose it was him owing *us* money, and a lot of his relatives was coming for a visit. We wouldn't press *him*, would we?"

"Of course not. That's what we must do, Jonas: sell the vanilla to Ah Sin."

Mama Ruau had the Tahitian's deep-seated belief in the sacredness of the obligations of hospitality toward kindred, and, although she had been most earnest in pressing Jonas to pay Dr. Blondin's debt, the family duty toward their coming relatives was one that came first. She had no doubt whatever that the doctor would understand this and agree that payment to him should be postponed.

The following day the sale of the vanilla to Ah Sin was made, but before paying Jonas the purchase price, the Chinaman insisted upon subtracting from it the sum of seventy-two hundred francs: the Tuttle bread

bill for a little more than two years past. In order to
obtain the loan of Chester's accordion, without which
the entertainment of their relatives was unthinkable,
Jonas was forced to repay the two thousand francs
owing to Emily Taio, the money borrowed for the
cockfight, thus earning the slender satisfaction of tear-
ing up his note. However, enough remained to insure
that the entertainment of their relatives would be on
the true Tuttle scale.

The week was a busy one for all. Everything, indoors
and out, was set to rights. Supplies of gasoline were laid
in, and the Tuttle truck made frequent trips north and
south on the Broom Road, borrowing from willing
neighbors the china, glassware, cutlery, and furniture
the family lacked. The old house scarcely knew itself
when the preparations were completed.

On the morning when the relatives were expected,
Jonas, dressed in a suit of white drill, starched to a
crackling stiffness, came down the front stairway to
the living room, where his mother, Effie, and others
of the family were waiting to view him before he went
into town to meet the steamer.

"Jonas!" Effie exclaimed. "You ain't going bare-
foot!"

Her brother glanced down at his feet. "I got to,"
he said. "Them canvas shoes you bought . . ."

"I won't have it! Mother, you make him wear
them! They're big enough; I know it! You ought to
be ashamed, Jonas! It's bad enough, your having no
collar. But what will our relatives think when they
see you coming to meet them in your bare feet?"

"Effie's right," their mother said. "For my sake, Jonas?"

Jonas seated himself on a bench and stretched out his legs. "Get 'em, then," he said. "Let's see you put 'em on me. I tried. They won't go, I tell you!"

The shoes were brought, of a size so enormous that Fana grinned at sight of them.

"If Jonas can't wear 'em," he said, "we'll order a couple of outboard motors from Montgomery-Ward and go fishing in 'em."

"Never you mind about that," said Effie, passing him one of the shoes. "Help me."

The two knelt before the head of the family, and after a struggle that brought beads of sweat to their foreheads, they managed to get Jonas's feet inside. The laces barely sufficed to tie the ends in hard knots, over the instep. "Now then," said Effie.

Jonas rose with a groan and immediately sank back on the bench.

"I can't walk in 'em, that's all there is to it," he said.

"Yes you can," said Effie, "and you're going to. We'll help you out to the car. You can sit in it and wait while the steamer docks."

Jonas's plan had been to meet his relatives in the old fish truck, but the womenfolk had overruled him. Even his mother had sided with the others in this matter. This was the first visit they'd ever had from their Rarotonga relatives, and no expense was to be spared in giving them a fitting welcome. Therefore, a Lincoln, the most luxurious car to be had at any of the

Papeete garages, had been hired for the occasion. It was to be theirs for the entire day at a cost of three hundred francs, which Jonas had been required to pay in advance.

With Nat supporting him on one side and Effie on the other, Jonas hobbled out to the car. Fana had been delegated by the family to go with his father to meet the steamer. He was wearing his serge suit, white shoes, sports shirt with an open collar, and a hard-brimmed American straw hat, set at a jaunty angle. Fana sat with the driver, and Jonas, with a sigh of relief, sank back against the well-polished cushions of the rear seat. Rarely indeed did he have an opportunity to ride as luxuriously as this and he was bound to make the most of the occasion.

"Now you bring 'em right out," said Effie, "just as soon as they're off the boat. Don't stop anywhere in town. We're all that anxious to see them."

"Better get one more demijohn of wine," Nat added, "so's to be sure to have enough."

Jonas waved his hand, and the car sped down the bumpy driveway.

A few minutes later Fana turned when his father laid a hand on his shoulder.

"I took 'em off," he said, with a glance at his feet. "I ain't going to be miserable this first time I've ever seen my cousins."

Fana laughed. "Don't blame you. You can sit in the car, like Effie said. I'll bring 'em off the steamer."

Reassured by his son's approval, Jonas leaned back once more to enjoy every moment of this smooth ride

to town. What a car! The houses scattered along the
Broom Road flashed by so rapidly as to give the impression that all the country between Vaipopo and
Tarahoi was one continuous settlement. The driver
sounded a long polite warning on his musical horn
as they passed through the latter village. There was
magic in the sound for Jonas. He could easily imagine
that it was his horn, his car, his driver; that the mortgage on Vaipopo had long since been paid off, and that
he was hastening to town for a triple purpose: to meet
his Rarotonga relatives; to receive a large shipment
of goods from Montgomery-Ward and Company, arrived by the last south-bound steamer; and to press
upon Dr. Blondin, whom he had heard was in financial
difficulties, a loan of twenty-five thousand francs. He
imagined himself walking up to the doctor's little house
and, after a quarter of an hour's conversation about
other matters, taking a huge wallet from his pocket and
slowly counting out on his knee fifty five-hundred-franc
bills. "There, Doctor," he said, as he placed the money
in his hands. "No, no! Don't say a word! I heard about
your having some trouble. Many a good turn you've
done me. Take this, and you don't ever need to pay
me back unless you want to." Then, leaving the doctor
speechless with astonishment and relief, he hurried
away to his Lincoln, waiting at the doctor's gate. "Drive
me out to Ellacott's shipyard," he then ordered the
chauffeur. "I want to see how they're getting on with
the new launch." . . .

"There she is," said Fana. "She'll be alongside the
wharf in another half-hour."

The dream faded. Jonas roused himself to find that they were passing the British consulate. Papeete lay before them, and across the lagoon was the *Maunganui*, the north-bound mail boat, the anchor chain rumbling out in a cloud of red dust as she halted in mid-harbor to await the doctor's launch.

"Stop a minute, Toni," Jonas called.

The driver drew up at the side of the road. Fana turned to glance at his father. "What for?" he asked.

"We got plenty of time," Jonas replied. "I like the view from here," but in order to give a more practical reason for the halt he got out and retired for a moment behind a fringe of bushes. He returned and stood by the car until he saw the government launch moving out from the landing steps by the post office. She was a quarter of a mile away, but Jonas could see Dr. Blondin in his white suit and sun helmet. While he was certain that the doctor would understand when he explained, later, the unexpected arrival of his Rarotonga relatives and the necessity for entertaining them in a suitable manner, he wished to avoid a chance meeting on this morning between the doctor, on his bicycle, and himself in the hired Lincoln. He had little fear of meeting Monsieur Dorme. His office was on the far side of the town, and he was too busy a man to waste time watching the monthly mail boat come in.

When the launch was alongside and he saw Dr. Blondin climbing the *Maunganui's* ladder, Jonas gave the order to proceed. "Go around the back streets, Toni," he said. "No use getting there too soon. And

stop on the road at the north end of the wharf, behind
Le Brunnec's sail loft."

"What's the use of that?" Fana asked. "Why not go
right along to the wharf?"

"Do as I say," his father replied. "It's shady behind
the sail loft. I'm not going to roast in the hot sun while
I'm waiting."

The chauffeur drove slowly along the inland streets
with their neat gardens, ablaze with color in the clear
morning light. As they passed the cross streets they
had glimpses of the crowds moving toward the wharf
to enjoy the great event of the month. The car was
halted at the place Jonas suggested, and Fana, accompanied by the chauffeur to help carry the luggage,
went along to the wharf.

It was quiet and cool behind Le Brunnec's sail loft.
Jonas stretched out at ease to await the coming of his
visitors, provoked that he could not have taken the car
directly to the wharf. He could then have seen the
crowds, and the steamer as she came alongside, her
passengers lining the rail. But always, for him, whenever he indulged in a little extra expense, there was
the need to keep out of sight as much as possible. Shopkeepers, garage owners, hotel proprietors — all Papeete,
in fact, seemed to take it for granted that the Tuttles
had no right even to a little pleasure in life. The moment anyone suspected that he had a few francs in his
pocket, he was sure to have boys with bills in their
hands chasing after him on bicycles, and presenting
them no matter where he might be. Well, someday . . .
If only the family might have a stroke of real good

luck, for once in their lives . . . ! He gave an exasperated sigh, thinking how nearly they came to it on the day of the *aturé* netting. There must have been forty or fifty thousand francs' worth of fish in that net; and then it had split just when they had them all but in! And there could be no repairing it. They would have to have a new net, and where they were ever to find the money . . .

With another sigh, Jonas put these unpleasant thoughts out of mind. It was wrong and foolish to worry about such matters on the day of his relatives' arrival. Everything was in readiness for them. Jonas smiled as he thought of the feasts and good times at hand.

What would his cousins be like? he wondered. He knew little about the Rarotonga Tuttles. At long intervals he had exchanged letters with Makitua, but he had never heard from Enoch, the older one. Enoch must be about his own age, and was a widower, like himself. Makitua was around forty-five. What was the name of his wife? Hapai, that was it. And their daughter, Hester, was the one who'd gotten married.

He went over the arrangements made for the accommodation of their guests. Enoch was to sleep at Paki's house. Jonas chuckled, remembering how Effie had been forced to go to Emily Taio to borrow the brass bed she'd lost in the cockfight. Paki would do nothing in the matter; he refused to buy back any of the lost furniture. Funny thing about Effie; since the day Paki had ducked her at the netting, she'd been like a different woman. She was proud of Paki now and boasted about how strong he was. Well, that's the way it was with women: they'd boss their men if they could, but what they wanted was to be bossed by them — made to toe the mark. That's how it was with Effie. She'd talk up to Paki as much as ever, but she knew now who was the head of the family.

Then Hester and her young man were to have the spare bedroom where his grandfather's furniture was, and the boys' room had been fixed up for Makitua and his wife. They would be a bit crowded while their relatives were here, but they could manage. It didn't seem to matter how many they had in the old house, there was always room for a few more.

Jonas gazed at the wall of Le Brunnec's sail loft. Good place to wait, this. No one could see him from the wharf. There was an old "To Let" sign on the wall; it had been there a year or two at least. And it would be there, more than likely, till the building fell to pieces. The building was a wreck, the upstairs part, anyway. Who'd ever want to rent it?

Here they came! Jonas straightened up quickly and got down from the car to meet his relatives. He was conscious of a little shock of surprise and misgiving when he first set eyes on them; it was like a faint chill at the heart. Fana felt it, too; Jonas knew it by the way Fana walked, by his expression, for all the smile that tried to hide it.

Enoch came in front. He was a tall bony man, with a long face and eyes whose glance seemed to be piercing through Jonas and on to the other side of Jordan. Jonas knew at once that he was a deacon of his church in Rarotonga. Everything proclaimed it, and he was dressed completely in black, with a band of crape around his hat, although the latter was, evidently, worn as a token of respect for his dead wife.

"*Kia ora na*, Brother Jonas," he said, in a deep bell-like voice, presenting his Tahiti cousin with a large limp hand as though he himself had no further use for it. Jonas held it for a moment, then relinquished it as unobtrusively as possible.

Makitua was more what he expected a Tuttle to be. He had a jolly face, and Jonas felt that he could, shortly, get on terms with this cousin. But Makitua scarcely opened his mouth. There was something subdued and apologetic in his manner, and when spoken to he would first glance at his wife. Hapai was a woman of character, that was plain at first sight, but Enoch was the undoubted leader of this expedition. The married pair were merely young people, having nothing in their characters to set them apart from others in that condition. The girl was slender and pretty, but dowdily dressed, like her mother, who seemed to have taken pains to make her daughter look as unattractive as possible.

Jonas felt ill at ease. He couldn't warm up, somehow, and his cousin Enoch made matters no easier when, having been asked to step into the Lincoln, he said: "One moment, Brother Jonas." He gave the others a commanding, mournful glance, whereupon all bowed their heads. Enoch then placed his long hands palm to palm and offered up a prayer of thanksgiving that they had survived the perils of the deep on their six-

hundred-mile voyage. Jonas felt constrained to bow
his head with the others, but as he did so he was thinking: "We won't need that other demijohn of wine
Nat wanted me to get."

Fana and the chauffeur returned with the rest of
the luggage, and Jonas was relieved to see that there
was no great amount of it. Perhaps his cousins planned
to return home by the schooner *Tagua*. This vessel
belonged to the Cook Islands Trading Company and
was now on the slip at Walker Brothers shipyard, under-
going repairs which would soon be completed. Jonas
reproached himself for hoping that Enoch-ma would be
returning by the *Tagua;* but then . . . well, he had
expected the Rarotonga Tuttles to be more like the
Tahiti ones. Maybe it wouldn't be so bad, later, when
they got to know one another better. But he hadn't
much hope of Enoch.

When passengers and luggage had been packed in the
car they started at once for Vaipopo. All the family
were waiting to receive them when they turned into
the driveway half an hour later. The old house was
scarcely recognizable under its charming decorations.
The veranda posts were wreathed in sweet-smelling
fern and the back walls hidden under a solid mantle
of green palm fronds. The open-sided cookhouse and
family dining room had been completely transformed.
The floor was strewn with coral sand, and the posts
that upheld the rusty iron roof were now pillars of
jasmin, gardenia, and bougainvillea blossoms, so that the
rickety shed was a bower of fragrance and harmonious
color. The table where the breakfast of welcome would

be served was covered with white cloths, much darned and mended, but spotlessly clean. The tableware, most of it borrowed, was of a dozen different patterns, but these served to lend a festive appearance to the board. The midmorning sunlight seemed to be inviting some ghostly and critical observer to note the reality beneath all this make-believe, but the womenfolk who had wrought the transformation were too intent upon giving the last touches of perfection to the table to take advantage of the opportunity. And then they heard the clear musical horn of the approaching Lincoln.

"There they are!" Effie exclaimed. "Tupa, you and Maitu stay right here and keep the fowls out. You can see them later." And with that the women hurried away to join the others on the veranda.

It had been arranged that Chester, Nat, Ru, and some of the other musicians of the clan were to play a very gay Tahitian song, while Hio and Tamara were to dance before their guests and place garlands of flowers on their heads and around their necks. The musicians were in readiness, led by Chester with his piano accordion. Hio and Tamara looked charming in their dancing costumes. Both were graceful girls, with well-deserved reputations as being the best dancers on the west side of the island. Mama Ruau stood at the head of the steps, her small bare toes peeping out from beneath the hem of her gown, which descended in voluminous folds from the high-waisted pleats. A smile of welcome already lit up her face as the car turned in from the Broom Road. Other members of the family, the men in white, the children scrubbed and tidy, the women in their best frocks of flowered print, were grouped around her and on the steps below.

The car came to a halt and the guests got down, Enoch leading the way, looking like a badly nourished crow in that assembly. He halted, facing the veranda, and raised both arms in a gesture of benediction, and at the same instant Chester and his orchestra struck into the lively opening strains of the song of welcome. Hio and Tamara glided forward like two young sirens intent upon bewitching and bedeviling an ogre, while two children approached with them, carrying the wreaths with which to bedeck the guests. So unexpected was the dance to Enoch, and the abrupt gesture of benediction to the Tuttles, that both proceeded at once, and, having started, neither could be arrested. Enoch's face was a study; his lips were moving in the words of his invocation but these could not be heard above the gay music of the fast-moving song. The two young matrons with their innocently wanton gestures danced more and more alluringly, as though determined to break the spell which this gaunt figure in black seemed determined to cast upon the house of Tuttle-ma.

Jonas stood behind the guests, holding his shoes in his hand. He was shaking with suppressed laughter, looking toward his mother with an expression that seemed to say: "It's too bad, Mama, but we can't help it now. These ain't our kind of Tuttles."

By this time all realized that the song and dance of welcome were not going off as they should have done. Enoch was bound to win. His lips were firmly set, and he stood in the same attitude, with his arms raised,

although now, it seemed, in malediction rather than
in benediction. Chester gave his fellow musicians a quick
glance and the music stopped. Enoch then let his arms
slowly fall and stood for a moment with head bowed.
Tamara took this opportunity to place a fragrant
wreath around his neck, and, rising on tiptoe, and drawing his head down a little more, she kissed him on
both cheeks. Meanwhile, the other guests had been
crowned with flowers. An awkward silence followed,
but Jonas was equal to the occasion. He remembered of
a sudden that he had his shoes in his hand. He passed
them to Effie, who gave him a sharp pinch on the hand
as he did so.

"Come along, Cousin Enoch," he said, heartily.
"There's Mother waiting to greet you."

The breakfast of welcome went off in better style.
There were twenty-two at table, some of the younger
people having been told off to help in serving the food.
Jonas had planned to place Enoch on his right hand,
but decided against this and asked him to take the opposite end of the table. Makitua sat at Jonas's right, and
Hapai, his wife, was placed some distance away, between
Nat and Chester. The young married pair sat on either
side of Mama Ruau.

There was food and yet more food, and the best *vin
ordinaire* to be had in Papeete at six francs the liter.
Enoch, observing Maitu approaching with a pitcher of
wine, turned down his glass. This was a gesture of re-
fusal unknown to any member of the Tuttle family.
Maitu turned up the tumbler. Enoch immediately re-

versed it once more; Maitu thought Jonas's cousin was
merely having a little game with her; therefore she
took up the tumbler and held it in her hand while she
filled it, setting it down with a pleased smile that seemed
to say: "I didn't suppose you'd even notice me. I'm
Tupa's daughter; I've always lived here, but I'm not
any real kin to Jonas-ma." Makitua's wife held her
hand over her own glass, shaking her head grimly as
Maitu offered to fill it. This was all very strange to
Maitu, but she was beginning to understand that the
Rarotonga *fetii* must differ from Jonas-ma.

Course after course came on, each one prepared and
served in the manner which had made the Tuttles
famous. Jonas observed that his guests did full justice to
the food. Enoch fairly shoveled it in, smacking and
crunching, and whipping up the *miti haari* with the
greatest relish. This pleased Jonas; he liked to see people
enjoy their victuals. Presently he caught Ru's eye. Ru
was helping to wait on table and stood for a moment
behind Enoch's chair. Suddenly his face took on an expression so perfect an imitation of Enoch's that Jonas,
who alone chanced to see it, sputtered, choked, and, if
he had not immediately grasped up his napkin, would
have deluged the entire company with a shower of
vin ordinaire. He was hard put to get his breath again.
The others watched him with concern, but Ru went
on about his duties with an air of complete innocence.
When he could speak, Jonas glanced at his mother.

"Excuse me, Mama," he gasped. "I was trying to
breathe and drink at the same time. I ought to know
better."

They had gone to the table at ten, and it was half-past two before the meal ended. Enoch rose with an expression of almost painful satiety upon his face, but Jonas was surprised to see that the gaunt frame looked as gaunt as ever. Where had he put all that food? he wondered. Makitua's little round belly looked half again as large as it had before. And he was in a fine digestive sweat, which was just as it should be. Hapai, his wife, hadn't done so badly either. She walked toward the house, leaning forward slightly to lessen the tension around her middle line. There was a set smile on her face, but her eyes looked glazed and accusing as though she blamed the Tuttles for having such good food, encouraging her beyond her capacity. But these signs of hearty eating were what Jonas liked to see in his guests.

It had already been arranged that they were to be given a drive around the island when breakfast was over. The car was waiting and Jonas helped his *fetii* in. Enoch and Paki, who had struck up an immediate friendship, got into the front seat with the driver; the young married pair had the pull-up seats, and Makitua, his wife, and Mama Ruau the roomy seat behind.

"Now drive slow, Toni," Effie cautioned the chauffeur, "so's our relatives can see things well. You all right there, Hapai?"

"*É, maitaki,*" Hapai replied.

"There'll be a full moon tonight," Effie added, "so it won't matter if you get home late." She gave the relatives a polite smile. "We're sorry we can't all go, but you just enjoy yourselves and don't think about us. We'll have a good supper ready for you when you come back."

When the car had gone, the others went round to the back veranda, always the coolest place in the afternoon.

"Fetch me a mat and pillow, one of you," Jonas said. When they had been brought and placed for him, Jonas stretched out on his back with a groan of relief. The rest of the family made themselves comfortable around him. Nat was asleep under a tree in the yard. There was silence for some little time. Chester was the first to speak.

"We went to all this bother for nothing: fixing up the house and everything."

"You boys didn't do much of it," Effie replied. "I don't see what right you got to complain."

"I ain't complaining," said Chester. "All I say is, they're a queer lot of Tuttles, if you ask me."

"Chester's still mad about this morning," Tamara said. She burst out laughing. "Wasn't it funny when Enoch started to pray just as we started to dance?"

At the memory of the reception fiasco, the rest began laughing as well, until the old house resounded with their mirth. Chester looked from one to another with a reluctant grin.

"It's all right to laugh," he said; "but they're here for we don't know how long."

"And we thought we were going to have such a good time with them," Hio added, still laughing.

"How long do you think they *will* stay, Jonas?" Fana asked.

"It's not for us to think about that," Jonas said.

"They're our relatives, and we must try to make them enjoy themselves."

"What happened to you at the table, Jonas?" said Ropati. "I thought you was going to choke to death."

"Ask Ru. Didn't none of the rest of you see? He tried his best to murder his father."

"Me? I didn't do anything," Ru replied, with an air of mild surprise.

"He was standing behind Enoch's chair," Jonas explained; "then he put on a face like Enoch's so's I wasn't sure which was which. You shouldn't have done it, Ru," he added, reproachfully.

"How was it, Ru? Show us," said Tamara, but Ru was not to be persuaded. He was an artist who required the inspiration of the moment for his imitations.

"Well, there's one good thing," said Ropati. "Paki's got a bosom friend at last. Him and Enoch hit it off wonderful together."

"Paki'll be wanting to move to Rarotonga," said Fana. "How'd you like that, Effie?"

"I suppose you think I'd go?"

"Maybe you'll have to," Ropati said. "He might take a paddle to you like he did at the netting."

"You leave Paki alone," said Effie. "And me too. Anyway, he's a better man than I thought he was."

Tamara laughed. "That's right, Effie. Stick up for your husband."

Effie had her reply ready. "And what about you? A fine wife you are, refusing to marry your husband, or even to live with him. If I was Fana I'd have something to say about that."

This matter was a sore point with all the Tuttles. Tamara had been Fana's wife in all but name for more than three years and was the mother of his two children. They had planned to marry since the early days of courtship but were still living apart, in their respective villages, because Fana had not yet provided the home, so long promised, on the beach at Vaipopo. Tamara, who had her mother's resolute character, was firm in refusing consent to marriage until the house should be completed and ready for occupancy. The cement posts upon which the house was to rest had long been in place, and some of the lumber for the dwelling was stacked away there, covered over with a few sheets of corrugated iron; but Fana, being a Tuttle, could not get on any farther with his plans for homemaking. He had often tried to persuade Tamara to bring their children and move in with the rest of the Tuttles; but she, knowing this would mean that a home of her own would never be finished, steadfastly refused. Fana was, therefore, obliged to divide his time between the Taios' place, at Tarahoi, and Vaipopo.

At this turn of the conversation, Jonas sat up and placed his pillow behind him, against the wall.

"Effie's right, there, Tamara. Now that you've come up for the day, why don't you stay with us for good? Just as soon as our relatives go we can fix you and Fana and the children up as comfortable as anything. You like it here; you know you do — better'n at your mother's house."

Tamara shook her head firmly. "There's no use going into all that again, Jonas. Fana knows how he can get me. I'm ready to marry him and live with him as soon as he gets our house built. And I won't come a day before."

Chester grinned. "You better have me in place of him, Tamara. Wouldn't t-t-t-take me long to have a house ready."

"Oh, wouldn't it?" Tamara replied, mocking him. "I wouldn't have you if you bu-bu-bu-built me three houses; not even if you were the last m-m-m-man in the world."

Jonas sighed. "Well, I guess we'll just have to wait a bit, then," he said. "But as soon as we get twisted round, Tamara . . . Your family's what's put us back, cleaning us out the way you did at the cockfight. I wouldn't have thought it of your mother, sneaking that strange bird in on us."

Tamara stooped and ruffled Jonas's hair.

"You old rascal," she said. "Now then, couldn't we have some music while there's a chance? Where's the Taios' accordion, Chester? And if Fana'll behave himself, I'll let him play the Taios' guitar."

CHAPTER X

THE Tuttles did their best to make the visit of their
Rarotonga relatives pleasant and memorable, but their
success was not at all in keeping with their efforts. The
boys blamed the failure upon Enoch, who seemed determined that everyone should breathe what Nat called
"prayer-meeting air" during the entire period of the
visit. The rest of the party were under his domination
and Makitua's wife seemed to glory in it. The young
married pair would have liked to enjoy themselves, but
were given no opportunity; they were not even permitted to dance the native dances. Jonas, the soul of
courtesy, who felt deeply his obligations as host-in-
chief, accepted the situation uncomplainingly, but
there could be no real gaiety in Enoch's presence. But
at last the visit came to an end: the relatives were sailing for Rarotonga on the schooner *Tagua*. Enoch's
prolonged and solemn farewell, interspersed with
blessings and Biblical quotations, did not disguise the
fact that he was as glad to leave as his hosts were to
see him go. Jonas's only comfort was that he had done
his best, and this was more than offset by the knowledge that all the money received from the advance
sale of the vanilla had gone in the attempt.

More than eight thousand francs had been spent in
the entertainment of his *fetii;* all he had left was three

hundred francs, little more than enough to buy three cases of gasoline. Fana and Ru, who had gone to town with Paki to see their relatives off, were to bring home this amount of gas, and the *Zimba* was to put to sea as soon as they returned. Jonas had told the boys, in confidence, of the mortgage Dr. Blondin had taken on Vaipopo. There was no alternative; he was forced to tell in order to bring home to them the gravity of their present situation. It had been a good move. They realized now that they must fish as they never had before.

While waiting for the return of the truck from town, Jonas walked into the valley to reflect in quiet upon the family situation. How was he to break the news to Dr. Blondin of the spending of the vanilla money, and persuade him to give them yet more time to pay their debt? Neither the doctor nor Monsieur Dorme would know that the money was irretrievably gone until the time of the public vanilla auctions, but that time was close at hand. And then — what?

Jonas was forced to put this question aside, unanswered. There was no facing it. His only hope was that, during the next two weeks, the boys might have such luck at fishing that he could go to Monsieur Dorme with enough cash to persuade the lawyer to grant him one more month of grace.

Vaipopo had never looked richer and prettier than it did on this particular morning. The stream, famous for its inexhaustible stock of shrimps and *natto*, murmured its way to the sea beneath overarching *mapé* trees — the Pacific chestnuts which contributed so abundantly to the family resources. The floor of the valley, composed of a deep soil rich in humus, was planted with groves of coconut palms, breadfruit, alligator pears, papayas, oranges, limes, bananas. Taro beds flourished in the swampy places. He passed the vanilla plantation whose splendid crop would soon be ready for picking, sighing as he thought of Ah Sin, who had bought for eighteen thousand francs a crop worth twenty-five thousand at least.

In a glade beyond he came upon his mother, engaged in planting a young breadfruit tree of a rare variety. The lad with her had dug the hole and partially filled it with humus; now Mama Ruau was on her knees, pressing the earth in firmly around the roots. She smiled at her son and went on with her work. Presently she rose, directing the boy to fetch water from the stream.

"For your great-grandchildren, Jonas," she remarked, glancing down at the young tree. "It's a *rotuma*, from Maupiti. It bears fruit in the dry season."

At his mother's words Jonas felt a sudden pang of fear, of deep apprehension, thinking of the mortgage he had so lightly given on his mother's land. For it was hers, by every law of right and justice. The fact that she had deeded the land to her children was nothing. Supposing they were to lose Vaipopo; that Monsieur Dorme were to insist upon full payment when due of the debt to Dr. Blondin? The lawyer had the right to foreclose and drive them out. The blow would kill his mother, and his would be the blame. But no, no, no! This could never be! Surely, Dr. Blondin would understand, once he had a chance to explain matters. He was alarming himself for nothing. Mama Ruau broke in upon these reflections.

"Jonas, have you noticed how thoughtless the young people are growing in these days? They care less for the land, now. When I was a child my father made each of us plant a breadfruit tree and tend it. He used to say that one tree would feed a man the year round if he made *tioo*."

"That fermented paste? Young people wouldn't eat it now," Jonas replied.

"I know they wouldn't; but it made strong men of our ancestors. Now we must have bread and sugar and all the other things that require money to buy. We neglect our lands and think only of crops that can be sold. . . . I wonder if you love Vaipopo as I do?"

"Of course I do, Mama."

"I don't think so, Jonas. You should have seen this place when I married your father. And now . . ."

"I love every inch of it," Jonas broke in, so fervently that his mother could feel his deep sincerity. "Just you give me time to get twisted round, Mama. We're going to have it looking better'n it ever did."

The old woman pressed his arm. "I'm glad to hear you say it, Jonas. I know how you and the boys feel about the sea. I love it, too, but the land comes first. Where would we be without our valley?"

As they were returning along the path by the river, Hio met them.

"They've really gone, Jonas," she announced. "Fana and Ru waited in town till they saw the *Tagua* well out to sea. Now we can be ourselves once more."

"Boys back, are they? Did they bring the gas?"

"Yes, and they went straight out fishing, as you wanted them to. I let Riki go with them."

Upon leaving Vaipopo, the Tuttle boys made a wide sweep to westward; then the *Zimba* was headed north and proceeded for three hours in that general direction, at a distance of five or six miles offshore. They came midway up the Moorea Channel, left Papeete behind, and when opposite the Point Venus light headed yet further out. And in all this great stretch of ocean the sea might have been as empty of fish as the sky was of sea fowl indicating their presence.

Nat was sitting aft with Chester, Ru was at the wheel, and Fana stood on lookout in the bow with Riki, Nat's eight-year-old son. The lad was a sturdy boy, already showing promise of his father's great strength and stature. Nat's glance rested upon him quietly, with the look of pride and deep affection which he was always careful that the lad himself should not see.

"Plenty of gas, Ru?" he asked.

"Hope so."

"What'd you put in?"

"Sixteen gallons."

Nat stared gloomily back at the receding land where Tahiti's deep gorges and winding plateaus stood out clearly in the afternoon sunlight. "Keep on out," he said. "We're not coming back till we got a full load. If we don't find 'em before dark we'll stop the engine and sleep out here."

His brothers were in the same determined mood. Their

father had made a strong appeal to them; they didn't mean to let him down in a pinch like the present one. They were bound to get fish, and tuna if possible. The market had been glutted with bonito, recently. The price was so low that receipts scarcely paid for fuel. But it was now midafternoon. There had been no sign of tuna or of anything else.

Nat rose for another glance around the horizon. He was about to resume his seat when his attention was attracted and held. He gazed steadily to the northeast.

"Ru . . ."

His brother glanced back.

"There they are. Tuna. Wait . . . keep her headed as she is for a little. Fana's seen 'em. He's hoping Riki will."

A moment later the child spoke eagerly to his uncle, pointing to the northeast. Fana bent his head to follow with his glance the lad's outstretched arm. He clapped Riki on the shoulder, nodding vigorously. The boy came running aft.

"Birds!" he called excitedly. "They're feeding! You can see 'em plain from the bow!"

Fana, who was approaching behind, gave his brothers a knowing glance.

"You're sure, Riki?" his father asked, his face lighting up.

"Of course he's sure," said Fana. "Didn't he point 'em out to me?" He put his hand on the lad's shoulder. "Riki *tané*! You're a real Tuttle! You'll be better'n your dad before you're ten years old."

"You really didn't see 'em?" the lad asked.

"See 'em?" said Fana. "Of course I did, after you'd pointed 'em out."

"What are they, Riki?" his father asked, in the tone of voice so flattering to a boy, as though he were speaking to an adult member of the craft.

"Tuna, I'm pretty sure," Riki said, knowingly. "I can tell by the way the birds act."

"We got to b-b-b-bring Riki with us every day, Nat," said Chester. "He's a born bird-spotter."

There was no hint of condescension in the manner in which his father and his uncles spoke. Riki felt that he was one of them: a seasoned offshore fisherman. He went forward again to his lookout post, as proud a lad as might have been found that day on all the vast Pacific. Ru followed his directions, altering the course at Riki's signals.

"He spotted 'em almost as soon as I did," Fana said, in a low voice. "He's a good kid. Chester's right: it was time we was breaking him in."

They made preparations at leisure, for the birds were still far off. Presently the lad gave a cry of disappointment.

"Look! They've sounded," he called back.

The birds had scattered and were now flying this way and that. Some settled on the water, taking flight again as the launch approached.

"What luck!" Riki exclaimed. "We were almost there!"

"No fault of yours, Riki. That's the way it goes, sometimes."

"Most times," Ru added.

"Slow her down," said Nat. "They ain't gone for good."

The *Zimba* now idled along at two knots, with both Nat and Ru scanning the sea, following the birds for direction. Fana got to his feet.

"Now, Riki: let's pretend we're right at the edge of a fine school. Here, take the gaff. You're on my side of the boat — see? You got to help me bring 'em in."

The boy seized the gaff and took his station.

"Now mind how you handle it," Fana warned. "Can't have you jabbing that hook into one of us. Keep it outboard. And look, Riki: I've got my short heavy rod. That means they're big tuna we're coming to: forty, fifty, sixty kilos. Don't waste no time hooking 'em in when I lift 'em. All ready?"

Riki nodded. Fana then pretended that he had his rod in his hands. Out went the lure. He gave a jubilant cry of warning; then, knees bent and leaning back at the same time, lips tightly set, he struggled with an enormous mythical tuna, his arms trembling under the strain of heaving it up. "Riki!" he shouted, and the lad gaffed it into the cockpit.

"Mind your work!" Fana shouted. "Don't look at me! I got another! Riki! Gaff him quick or we'll lose him!"

So real did Fana make the sport that his nephew could almost believe in the huge fish they brought over the side: hear the hard drumming of their tails in their death throes, feel the blood spattering over his bare arms and chest. Presently his uncle brought in his imaginary rod and sat down, panting realistically.

"Good boy, Riki! That's the way to handle your gaff. But I thought we was going to lose that second one and he's the best of the lot. What's he weigh, Chester?"

"All of s-s-seventy kilos," his brother replied, judicially.

The boy grinned. "He wouldn't weigh that on the market scales."

"Maybe not, Riki. I've seen bigger ones that seemed to weigh a lot less on them scales." Fana felt of his nephew's hard biceps, shoulder and stomach muscles. "You'll be heaving 'em in in a few more years," he added. "Then, with the five of us at work out here, we won't leave nothing but skipjacks for the Taios."

Nat, who had gone to the bow, called back: "Get going! They're up again."

The last dull glow of departing day was fading as the *Zimba*, splendidly loaded, turned in a wide arc and headed for the distant land. They were a good twenty-five miles from Papeete; even Point Venus light was below the horizon, but the land lay in massive shadow before them. The sea was still dead calm and the eastern sky now bright with stars.

Nat, Fana, and Chester were resting after the exhausting work of the past hour. There was nothing mythical about *these* tuna. Ru was clubbing the fish still alive, and Riki sat proudly at the wheel, humming to himself as he steered. The brothers stripped, sluicing one another with sea water. They got into their sweaty, bloodstained trousers once more, for it would be useless putting on fresh ones until the fish had been cleaned. Ru went below to fetch some bananas and baked yams, which he passed around. They ate their supper in silence. All were deeply content, for they were homeward bound with a load that brought the *Zimba's* freeboard down to sixteen inches. The peace of mid-ocean and the glory of the cloudless sky, powdered with the southern constellations, had its effect upon them all. Fana joined Riki in the song he was singing, one with a refrain that seemed to have in it the loneliness and beauty distilled from the experience of countless Polynesians before their time.

Nat brought out a book of cigarette papers and a packet of fine-cut native tobacco. By the light of the lantern he peered into the packet, feeling of it with thumb and forefinger.

"There's enough left for a couple of smokes all round," he announced. "I'll save mine till later."

"I'll have one now," said Fana, and Nat passed him the tobacco.

"Make one for me," said Chester. "I been smoking ready-mades so long I c-c-can't roll my own any more."

"We won't be smoking this Moorea shag long," said Fana. He glanced at the heap of tuna upon which his bare feet were resting. "What a killing! We got a bigger load than we had the time the Taios sold 'em for us."

"They ain't home yet," said Nat.

"What do you think, Ru?"

"I ain't thinking. I'm hoping. I'd like to see the light coming up. We're to hell and gone off."

"It's always the way," said Chester. "The b-b-b-bloody tuna seem to know how the *Zimba's* fixed for gas."

"Didn't know today, for once, anyhow," said Ru. "But they sure gave us a chase. Well, maybe we'll get a breeze."

Chester grunted. The stars were reflected in the sea and the long ripples moved out from the *Zimba's* bow in glassy curves.

"What'd you say we had when we started, Ru?" Nat asked.

"Around eleven gallons by the stick. And Fana put in five more. We're all right."

He had scarcely spoken when the *Zimba* began to choke and sputter and stammer an indignant protest to her engineer's last remark. A moment later the engine stopped dead.

No comment was made. The others waited while Ru examined the machine with swift expert movements. Then he went forward to the gas tank with his measuring stick. Returning, he held out the stick to Nat. Not more than a sixteenth of an inch at the end was wet.

"Something's wrong," Ru said. "We've been throttled down half the time. We ain't used any sixteen gallons."

"I know we ain't," said Fana.

Nat glanced up. "What do you mean by that?"

Fana made no attempt to shift the blame. "It's my fault," he said. "I forgot to put in the other five."

Chester's comment was approved of by the other brothers. "You G-g-g-God-damned careless b-b-bloody idiot! There goes our f-f-f-fish!"

"It's Ru's fault as much as his," said Nat. "He might have known better than to trust him. Get out the oars! We're only twenty-five miles out. By God, you can *row* us home!"

Ru and Fana knew better than to protest when Nat spoke in that savage tone of voice. Without a word the two younger brothers got out the oars, dropped the oarlocks into place, and began their heavy hopeless task. Strongly and steadily they pulled, and the *Zimba* moved on at about one knot.

At ten o'clock, Chester went forward for the second time in the past two hours.

"Let me spell you, Ru," he said.

The lad shook his head grimly. A quarter of an hour later, when he felt he had punished them as they deserved, Nat himself went forward. "Knock off," he said, gruffly.

The oars were drawn in with alacrity. "I wouldn't have cared if you'd said that an hour ago," said Fana.

Riki was sitting on the wheelbox, staring gravely down the companionway where the engine could be dimly seen. He broke a long silence. "What is it, Ru?" he asked.

"What's what?"

"Gas."

"I'll tell you that, Riki," said Chester. "It's what Fana left five gallons of in the boat shed, enough to have taken us right into Papeete harbor in time for market."

"Shut up!" said Fana. "I said it was my fault, didn't I? That's enough. I don't want to hear no more about it."

"But I want to know where it comes from," said Riki. "How do they make it?"

"It comes out of the ground," Ru explained.

"Yes, of course," Riki said, scornfully. "Just like water, I suppose!"

"That's right; it does, Riki," Chester replied. "I've seen lots of oil w-w-w-wells in America; but the oil's way down below the water. Th-th-th-thousands of feet. It ain't gas when it first comes up. They what you call refine it."

"Then they put it in five-gallon tins for fools like your Uncle Fana to leave in the boat shed when we go to sea," Nat added.

"If it comes out of the ground, why couldn't we dig for it on Tahiti?"

"It wouldn't be on our land, that's sure," said Fana. "If ever they was to find it, it would all be under the Taio place."

Nat rose and removed the clasp knife from the chain at his belt. "Come on. Get to work."

"What's the use?" Chester asked. "They'll all go bad on us before we can get 'em to town."

"We'll clean 'em anyway," said Nat. "We can sell 'em to the Chinamen for pig food."

"That's right: at half a franc apiece. G-g-g-good old Fana! He's sure done well by us today!"

All of them set to work, slitting open the bellies, making the tuna ready for market. They worked even more rapidly than usual, anxious to be done with a task which all knew was a useless one. The fish would be rotten before they could get them to Papeete.

The hours wore on to midnight. The three younger brothers went to the small cabin in the bow to sleep. Riki, wrapped in a quilt, stretched out on a seat in the cockpit, his head on his father's knee. The sea was still glassy calm; the *Zimba* lay almost as motionless as though at moorings under the boat shed in the shallows of Vaipopo lagoon.

Nat stared quietly down the companionway. At sea he slept little, except for an occasional nap in the daytime, when they were cruising, with no fish about. The Tuttle boys had spent many a night at sea, and it was always taken for granted that Nat would be on watch until dawn. He could sit hour after hour, alert for any change in weather, but otherwise scarcely more animate than the *Zimba* herself.

Riki was roused with difficulty from the deep slumber of boyhood. When at last he opened his eyes the sky was as black as the sea itself. Spits of rain struck his face, and the *Zimba* was wallowing with an uneasy motion. His father was bending over him, shaking him by the shoulders.

"Riki! Riki!"

The boy sat up, rubbing his eyes.

"Go below," his father said. "It's going to rain hard before long. You'll get soaked out here. Tell Fana I want him."

Gathering up his quilt, the boy, scarcely awake, went to the tiny cabin, where he slumped down beside Ru, on the floor, and immediately fell asleep again. After waiting a few moments, Nat himself went to wake Fana, shaking him roughly half a dozen times before he could bring him to consciousness. His brother followed him out and was soon thoroughly awake. Rain, driven by the rising wind, was lashing across the sea in slanting sheets. He turned quickly to close the companionway hatch. Nat flashed on his pocket lamp and handed it to his brother.

"Get the steering sweep."

Fana knew what that meant. The wind was coming straight off the land. There would be no sailing home. He drew the long oar from amongst the fishing gear lashed along the side of the launch. Nat ran it out through its loop of two-inch rope. He heaved the *Zimba* round to head into the sea, which was growing rougher each moment.

"Over with the tuna," he ordered.

"Hell, this ain't nothing," Fana replied.

"Do as I say. I know what's coming. Leave three or four."

Nat was never wrong in his estimates of wind and weather. Fana knew his every tone of voice, and the way in which he now spoke convinced him that they were in for a bad time. He tied the flash lamp where it could throw its tiny circle of shadow-centered light into the cockpit and set to work heaving overboard the tuna they had labored so hard to catch a few hours earlier. As she was lightened the launch pitched more violently, throwing up clouds of spray that felt warm to their bodies after the colder rain.

The first pale light of day showed dead to windward as Fana completed his task. Presently the companionway hatch slid back and Ru and Chester appeared. The four men were shadows to one another in the ghostly light.

"Where's Tahiti?" Chester asked.

"Right where this is coming from."

Nat heaved and pulled strongly to keep the launch headed up. They could scarcely see him in the spray that flew over them, but they heard his voice plainly enough as he added, to what Fana had just said: "And where we'd have been ashore since midnight with that extra five gallons!"

"Nat! Don't forget we got Tetiaroa somewhere to leeward," Ru shouted.

There was no reply for a moment; then Nat's voice was heard again coming out of a cloud of rain and spray: "What do you want me to do — move it out of the way?"

Tetiaroa, a long, low coral island, lay twenty-eight miles north of Tahiti. When the *Zimba* had run out of gas they were half a dozen miles southeast of the island. They could not know how much they might have drifted during the night, and in the dim light of dawn, with the rain driving over them, they could not see fifty yards.

"If we hit we'd have a bare chance," said Chester. "There'll be a hell of a surf along the west side. Might carry us right over the reef."

No reply was made to this remark. Nat was having all he could do to keep the launch headed into the seas. They now had all the light they could hope for, and it diminished rather than increased as the morning advanced. Riki was again on deck, crouched in the cockpit with his back to the wind.

"All right, Riki?"

The boy smiled faintly.

"Not scared, are you?"

He shook his head, resolutely.

"That's the boy, Riki," said Fana. "You'll be out in a lot worse than this, tuna fishing."

"What is it you're looking for?" the boy asked.

The brothers exchanged glances. Riki was no coward. They wouldn't baby him. It was Fana who spoke.

"Tetiaroa's somewhere to leeward. You got the best eyes of the lot, Riki. Keep 'em peeled, will you, off in that direction?"

The lad got up at once and kneeled on the seat, facing aft. Fana put his arm around him. Now and then he glanced up at his father, as though for reassurance. He saw nothing there to worry him.

It was at times like this, in such situations, that the Tuttle boys were seen at their best, with none to see them save an occasional lonely gannet, or frigate bird, scudding down wind. It was now blowing half a gale, and the low dirty clouds flying past seemed almost within reach. Despite the increasing tumult of wind and sea, all heard at the same moment the roar that meant breakers. Riki gripped his uncle's arm, but Fana laid a hand quickly over his lips. He put his mouth close to the boy's ear. "I heard, Riki. Mustn't rattle your father. It's all right. We're going to miss it."

Ru and Chester were gazing steadily in the same

direction. There was no change in Nat's expression. He had no time even for a quick glance.

"Chester!"

"Yes?"

"Let me know what you see."

"All right. Nothing yet."

At last, through a momentary rift in the clouds, all four watchers saw, a quarter of a mile abeam, a long point of reef where the seas were piling up in an appalling fashion. Beyond they had a glimpse of a stretch of beach where half a dozen tall coconut palms were bending to the gale, their tattered fronds streaming out horizontally. Fana gave a yell of delight.

"We're clear!" he shouted.

"Sure?" Nat asked.

"It's the *motu* at the west end, with the seven palms!"

"How's that for luck, Nat?" Chester yelled.

His brother had no time to reply. All his strength was needed in keeping the *Zimba* headed up.

"Fana!"

"Yes?"

"Get sail on her — just a goose wing! We got to scud."

Gradually the wind shifted from south to east, increasing in force, and for twenty hours the *Zimba* ran before a gale which drove her far beyond any fishing grounds with which she was familiar. Dawn was breaking once more when the wind began to abate, and by the time the sun was three hours high, only the long swell, gradually subsiding, was left to remind the Tuttle boys of what they had passed through. The *Zimba* was a splendid sea boat, and once they were running, their only anxiety had been on account of the sail. Fortunately, the weakest part of it was that reefed down. They blessed the sail as they blessed the *Zimba* herself. Neither had been found wanting in a storm which all admitted was the worst they had ever experienced in so small a boat. Although no one spoke of it, there had been one moment of great danger: when they bore off to scud. For all Nat's care to choose the right moment, a sea had caught them broadside-on, and only the exertions of all of them had saved the launch from floundering.

At midday, the sun was shining in a cloudless sky, and a faint breeze, still from the east, wrinkled the surface of the swells. Around the entire circle of the horizon there was no land in sight.

"Might be a hundred miles," Nat was saying. "That's my guess, anyway. That bit of sail wouldn't do much, and there was the drag of the propeller. When it was blowing hardest I doubt if we did more than three knots."

"Call it three," said Fana. "Where'd that bring us?"

"Where we are now," said Chester.

This seemed as good a reply as any to Fana's question. They knew the seriousness of the situation. With no gas for the engine, and what little breeze there was dead against them, there was nothing they could do but wait and hope. They had a full five-gallon demijohn of water, and about half a gallon in a smaller one. For food they had only the four tuna caught more than thirty-six hours earlier, and half-a-dozen bananas. Two of the fish were thrown overboard; the other two they decided to cook at once to preserve the flesh as long as possible. Fana and Ru attended to this. The primus stove was brought on deck and they cut the fish into steaks, using up all their lard in frying enough to fill an empty biscuit tin.

"Tuna steak!" Fana called. "Nice tuna steak, only a little rotten. Who wants it?"

"I do," said Nat.

"We better all fill up now before it goes too bad," said Chester. "Bring the vinegar, Ru."

They had only half a bottle of vinegar, and Nat insisted that they use it sparingly at this first meal. They would have greater need for it later.

"There won't be any later for me," Ru said, making a wry face as he chewed. "I'll go hungry."

"Tell us that day after tomorrow," said Nat. "Rotten or not, you'll be glad to eat it. How's it go, Riki?"

The lad smiled. "I can get it down, all right."

"That's the boy," said Fana. "You'll be a real fisherman before you're through. What about the bananas, Nat? We got six left."

"Better eat 'em now. They'll go rotten in no time."

Fana went to fetch them. "One apiece for us and two for Riki," he said. "If I was you, Riki, I'd save that one for tomorrow. It ain't so ripe as the other. You'll be wanting it bad then."

Having bolted the fish, they took their time over the bananas. Then Fana ransacked the cabin, hoping to find a forgotten packet of tobacco. He had no luck.

Nat stretched out on the floor of the cockpit. The midday sun baked them, and the faint breeze died away. They were silent for some time, each man engaged in his own reflections. With an exasperated sigh, Fana rose to scan the horizon, and took his seat again.

"Who's noticed anything funny?" Ru asked.

"What do you mean — funny?" Nat said, morosely.

"It's about Chester."

"Well, spit it out. What is it?"

"He ain't stuttered since yesterday morning when we just missed the Tetiaroa reef."

"How do you know?" Chester replied, his face brightening. "I must have."

"Not once. I could swear to it."

"Don't believe he has, at that," said Fana.

"That reef must have scared it out of me," Chester replied. "We didn't have more'n f-f-f-four hundred yards to spare."

"There you go again," said Nat. "What'd you tell him for, Ru? He might have been cured if you hadn't spoke."

"There ain't no chance of that, I guess. I t-t-t-took some treatments once when I was in America. Cost me twenty-five du-du-du-dollars. Didn't do a damn bit of good."

There was another long silence.

"Say we're a hundred miles off," said Fana, continuing his reflections aloud. "We can probably . . ."

"Shut up!" said Nat. "If you want to do some figuring you can tell us what we know: where we'd be now if it wasn't for you! Home — that's where, with four or five thousand francs for the tuna we had to feed to the sharks." He glanced at Riki to make sure he was asleep. "I know what they'll be thinking at Vaipopo in a day or two," he added, in a low voice. "And by God, it may be so before the week's out."

"What about rowing?" Chester asked. "Might do a mile an hour."

Nat shook his head. "Not now. Make us too thirsty. We'll wait till sundown."

Half an hour later, Chester, Nat, and Ru were all asleep beside Riki, in the shelter of the sail which had been rigged for an awning over the cockpit. Fana sat with his chin in his hands, staring at the planking between his bare feet. He could imagine the scene at home. At this very moment Jonas would be out with the Taio boys, in search of them. They would probably go to Moorea first, thinking they might have run into Cook's Bay or Afareaitu. Not finding them there, they would make the circuit of Tetiaroa, in wide zigzags, going and coming, to cover as great an area of sea as possible. By tomorrow all the Papeete fishing fleet would be out in search, but they would never come this far. And by the end of the week hope would be given up. A picture as vivid as reality came into his mind, of the family gathered at Vaipopo awaiting Jonas's return. All the village would be there. He saw Hio, Nat's wife, with her head in her arms, Mama Ruau trying to comfort her, and Tamara sitting on the steps beside them, their two children on her lap. He saw the Taio truck coming up the road at dusk, Jonas in the front seat beside Emily and Moa Taio. He heard Hio's despairing cry: "No news, Jonas?" and the wild outburst of grief that followed.

Fana raised his head quickly as a faint breath of air fanned his cheek. To starboard, as the *Zimba* lay, the glare on the sea was vanishing beneath a film of blue wind-rippled water, deepening as he gazed. He threw a hasty glance at the sun, then, scarcely able to believe, sprang to the compass for confirmation. West — due west! The *Zimba* began to rock gently.

With eager fingers he began to cast loose the sail awning, shaking Nat vigorously with his foot at the same time. "Nat! Nat!"

His brother opened his eyes and stared vaguely at him.

"Wind!"

"Where from?"

"Fair as anything!"

Nat jumped to his feet, and the two brothers worked rapidly.

"Won't last," Nat said, as they were bending on the sail, as if to prepare himself for any disappointment to come.

"The hell it won't," said Fana. "We've had west winds many a time, two or three days at a stretch."

"Take the wheel."

"What course?"

Nat reflected. "Make it east-by-north."

"Just what I was thinking." Fana ran back while his brother stood waiting. The *Zimba* came round slowly, gathering way as Nat paid out the sheet and made it fast.

"Shall we let 'em sleep?" Fana asked, with a glance at the others.

Nat smiled. "Might as well. Chester'll have something to stutter about if this holds."

"Hold? Sure it will," Fana said, jubilantly. He glanced over the side. "We're doing a good three knots."

The sun was near to setting when Chester awoke. Ru and Riki had been up for an hour past. Fana grinned at him.

"No, you ain't dreaming," he said.

Nat, who was in the bow with Riki, called back: "Swing her over, Fana!" He pointed with his outstretched arm a little to the east of the course they were on. Fana gave a cheer as he obeyed the order, while Ru and Chester ran forward. As the *Zimba* rose to the swell, they saw what Nat and Riki had seen: a tiny blue triangle pricking the eastern horizon. Chester wouldn't believe in it until he had confirmed the view, unmistakably, a moment later.

"B-b-boy! Don't that look wonderful! Riki, have a good look. You won't see Tahiti this far off many times in your life."

"How far is it?"

"A good eighty miles," his father replied.

"*Au-é, Tahiti-Nui 'ti é!*" Ru exclaimed joyfully.

"We ain't there yet," said Nat.

CHAPTER XI

THEY had the breeze all night, and throughout the next morning it was blowing as sweetly as ever, from the same quarter, under the same cloudless sky. No one spoke of their luck, but they blessed it in their hearts. Aorai and Orofena, Tahiti's six- and seven-thousand-foot peaks, were now well above the horizon. Fana could see the saddle on the higher mountain beneath which he had once camped with an American traveler who wished to be the first who had ever climbed Orofena.

"You see that little niche above the saddle?" Fana was saying. "Maybe you won't believe this, Chester, but the main ridge there's just wide enough to straddle. Goes down a thousand feet on both sides, straight as a wall. We went along mighty careful, believe me! Then we come to a place where it widens out a little. The wind was strong enough to blow us off if we'd tried to stand up. We had a wonderful view for a few minutes; we could see the valleys all round, and Mehitia and Maiau off to sea. Then the clouds closed in again and it began to rain. Cold? I ain't been so cold in my life as I was that afternoon.

"Then we come to a big step, eighteen or twenty feet high. All there was on it was a few tufts of grass and fern; not a niche to get two fingers in. There was no way past it and no way up. We was bitched. I knew it and the *popaa* knew it, but we didn't say nothing for a while. Our camp was about fifteen hundred feet below. We had a little tent there, on a ridge just wide enough to pitch it on. It would take us a good three hours to reach it if we was going back. If we wasn't, we'd have to sit astraddle of that ridge till next morning, freezing in the rain and wind, not daring to sleep even if we could have. The *popaa* was crazy enough to do it, too. I was bound to stay if he did. He sat there, freezing and thinking, for half an hour. He was a skinny chap, and I knew he must be even colder than I was. Finally he said: 'Well, Fana, what do you think?' 'I ain't got no brains left to think with,' I said. 'What little I had is froze solid.' 'There's nothing more we can do tonight,' he said. 'Are you game to sit here and wait till morning?' 'If you are,' I said. He thought a while longer, then he said: 'Probably mean pneumonia for both of us.' I told him I'd take the chance if he wanted to. 'You're married, ain't you?' he asked me. 'No,' I said, 'but I got a wife and baby.' 'Then we're going down,' he said. All he wanted was an excuse. So we turned round and went back to the place where we had to let ourselves down a wall steep as the side of a house. I don't think we could ever have got up it again. We got to our camp long after dark, but he had a flashlight. Then we drank half a cup of neat rum apiece and got into our blankets. I wasn't warm again for two weeks."

Nat grunted. "What'd he want up there, anyway?" he asked.

"Nothing; that's the funny part. To get up; that's all, and come down again."

"*Popaas* are all like that," Chester said. "They're crazy, that's all you can say about 'em. Look how some that come to Tahiti to fish pump in tuna with a rod and reel. They like to make work for themselves. Must be because they're all rich and have nothing to do at home."

Riki was gazing intently off to starboard during this conversation.

"What do you see, Riki?" Chester asked.

"I don't know what it is. There's something off yonder."

Fana rose to gaze in the direction of the boy's outstretched arm.

"There! You see?" Riki asked, as the *Zimba* rose to the swell.

"Sure I do! You got better eyes than your dad."

"What is it?" Ru asked.

"Hard to tell. Might be a floating tree."

Nat rose for a look. "It's standing straight up," he said, after a careful scrutiny. "Never saw a tree float like that."

"I have," said Fana. "Depends on the kind of tree and how heavy the butt is. Bear off a little, Ru. Let's have a look."

"The hell with it," said Nat. "We ain't going off our course to look at a tree."

"We'd better," Ru urged. "If it *is* a tree, there's sure to be fish around it. I can't eat no more of that rotten tuna."

"Nor me," said Chester. "How about it, Nat? It won't take us more'n an hour off our course."

"Go on, then," his brother replied, grudgingly. "But I'm telling you! You'll change our luck. We got a fine breeze, but wait and see! It'll die on us for this."

There was no indication of Nat's prophecy coming true during the next two hours. The breeze held as fresh as ever. At first they watched in desultory fashion from the cockpit. All were puzzled for a time, although Fana held to his first opinion: it was a tree, he thought, with two ragged limbs, high up, sticking out at right angles. Presently Riki shinned up the mast for a better view. He slid down, his eyes bulging. "It's a ship," he announced. "I could see her, plain!"

Fana corrected him gently. "It can't be a ship, Riki. But maybe it looks like one from up there."

"I *know* it is," the boy replied, with such conviction that even Nat was interested. "Ru, you're lightest," he said. "Go up for a look."

"It is, sure as the world!" Ru called down. "She's only got one mast."

Gradually the hull came up until all could see it whenever the launch rose to the swell. Chester had gone to the bow and stood gazing ahead for a full quarter of an hour, his hand shading his eyes. He came back, sputtering and hissing, unable to make an intelligible sound. Nat gave him a resounding thump between the shoulders, and like a pump half-primed, jetting water mixed with air, the words came at last.

"It's the *Ch-ch-ch-ch* . . . It's the *Ch-ch-ch-Charlotte*," he said, and immediately became unintelligible again, straining and spitting in his effort to say more.

"The *Charlotte?* What's that?" Fana asked.

"Du-du-du-don't you remember? It's the b-b-b-barque I was on!"

The others stared at him. "You're crazy!" Nat said. "You told us you left her way north of the Marquesas."

"I'm telling you it's the *Ch-ch-ch-Charlotte*," Chester repeated. "Don't you think I nu-nu-know my own ship?"

"Maybe he's right at that," Fana put in, eagerly. "It's all of six months ago you left her, wasn't it? She might have drifted down here by now."

"Might have?" said Chester. "G-g-g-God damn it! Th-th-there she *is!*"

His excitement was now shared by the others. They stared and stared as they approached, scarcely believing in what they saw. They were within a mile of her now, and a forlorn and lonely sight she was in that empty sea. Only the foremast stood, and from a single yard, which hung at an angle, a few rags of canvas flapped in the breeze. Seafowl wheeled about her, and small waves lapped her hull, falling back in showers of spray.

"What about it, Nat? Sorry we came?"

His brother replied with another question. "What'd I say about the breeze? Won't have enough to take us alongside."

The others glanced back in surprise. So keen was their interest in the derelict that only Nat had noticed how slowly they were moving. The breeze became lighter and lighter and the *Zimba* lost steerageway. The sweeps were gotten out at once. Nat took one and Fana the other and they pulled mightily. The derelict had been lying with her stern toward the distant land, but as they neared she began to swing around, very slowly.

"Look!" said Chester. "She's been hunting f-f-for me all this time. Now she hears my voice, she's coming round the wu-wu-way she ought to go!"

"What'd you tell us she was loaded with?" Ru asked.

"Water, mostly, from the looks of her," said Fana.

"Lumber. Thousands and thousands of feet. And two hundred fifty-gallon drums of gas."

Nat and Fana stopped rowing, staring at Chester incredulously. "Two hundred *drums?*" said Fana.

Chester nodded. "I ain't sure it wasn't two-fifty."

Ru gave a yodel of joy. Nat spit on his hands and grasped his oar again. "Come on, let's get alongside."

They passed under her stern where the name

CHARLOTTE

VANCOUVER

seemed to be repeating itself soundlessly in the wide air of mid-ocean. The *Zimba* accosted her with a gentle thud, and four pairs of hands drew the launch along to the waist of the barque, where Chester scrambled aboard. The launch was made fast, bow and stern, with a couple of worn-out tires as bumpers, whereupon the rest of them shinned up the side. The seafowl, perched on the foresail yard, which was white with their droppings, took the air, circling over the ship with faint harsh cries, as though in protest at this invasion of a sanctuary which they had claimed long since. Indeed, the old vessel seemed to belong to them and to the sea more than she had ever belonged to the world of men. A booby, resting on the deck, remained where he was, with an air that said, unmistakably: "Be off! We found it first." He snapped his beak indignantly as Nat took him up, teased him for a moment with his forefinger, and tossed him into the air.

Fana glanced around wonderingly. "You must have gone through it, Chester, in that storm."

"Didn't I t-t-tell you? Right where you're standing is where the mate was, last time I saw him. He went in a sea that swept clean over us. It was the s-s-s-same time we lost the galley, cook and all. There was half an hour about then when we thought it was f-f-finish for the lot of us."

"How big a crew d'you have?"

"Eleven, with the cook. She's only three hundred and fifty tons, the *Charlotte*."

"Where's the drums of gas?" Ru asked.

"Come on."

The hatches were still safely in place, although the tarpaulins over them were worn and tattered. They knocked out the wedges around the fore hatch and lifted off three heavy planks. A warm, almost stifling odor of oil, lumber, bilgewater, and tar greeted them as they peered into the gloom below where, presently, they could see a jumbled mass of twelve-inch boards that had been laid over the drums of gasoline.

"It ain't hardly budged," Chester exclaimed, jubilantly. "Look, Ru! Can you see? Drums and drums and more drums! See how they're shored to keep 'em in place? That was done in Frisco, and a good job, too."

Fana heaved a sigh. "I could sit here all day," he said. "Don't it smell good?"

"There's probably a few of 'em busted," said Chester. "We got to be awful careful about matches. All the gas is forward. We can do our cooking aft."

"What's there to cook?" Nat asked.

"The old man laid in any amount of tinned stuff; and he didn't keep it all for himself and the mates, neither. We lived about as well, forward, as they did aft. I never tasted better salt beef and pork than we got aboard here. All prime pieces; no shins and lumps of gristle and fat such as I've et times enough on other ships. If the tinned stuff's gone bad we can live high on the salt beef."

Chester had said nothing of the *Charlotte* and his voyage aboard her since the brief account given to the family on the night of his return home. His brothers had not bothered to question him further, but now they inquired about everything, down to the minute details. They remained for some time around the hatch, breathing the, to them, delicious fragrance of gasoline while they listened to his recital. At last Nat said: "What about something to eat? Where's all that salt beef you was telling us about?" He glanced at the sea, which was again glassy calm. "What'd I say about the breeze?" he added. "We're stuck here, right enough."

"Stuck?" said Ru. "With all that gas in the hold?"

"That's right." Nat grinned, sheepishly. "I can't seem to get it through my head about the gas."

Chester, who had preceded them aft, beckoned. They

pried open the companionway hatch and Chester led
the way down to a spacious cabin with a dining table
in the center, two swivel chairs on either side, and a
larger one at the end. A fine brass lamp, now dull and
green with mold, hung over the table. The walls were
paneled in oak, ornamented with faded gilding, and
behind the captain's chair two paintings of sailing
ships that looked as old as the *Charlotte* herself were
let into the paneling. Chester tried a door on the right,
but that was locked.

"It's the old man's cabin," he said. "The mates' is on
the port side. The storerooms is along this passage."

The door here was fastened only with a sliding bolt.
Chester opened it and his brothers gazed about them in
silence. Shelves loaded with supplies ran around the
walls, with roomy lockers beneath. An adjoining
storeroom was half filled with food in cases and barrels.

"Things ain't in such a mess here as you'd expect,"
said Ru.

"You should have seen it right after the storm,"
Chester replied. "But we was three weeks aboard, afterward, trying to get to the Marquesas. The ones not on
watch was kept busy cleaning up and setting things
to rights, below. That's when all them battens was put
acrost the shelves." He was silent for a moment. "I
can't help thinking about our cook," he said. "He used
to be in here a dozen times a day, getting things for the
galley. He knew more songs. He had a good voice, too.
There was one he used to sing half the time, about
another Charlotte. It had a fine swing. Went like
this: —

"Oh, Charlotte,
The harlot,
She'd been most everywheres:
From London down to Singapore,
New York and Bonus Airs.
And every port where Charlotte went . . ."

Chester broke off, remembering that Riki was with them. The lad was listening with interest. "What's a harlot?" he asked.

"Nothing so much, Riki. It's just a word the *popaas* use."

"What's it mean? Is it a kind of a ship?"

"That's right. It's a . . . it's an old hooker like this that's been around the world a lot and finally goes adrift, nobody knows where. Now then, let's see what we got here."

They brought up food and more food from the storerooms, nor was there any lack of water on board. The *Charlotte* had two 400-gallon tanks, forward, and another, of 200 gallons, aft. The water in them was anything but fresh, but still drinkable; meanwhile they had their own supply from the *Zimba*, ample for the moment. They found that a good deal of the tinned food had gone bad, the tins having rusted through, but enough remained to give them a wide choice of such delicacies as sardines, beets, salmon, tinned peaches and pears; and they found one case which proved to be filled with English plum puddings. The salt beef, pork, and salmon were all that Chester had claimed, and there were mustard pickles to give them an extra relish. A makeshift galley composed of a piece of sheet iron and a biscuit tin was set up on the quarter-deck. While Ru was preparing the food the others followed Chester to the forecastle. To his surprise and relief, Chester found that the crew's quarters were as dry as when they had abandoned the ship. Lashed to the top bunk on the port side was a large sea chest.

"That's mine," said Chester, "and just where I left it!"

He cast off the lashings, and with Nat to help him the chest was carried on deck.

"I got a lot of stuff in here," said Chester. "Remember how you kidded me the night I got home with my franc and a half? I'll show you why I didn't have any more."

He raised the lid to reveal a guitar in a leather case. He drew the instrument from the case. The frets were of mother-of-pearl and the sounding board was beautifully inlaid with the same material. "This is yours, Fana. I didn't want to tell you I bought it because I thought it was gone for good. It's got a wonderful tone. I got it in Honolulu. It's a lot better than the one you lost at the cockfight."

Fana handled the instrument with an air almost of reverence. "Chester *tané!*" he exclaimed. "What'll I say?"

"Don't say nothing," his brother replied. "We can have some real music with a guitar like this. There's a lot of extra strings in a waterproof box. These is kind of rusty. I didn't forget you, Riki," he added, handing him a fine harmonica. "Set your lips to that. And look, Riki; it's a double one: key of G on one side and key of A on the other. I got one just like it for Tupa."

He then brought a lacquered box containing a shawl with flowered designs embroidered on black silk. "This set me back plenty," he said. "It's for Mama Ruau; I got it in Shanghai. There's three others almost as good for Hio and Tamara and Effie. I won't take the other things out now. We got plenty of time."

If ever a meal was enjoyed by hungry men it was that to which Ru now called them. They rigged the fore-hatch tarpaulin for an awning, over the stump of the mainmast, which had broken off at a height of six or seven feet. In the shade of the awning they reclined at ease, eating until they could hold no more. At last Nat lay back with a groan of content. "The rest of you can do what you've a mind to," he said. "I'm going to stay right where I am, for a couple of hours, anyway."

"Sure, why not?" said Fana. "There ain't no hurry. My idea is, we might as well stay on board three or four days and take it easy."

Chester said nothing. He was enjoying, in secret, the luxury of anticipation. He could see, from the way in which they spoke, that his brothers had no conception of the nature of their find as it concerned themselves. He had an announcement to make, but he put it off from moment to moment, waiting for just the right opening.

"I don't know about that," said Nat, replying to Fana. "They'll be awful worried about us at home. The weather looks settled enough, but you can't be sure about it this time of year. We ought to go while we got a calm sea."

"Go where?" said Chester.

"Home — where else?"

"We'll have to call at Papeete first," said Fana, "to notify the harbor master. They'll want to send a boat right out to tow her in." He gave Nat a contemptuous shove with his foot. "What about changing our luck now?" he said. "If we'd listened to you we'd be rowing the *Zimba*, with empty bellies."

"Don't take so much credit to yourself," said Nat. "We got Riki to thank for it. What do you think they'll give us for finding her, Chester?"

"Nothing," said Chester.

"What!" said Fana. "They're bound to. Shouldn't wonder if we got ten or fifteen thousand francs, four times as much as them tuna would have brought us."

"I s-s-s-said, nothing," Chester repeated, beginning to stutter violently in the excess of his pleasure. "Th-th-they ain't got the right to."

"The hell they ain't! Why not? You mean, all they'll do is say 'Thank you'? The owners can't be as low-down as that."

"You p-p-p-poor idiot, don't you know nothing about marine law? Th-th-th-the owners d-d-d-don't own the *Charlotte* now."

Nat raised his head to give him a puzzled glance. "What you talking about? Who does, then?"

"The ship and everything in her, every gu-gu-gu-gallon of gas and every f-f-f-foot of lumber, belongs to us."

If Chester expected his announcement to make an immediate stir, he was disappointed. Fana's only response was a wry smile. Ru said: "Sure. Ain't we lucky!" and Nat said nothing at all. Chester hadn't counted on this. He now settled down to convince them, and little by little he succeeded; the incredible truth dawned upon them at last. Nat sprang to his feet with a whoop of joy that startled into flight the terns and gannets that had again settled on the foremast yard. Fana took his brother by the shoulders. "You're dead sure, Chester? It's ours, ship and all? There ain't no doubt about it?"

"Ship and all," said Chester; "but we got to get her into port, somehow, without help. If we was to take a tow, whoever owned the boat that towed us would have a big cut in the cargo. Half anyway, and maybe more." He smiled. "Guess you won't want to be going to see the port captain after all."

Ru was doing some mental arithmetic. "Two hundred and fifty drums," he said. "That's twelve thousand five hundred gallons; enough to keep the old *Zimba* going day and night for about a year and a half, if we wanted to."

"The 'old' *Zimba*?" said Fana. "We're going to have a *new* one that'll make the Taios' *Hina* look like nothing at all."

"Sure," said Ru, "but it's the old *Zimba* that's got to get us home."

"What I'm wondering is if she's gu-gu-got power enough to move her."

"She's got to have!" Nat turned to glance at the

distant outline of Tahiti, pale blue against the sky.
"We ain't more'n thirty miles off. We'll keep her at it
if it takes a month."

"It's too bad we can't let 'em know at home," said
Ru. "They think we're dead by now. Lost at sea."

"That won't matter," said Fana. "I'd just as soon
Tamara did some crying over me. I've been crying over
her long enough, you might say, trying to get her to
bring the kids and move in at Vaipopo. I'll bet she won't
need no more coaxing when she knows what we've
got here. First thing I'll do is finish our house."

"We ain't there yet," said Nat. "The first thing
we're going to do now is get the *Zimba* started."

They lost no time in rigging a block and tackle over
the fore hatch, and one of the drums of gasoline was
hoisted on deck. For the first time within memory, the
Zimba's tank was filled to capacity: a full forty gallons.
A fifty-fathom towline, of good Manila, was made fast
to the bitts. Ru and Fana were in the launch. The engine started at the first whirl of the flywheel.

"That's the girl, *Zimba!*" said Fana. "You hear her,
Nat?" he called. "She's as anxious to get home as we
are."

"Easy! Head off north till we get her swung around."

They watched anxiously as the *Zimba* took up the
slack. For ten minutes she seemed to be tugging in
vain; then, with infinite slowness, the *Charlotte* began
to turn. Nat hailed the launch, raising his arm for
straight ahead; then, with her nose toward home and
her throttle wide open, the *Zimba* settled down to her
work. Chester and Nat were leaning over on either

side of the bowsprit, their eyes fixed on the water. It was a tense moment for all. "Is she moving?" Fana yelled. Nat shook his head. "Can't tell yet." A moment later he dropped an empty tin over the side, right against the bow. The tin rocked gently where it had fallen as if it meant to rest there forever. Presently Nat gave a jubilant shout. There was no doubt of it: the *Charlotte* was moving. "Give her all you've got, Ru," he called.

"I have. Does she feel it?"

"She's on her way! We'll do a quarter of a knot, once we get going."

"*Aué, Tahiti é!*" Fana yelled, waving his arm at the distant land.

"Look at him," said Chester, with a contented grin. "Fana's home already."

CHAPTER XII

JONAS was the last of the family to give up hope of the boys' return. Four days had passed, with no news, and the womenfolk abandoned themselves to grief. Friends and neighbors came in to mourn with them, to comfort them as best they could; but when a schooner arrived from the Leeward Islands, bringing word that the *Zimba* had not been seen or heard of there, the truth was brought home to Jonas himself: his boys were lost, and little Riki with them.

Nevertheless, he continued the search four days longer before sending out word of the memorial service to be held at Vaipopo. To postpone it further would have been useless, and to have dispensed with it altogether, a breach of custom unthinkable in a family of Polynesian blood. Therefore, much as they dreaded the ordeal, preparations were made for the reception of guests whom they knew would come from every district the island around.

Paki was a friend in need at this time. Knowing that Jonas was without funds, he had given Effie, unasked, five hundred francs with which to provide the refreshments of coffee, bread, and butter to be served at midnight. Then, having assisted with the preparations throughout the day, he had gone to Papeete at sunset, as the first guests were arriving. He made a gruff excuse to his wife, but Effie knew the reason for the hasty departure. Paki's grief at the family's loss was deep and sincere, and his affection for Ru in particular bordered on idolatry. He could not bear the all-night ordeal of the *himiné*, and as he was not blood kindred of the Tuttles, he was justified in escaping it.

Jonas was never more the head of the family than now when his help was needed most. He sustained and comforted them all. Hio, who mourned the loss of both husband and son, was the last to recover from the exhaustion of passionate grief, but as their guests began to arrive, she took her place with the other members of the family to receive them. Never in Vaipopo's history had there been a greater gathering to do honor to the memory of the dead. There was not room for more than the kindred and intimate friends in the living room, where the singing would take place; the others gathered in silence on the verandas, or in groups scattered over the lawn between the road and the house. A table with two lamps upon it stood at one end of the living room. Tearo, pastor of the Vaipopo church, sat here with Jonas on one side and Mama Ruau on the other, while ranged in rows of chairs behind them were the other relatives. Two-score of singers, men and women, sitting crosslegged on mats, occupied the rest of the room. The night was cloudless and profoundly still, and the silence within the room itself was broken only by an occasional muffled cough, whispered word, or the fretting of an infant in its mother's arms.

Of a sudden a woman began the singing in a clear, high-pitched voice; the others joined in until the old house seemed to shake with the wild and melancholy music of the opening song of lamentation. Tears sprang into Mama Ruau's eyes, but she maintained her self-control. Hio, and Tamara, Fana's wife, bowed their heads in their arms and wept unrestrainedly. Jonas, his lips tightly set, gazed before him into the shadows of the far end of the room until at last the song came to a close in a long-drawn note sung in unison, dying slowly away to silence.

Despite the melancholy of the music, there was comfort in it, for the womenfolk, at least. It softened — how, they could not have explained — the bitterness of sorrow, and after the relief of fresh tears they listened as did their men, in stoical silence. It was necessary that they should remain as auditors until midnight, when would come the break in the service for refreshments. Shortly before this time, Tearo, the native pastor, rose from his chair and spoke with dignity and simplicity to the bereaved family, offering, on behalf of their neighbors and friends, what comfort might be found in the assurance of their sympathy and affection, and speaking to Jonas's sons as though they were present in the room, viewless spectators of what was taking place there. Then Jonas rose in his turn, and in the same simple manner spoke as follows: —

"My friends and neighbors: I wish to thank you on behalf of our family, for your words of sympathy and comfort, expressed through the lips of our pastor. Our four sons are gone — Nat and Chester and Fana and Ru, and our little grandson, Riki. It was the will of God that they should be taken: that we must believe. A lonely

family we shall be now, without them, but we shall
bear our loss with what strength we can find. There
is no more to be said."

Dawn was an hour distant when the singing came to
an end and the guests began to take their leave. Jonas,
his mother, and Effie stood on the veranda while the
others filed past to shake them silently by the hand.
At this time Dr. Blondin, who had been waiting outside, with other members of the European colony,
came forward to speak to the family. Jonas had not seen
the doctor since the day when he had come to Vaipopo
with Maître Dorme. Deep though his sorrow was, he
felt constrained to mention the vanilla money and to
explain why it had not been paid, as promised. Dr.
Blondin immediately protested.

"Jonas! Don't speak of it, I beg of you! It doesn't
matter."

"But I wanted you to know, Doctor," Jonas replied,
as he walked with him to the road where the doctor's
car was waiting. "I don't know what I'll do now," he
added, in a heartsick voice.

"Say no more, old friend." Blondin pressed his hand.
"You have sorrow enough to bear, God knows! Far be
it from me to add to your burden. I'm leaving at daylight for Mangareva," he added. "They have an epidemic of influenza there. I may be gone a month, perhaps longer. Come to see me when I return, Jonas, but
promise, meanwhile, that you will think no more of the
money affair. You know me of old. I would be the last
man in the world to press such a matter at a time like
this."

Jonas returned to his duty at his mother's side. He felt the genuineness of the sympathy of all these friends who had come to mourn with him the loss of his boys. Tears trickled down his cheeks as he bade them farewell, but he maintained his composure until the last of them had gone; then, excusing himself to his mother, he walked down the steps and vanished in the darkness. He went on to the beach and seated himself near the boat shed, looking out over the starlit water where the little waves were lapping so cheerily around the barnacled piles. He was never to see his boys again — never, never, never. There would be no mornings in the future when he would come down here to await their return from market. Of a sudden, he put his head in his arms, and with no one to see him gave way to his grief.

Dawn was breaking when he returned to the house. A few old friends had remained to help the family through the day to come: through the period of blankness that lies between the door shut upon the familiar life of yesterday and the door yet to open upon the uncertain life of tomorrow. Emily Taio was there, and a loyal friend she had been through this dark time — a comfort and support for the womenfolk; and had not her own daughter, Tamara, suffered with them? Jonas had realized more clearly than ever, during the past week, the strength of the tie that bound Tamara to her husband's family. She seemed to belong more to them than to her mother's people.

He halted by the cookhouse where some of the women were clearing up the dishes on which the midnight refreshments had been served. Tupa came forward at this moment, wanting to find some words of comfort for the head of Tuttle-ma.

"There's three kilos of sugar left from the supper," he said, gruffly, "and two tins of butter Effie brought ain't been opened. And we won't need no bread till tomorrow."

Jonas nodded, without speaking, and went on to the house. The relatives were gathered in the living room that looked so bare and forlorn, now that the guests were gone. The lamps still burned on the table, but the light of early morning was already in the room. He seated himself beside Tamara, taking the girl's hand. She glanced up at him, her lips quivering.

"I'm coming to Vaipopo with the children, Jonas," she managed to say. "I'll come to stay, for good, if you want me."

"We've always wanted you, Tamara," he replied. "It'll be a comfort, having you. It's all right, Emily?"

Tamara's mother nodded.

"If only I'd come when Fana was here," Tamara went on. Then tears blinded her eyes, and she could say no more.

Jonas was about to reply when a car driven at headlong speed turned in at the gate and drew up in front of the veranda with a screaming of brakes. Manu, one of the chauffeurs of the Tiaré garage in Papeete, sprang out, rushed up the steps, and halted at the doorway to the living room. He stood gaping at its occupants, unable to speak at first; then he managed to blurt out: "They're two miles off the passage! Moa sent me out!

They're coming awful slow! I can get you to town long
before they are!"

Emily Taio replied. "What are you saying, Manu?"
she asked, in a puzzled voice.

"They got an old ship in tow. Nobody knows what
it is yet, but they're all there — all five! Moa could see
'em plain through the telescope at the Bougainville
Club! He ran up there to look, and he knows it's them!"

The family looked at him in silence, not in the least
understanding what he was trying so hard to tell them.
Emily spoke again.

"Moa could see who? What has he sent you out here
for?"

Manu struggled hard to deliver himself of his astound-
ing and joyful news, and at last succeeded. "The *Zimba!*"
he shouted. "They ain't drowned, Jonas! They ain't none
of 'em drowned! And they're towing in an old ship,
like I said!"

The effect of the announcement was stupefying.
Jonas sprang to his feet and seized Manu by the shoulders.

"The *Zimba?*" he exclaimed, his voice trembling.
"You're sure, Manu? There ain't no mistake?"

"Sure as I'm telling you! It's them, Jonas! I didn't
leave till Moa'd seen all the boys through the telescope,
and Riki too. Everybody in town's down at the waterfront."

Within five minutes, it seemed, the news had spread
through all the village, and friends and neighbors came
thronging back to have it confirmed, but by that time
Manu's car was racing toward Papeete once more, with

Jonas, accompanied by Effie and Emily Taio, in the rear seat. As they approached Emily's place, at Tarahoi, she leaned forward. "Wait, Manu!" she shouted. "Stop at my place!"

"You won't be long, Emily?" Jonas inquired, anxiously.

"We're not going to town in the car," she replied. "I've got a better plan. The launch is here. We'll go out to meet them."

"There won't be time," Effie said. "I'm going in the car."

Manu now drew up at Emily's gate. "There's plenty of time to meet 'em in the *Hina* if you want to," he said. "The *Zimba's* barely moving with that old ship dragging after her. They won't have her inside the passage for a long while yet."

Jonas was so excited as to be incapable of making a decision, so Emily made it for him. "You come with me, Jonas. We'll see the boys long before Effie does." And so it was decided, but Effie was firm in her decision to go on by car.

Ten minutes later, the *Hina,* with Jonas and Emily on board and Emily's son Tihoti at the wheel, left the Taios' boathouse and headed for sea at her full twelve-knot speed.

At the hour when the *himiné* guests were being served with midnight coffee at the Tuttle homestead, the *Zimba,* with the *Charlotte* in tow, was headed diagonally across the Moorea Channel, five miles off the passage into Papeete harbor. Nat, Ru, and Riki were in the launch, and Chester and Fana on the derelict, and they could see afar the twinkling lights of the town which they had been approaching with infinite slowness for eight days past. The weather during this time had been all they could have wished, with a breeze so light that it did no more than take the glare from the surface of the quiet sea. They had worried about the current they would find in the Moorea Channel; sometimes it flowed to the westward and sometimes in the opposite direction, and it was impossible to know, beforehand, which it would be. But once they were well in it they found that it favored them: they were now moving at better than half a knot. Chester and Fana were jubilant as they stood in the bow of the *Charlotte* gazing toward the sleeping town whose lights beckoned them so cheerily.

"And there ain't nobody seen us," Fana was saying. "That's the best part of it. I been hoping all the way we could get right inshore at night, like this."

"It's funny we ain't seen none of the bonito boats," Chester said. "They must be fishing off Tiarei and Hitiaa. . . . Don't she run sweet?" he added, with a nod toward the *Zimba*. "That old Frisco Standard ain't never going to wear out, if you ask me."

"We got Paki to thank for a lot. There's nobody on Tahiti knows more about engines; he's sure kept it in fine shape."

"It shows what the *Zimba* can do wh-wh-when she's got all the gas she needs," said Chester. "She's only stopped that one time — day before yesterday, wasn't it?"

Fana grinned. "Guess she knows as well as we do what she's got behind her. She won't go hungry no more if she gets that gas in. Twelve thousand gallons!" he added, incredulously. "I can't hardly believe it, Chester."

"What about Jonas?" said Chester. "He won't be able to get it through his head even when we show him all them drums."

"Come on, *Morning!*" Fana exclaimed. "Shouldn't wonder if they've had a *himiné* over us before this. Wouldn't you like to see 'em when they get the news?"

They were interrupted by a hail from Nat. The launch was slowed down to take on gas. Fana and Chester drew her alongside; the gas was ready and waiting and the *Zimba's* tank quickly filled. Then Chester took Nat's place on the launch and the towing proceeded.

Slowly the hours of darkness passed; dawn was in the air, and little by little the island, now so close at hand, emerged from the shadows until it stood out in clear silhouette against the eastern sky.

"They'll be spotting us from shore any minute now," said Fana. "They probably got the telescope at the Bougainville Club trained on us already."

"Hope the Taio boys are in town," said Nat. "They'll be sure to send word out home, soon as they know it's the *Zimba.*"

They paced restlessly up and down, keeping their eyes fixed on the distant port. They could now make out the red spire of the native church on the beach opposite the harbor entrance, and, as the light increased, pale blotches of color, that were houses, began to appear amongst the trees along the waterfront. Nat stretched out his arm.

"There's a schooner coming. Looks like Knudson's."

They could see her plainly, a moment later, heading out through the pass under power, at full speed. Chester had seen her too, and was shouting to them from the launch.

"Remember what I said," he called, through his cupped hands. "No tow!"

Fana waved in response. Knudson, a half-caste Norwegian, was a man as big as Jonas Tuttle himself, whom he resembled in a superficial way, but the characters of the two men were vastly different. Knudson was a hard, shrewd man of business, the owner of two schooners, and one of Papeete's richest merchants. The Tuttle boys could make him out at the wheel of his vessel, and a little later he passed directly in front of the *Zimba* and not twenty yards ahead, making the little launch rock violently in the wake of the schooner. Then he turned in a wide circle and closed on the *Charlotte*, waving his hand to Nat and Fana as the engine was put in reverse.

"Thought you boys was drowned," he shouted.

"Drowned? We been fishing," Fana called back. "What do you think of our tuna, Knudson?"

"Where'd you find it?"

"We ain't telling. Might be more in the same place."

The schooner was alongside now, and the mate, a burly Tuamotu man, leapt on board the derelict. Knudson nodded to one of his sailors, who cast a line to the mate by which the latter drew up a stout hawser and proceeded to carry it forward. So rapidly was this done that the Tuttle boys had scarcely time to protest.

"Hey! What do you think you're doing?" Fana shouted, as the schooner moved slowly away, forward.

"It's all right, boys," Knudson called. "Give you a tow in."

"Cast off!" Nat shouted. "We ain't asking for no tow."

"Don't be a fool," Knudson replied. "You'll never get her in alone. Make fast there, Kola," he called to his mate.

Chester was shouting and gesticulating from the launch, but he needn't have worried. Nat's temper blazed up in sudden flame. He ran to the bow, seized Knudson's mate by the belt, and lifting him in his arms tossed him into the sea, where he fell with a mighty splash. Meanwhile, Fana had cleared the towline and thrown it overboard, after the mate.

"Thanks for nothing, Knudson," he shouted. "Whose ship is this, yours or ours?"

The trader had not expected this reception. Himself part native, he knew how far bluster and a peremptory manner would, commonly, carry him in dealing with other natives. He was in a rage as he fished up his mate and brought the schooner alongside again; nevertheless, he managed to conceal his feelings.

"You boys crazy?" he said. "You'll never get her through the pass without help."

"Mind your own business," Nat replied. "We're doing all right. We ain't asking for no help."

On the launch, Chester was waving his arms and

shouting with delight. Knudson controlled his temper.

"All right. No offense, Nat," he called, genially. "But I'm going to stand by when you reach the passage. Want to see you boys get safe in with what you've got there." As the schooner drew away he turned to call back: "They've sent word to Jonas-ma. I'll fetch him right out when he comes."

"Maybe we ought to take a tow, at that," Nat said anxiously as he gazed after the receding schooner. "He's right about the pass. We don't want to pile her up on the reef."

"Don't worry," said Fana. "We'll get her in, and old Knudson ain't going to have nothing to do with it. . . . Nat! Look what's coming!"

The sun was just rising and long shafts of golden light struck across the sea, revealing boats of every kind coming out from the distant harbor: schooners, launches, reef boats, canoes — whatever had man or engine power to propel them; sailing canoes as well, for these could move in the lightest of breezes. It looked as though all Papeete were on the way to greet them. It was a happy moment for the Tuttle boys. Had they returned bringing only the *Zimba* and themselves, they would have caused excitement enough, but with a derelict in tow — Such an event had not happened before. A ramshackle launch, loaded with friends from the fishing fleet, was the first to reach them. It slowed down by the *Zimba*, the men in her shouting boisterous greetings in both directions at once.

"What's all this, Chester?" one of them called. "Coming back to horn in on the fishing, are you?"

"And us thinking you was out of the way for good!" another shouted.

"You boys want any help getting that tuna to market, call on us."

"What's he weigh, Nat?"

"If you got any extra hooks like the one you caught him with, pass 'em along, will you?"

Chester sputtered out jubilant replies, and Ru stuck his head out of the companionway to wave his hand. A flotilla increasing in numbers gathered round them. They had offers of help without number, although there were no more Knudsons with attempts to take the *Charlotte* out of their hands.

"She ain't hardly moving, Nat! Better let us give you a hand!"

"Cast her loose, boys! Sea water ain't worth nothing."

"Sea water?" said Fana. "Wait till you see what we got down below!"

"What is it? Cement?"

"Gas," said Fana. "Two hundred and fifty drums. Maybe three hundred; we ain't sure yet. And all the rest lumber."

The news spread circle-wise, with the speed of sound, and so fast does rumor travel in Polynesia that, long before the *Charlotte* had been inched along to the harbor entrance, it was known in Tahiti's farthest settlements that the Tuttle boys were home, having towed in an abandoned vessel containing thousands of drums of gasoline and enough lumber to provide for the island's needs for years to come. The cargo was estimated as worth millions of francs.

Jonas and Emily heard it half an hour before they reached the *Zimba*. As the *Hina* passed the district of Faaa, the news was shouted to them by a native fishing from a canoe outside the reef. If anything could have added to Jonas's excitement, such an announcement was qualified to do so.

"Gasoline!" he exclaimed. "Must be so, Emily! That's what a sailing ship would be loaded with: gas and lumber!" He thrust his head down the companionway. "Tihoti, you got her full on? Don't seem like we're going good."

"What do you expect, fifty miles an hour?" Tihoti replied. "We're doing twelve knots."

"Yes, I s'pose we are. *Aué*, Emily . . ."

"Now just you keep calm, Jonas," Emily broke in. "We'll get there. And I wouldn't be too sure about the gasoline. You know how news gets spread around. There ain't ever a quarter of it true."

"I know, but there's always some truth in it. What in the world can it be, this ship they've found?"

Jonas had already asked the question half a dozen times since the launch left Tarahoi, but he was too excited to remember.

"What I said, Jonas. Wait and see. I'll be surprised if it ain't the vessel Chester was on. She's had time to drift a long way from where they left her."

When they had rounded the last point on the Faaa coast, the sight of the flotilla offshore with the derelict in their midst burst upon their view. Jonas cupped his hands around his eyes as he gazed.

"I can't hardly believe it, even now," he said, in a

trembling voice. "You don't know what I been through, Emily."

"It's past and done with, Jonas. Thank God for that!"

"Looks like everybody in Papeete's come out to meet 'em. Can't even see the *Zimba*."

Jonas's old lighthearted manner returned to him now. It wrapped itself around him like an invisible garment. Tears glistened in his eyes and his round face beamed with happiness.

"Must have been a dream I had, about the *himiné*," he said. He chuckled. "I was thinking about that five hundred francs we spent for the refreshments. Seems like the Tuttles never get the good of their money. Well, I'm just as glad we didn't, for once."

They approached rapidly, and Tihoti Taio throttled down the engine to weave his way amongst the craft surrounding the derelict. Jonas waved in response to greetings that came to him from all sides. The *Hina* came alongside where Nat and Fana, with Riki beside them, were waiting for their father. The derelict was crowded with people, and the Tuttles were not the family to display their deeper feelings in public. The meeting of Jonas and his sons had the friendly casualness of every day; it was as though the boys had returned from an ordinary fishing trip; but Jonas got rid of some of his pent-up emotion by lifting Riki in his arms and hugging him close.

"We wasn't expecting you to bring home any fish as big as this, Riki," he said, as he set the lad down.

"Riki was the one that found it," Nat said.

"So he did, Jonas," Fana put in. "We'd probably none of us have seen it if it hadn't been for Riki."

"And you been towing her all this time?"

"Over a week," said Nat. "The *Zimba's* run smooth as anything. We only had one breakdown, and Ru fixed that in no time."

"Well, you'll have another if you don't clear off all this crowd," Emily Taio said. "You got enough of a load without them."

"*Parau mau!*" said Jonas. "What you boys thinking of to let everybody in Papeete come on board?" He glanced quickly over the side. "Don't believe she's moving an inch."

Jonas now took command, scattering adults, youths, and small fry to all sides. "*Haeré outou!*" He waved his arms, driving them before him. He snatched a cigarette from the lips of one youth and gave him a smack on the behind that nearly lifted him from his feet. "You want to blow us up?" he demanded. "Don't you know this ship's full of gasoline?" In three minutes he had the vessel cleared and all the skiffs and canoes driven well away from the side. The boys watched him admiringly. They liked to see their father in one of his determined moods. He got things done, and done quickly.

Nat and Fana led him to the forward hatch, which was open. "Have a look, Jonas." Their father peered into the gloom below. "Can't see nothing, boys, with all this glare. Is it . . . ?"

"Gas," said Fana. "Two hundred and fifty drums sure, and probably a lot more. And all the rest's lumber."

"Twelve thousand five hundred gallons," Nat added. Their father stared at them. "Twelve thousand five hundred gallons," he repeated, softly, in an awe-struck voice. These were astronomical figures to Jonas, with respect to gasoline. Fana helped him to a realization of the vastness of the quantity by saying: "Ru was figuring it out. If we was to keep the *Zimba* running every minute, day and night, we'd have enough to last us nearly a year and a half."

"But it ain't ours, is it?" Jonas asked, incredulously. "Don't it belong to the people that owns the ship?"

"That's us, Jonas. We found her, didn't we? There wasn't a soul on board. Chester knows all about the law. He says a ship abandoned at sea belongs to whoever finds her."

"Don't know about that," their father said, doubtfully. "What do you think, Emily?"

"It's so, I'm pretty sure," said Emily. "Anyway, the biggest part will be yours."

"Old Knudson was out here in his schooner first thing this morning. He was bound to give us a tow whether we wanted it or not."

"You ought to have took it, boys. The *Zimba*'s barely moving her."

Emily shook her head. "The boys were right. I don't know the law, but I know Tom Knudson. You can be sure he'd fix it so he got a big share for bringing you in."

The tension increased as the morning advanced. Everyone knew that the Tuttles were determined to accept no help. Not a boat returned to harbor; all wanted to see what would happen when the pass was reached.

When directly opposite the entrance and about a mile distant, the derelict was brought slowly around until the launch and her tow were in perfect alignment with the two guiding beacons on shore. Jonas paced the deck nervously, glancing over the side at every moment to make sure they were still moving.

"I'd feel a lot better if Paki was out here," he remarked, nervously. "Can't make out where he's gone to. He was in town last night. And what's become of Effie?"

"She'll be looking for him," said Emily.

As they discussed this matter, Jonas decided that Paki must have spent the night in the Taunoa quarter, where many of his Low Island friends stayed during their sojourns on Tahiti. This would account for his not having heard the news. Presently they saw Knudson's schooner coming out from the harbor once more.

"There they are," said Jonas. "There's Paki and Effie on Knudson's boat. What'd they want to come out with him for?"

"Probably no other way to come," said Emily.

The schooner swung round by the derelict, about forty yards distant, and moved with it, the engine idling.

"Jonas!" Knudson called. "You better let me give you a tow. There's a strong current coming out the pass."

"Don't you take it," said Fana. "He ain't offering it to help us."

"Much obliged," Jonas called back. "Guess we'll make it all right. Go along by the *Zimba,* will you, Tom? Let Paki off on her."

Knudson made no reply. They could see Paki urging him, but the schooner remained where she was.

"Ain't that Knudson for you?" said Emily. "He won't let Paki come."

"What are you fretting about, you and Jonas?" said Nat. "Ru's doing all right."

Their father shook his head anxiously. "I know, but I'd like to have Paki on hand, in case anything happens the last minute."

His fears were justified a short time later. The *Zimba's* engine had stopped. Jonas's heart smote him as he ran to the bow of the *Charlotte*. Nat and Fana were both shouting to Chester, and the fleet of boats drew in closer to the launch. The line was now slack as the *Charlotte*, with glacier-like momentum, continued to move forward. Soon the launch was right under her bow, and those aboard the derelict could see Ru at work below. He thrust out his head for a moment to see how they lay with respect to the reef, then resumed his work with desperate haste while all three of his brothers were making suggestions as to the possible cause of the trouble. At last he lost patience. "Shut up!" he yelled. "How do you expect me to work with all of you yapping at me at once?"

"We ain't got no time to lose!" Nat warned.

"Can't you find what's wrong? Maybe it's the feed pipe."

"Make it fast, Ru! We'll have to take a tow if you don't!"

"We're out of line for the pass already!"

The boys were too worried to heed Ru's protests and rattled him all the more. Meanwhile, Jonas was in de-

spair. He shouted to Knudson, who was about thirty
yards distant, begging him to let Paki off on the launch.
Paki, too, was pleading with the trader; but seeing it
was useless, he threw off his hat and coat, leaped into
the sea, and swam for the *Zimba*.

Everybody was shouting at once as Paki reached the
side of the launch. Chester gave him a hand up and he
ducked below.

"What you tried, Ru?" he asked.

"Most everything," the boy replied. "Can't find
what's wrong."

After a quick glance over the engine, Paki seized a
wrench and unscrewed the plug over one of the valves.
"Kerosene," he snapped. Ru handed him the can and
his uncle squirted in a small quantity. "After all I've
taught you," he said, witheringly; "and you can't fix
a stuck valve!" With a chisel and hammer he tapped
the head of the valve, which immediately snapped into
place. Thirty seconds later he had the plug on again.
"Bar it over," he ordered. Ru obeyed, and the *Zimba*
sprang into life as though as eager as the boys themselves to make up for lost time.

And, certainly, there was none to spare. The derelict
was within one hundred yards of the reef before the two
shore beacons were in line again from her bow. Knudson stood by, hoping that his help would yet be needed,
but the *Charlotte* had, seemingly, a desire within herself
to ride peacefully in a harbor once more. She followed
the little *Zimba* down the precise center of the passage
and across the lagoon to the buoy, where she was made
fast just as the Papeete shops were closing for eleven-

o'clock breakfast. The waterfront was thronged with people witnessing this memorable event, and cheers went up when Fana climbed the *Charlotte's* foremast and tacked up a French flag which Jonas had sent for, ashore. Launches went back and forth, ferrying visitors eager to see the vessel. Leaving Paki and Effie in charge, Jonas went ashore with the boys, and they had no more than reached the steps by the post office when the superb Lincoln car from the Tiaré garage drew up before them. After greeting the boys, Tutu, the chauffeur, threw open the back-seat door. "Hop in, Jonas," he said. "Where to? Home?"

"You'll have to charge it, Tutu. I ain't got a franc on me."

"No hurry about that. The car's yours, long as you want it. The boss said so. Guess you could buy twenty cars with what you got in that ship."

"Coming home with us?" Fana asked his father.

"I'm going to stay right on the *Charlotte*," said Jonas, "but there's one thing I want to do first. Tutu, drive us up to Doc Blondin's!"

It was only three blocks to the doctor's office. Jonas hurried up the steps and rang the bell. Old Maria, the housekeeper, came to the door. "The doctor ain't here," she said. "He's gone to Mangareva."

Jonas remembered, then. "What's this I've got for a head?" he exclaimed. "Of course he has! He told me he was going, himself!" He hurried back to the car. "Now you boys go right on home, just as fast as Tutu can take you," he said. "They're all waiting for you out there."

CHAPTER XIII

FROM the moment he came ashore, after his unsuccessful attempt to establish a claim on the derelict, Tom Knudson had been as busy as the Tuttles themselves. He obtained from Lloyd's agency a copy of the *Charlotte's* manifest, forwarded from the Marquesas at the time the vessel was supposed to be lost. In the retirement of his office he checked this over carefully, canceling the items that would have been ruined by sea water, and estimating the value of the remainder of the cargo. The lumber, thousands upon thousands of feet of clear pine and tongue-and-groove, would be improved for a soaking, from a local point of view, for Tahiti merchants believed that such lumber was rendered proof against white ants. The oil in drums would, almost certainly, be intact. His view of the *Charlotte* had convinced him that the vessel herself was worth a lot of money; but leaving this out of consideration, her lading, putting the lowest estimate upon it, might easily bring between seven and eight hundred thousand francs.

Satisfied of this, Knudson left his office and was on his way to the Bougainville Club when he met Robert Tyson, the British consul, and Monsieur Verdier, the harbor master, a rosy-cheeked, blue-eyed Breton. The derelict was now safely in port, tied up at the buoy in the lower harbor.

"We're going out for a look at her, Tom," the harbor master said. "Want to come along?"

The government launch was moored by the sea wall below the Club. Boarding her, the three men steamed out toward the derelict.

"Understand the Tuttle boys spurned your offer of a tow?" Tyson remarked, drily.

"You'd have offered it yourself, in my place, Mr. Tyson," Knudson replied. "It's just bull luck they've got her safe inside."

"Of course. And now that she is in, who does she belong to? What's the procedure?"

"You ought to know that," said Knudson. "She's a British ship."

"In my opinion, it will call for an Admiralty court."

"I remember one point," the harbor master remarked. "If they've found so much as a dog or cat alive on board, we can't call the vessel abandoned."

"Not much chance of that, after all these months," said Tyson.

"I'm kind of stumped, myself," the trader remarked. "The law ain't clear, not to me, anyhow. But if she's abandoned, I reckon the Tuttles own her outright. Lucky devils! I was in the Marquesas with my schooner six weeks after the captain came in to Taio Hae with his crew. He was still there, and had just chartered the *Tereora* to go out in search. I went on a search of my own. Spent three weeks looking for her. Cost me close to twenty thousand francs."

The consul smiled. "That must have hurt. You can't have all the luck, Tom. I'm glad the Tuttles found her. What a time they'll have now! It's a pity Doc Blondin can't be here to see it."

"Where has he gone?" the harbor master asked.

"He left on the *Tooya* just before daylight; for Mangareva. Having a flu epidemic at Rikitea. There's Jonas. Look at the breadth of that smile!"

The launch came alongside and the harbor master with his companions climbed aboard the *Charlotte*.

"A great day for you, Jonas," said the consul, giving him a warm handclasp.

"I was hoping you'd come out, Mr. Tyson," Jonas replied. "Good morning, Mr. Verdier. Well, Tom, my boys got her in all right!"

"Gone straight home, have they?" Tyson asked.

Jonas nodded. "I wanted 'em to get there just as quick as they could. You don't know what we been through, Mr. Tyson."

"I can well imagine it. And to have the boys come back with *this!*"

"You mind if I have a look below, Jonas?" Knudson asked. "I've got a flashlight with me. Like to see what shape the cargo's in."

"Go right ahead," Jonas replied heartily. "Ain't had time to do it myself, yet." He smiled happily. "Don't know whether I'm coming or going, that's the plain truth."

"I shouldn't think you would," said Tyson. "Only twelve hours ago, Jonas, I shook your hand in another fashion."

"Did you?" said Jonas. "I didn't even remember you was out to the *himiné*."

"I don't wonder."

Knudson took off his coat and disappeared down the forward hatch.

"It's just as well the boys didn't take a tow from him, Jonas," the harbor master said. "He'd have been entitled to a big cut in the cargo."

"That's what they thought. Chester says the ship and everything in her belongs to us. First thing I want to do is to get some of them drums of gas right out to Vaipopo. That's always been our trouble." He sighed, luxuriously. "Guess we got enough now to last the rest of our lives."

"You can't touch anything at present," the harbor master said.

Jonas looked at him blankly. "We . . . we can't take none of the gas?"

"Tyson and I are not sure how the law stands. Everything may have to be sold at public auction. I'll put one of my men aboard as shipkeeper for the present."

"You understand, Jonas," the consul put in: "the legal complications have to be straightened out. But you can be sure that a big share of the money from the sale of the cargo and ship will go to your boys. Perhaps the whole of it."

Jonas concealed his disappointment as well as he could. "I never thought of that. How long d'you suppose it'll take?"

"It's hard to say, offhand. Meanwhile, everything on board must be left as it is."

While Knudson was in the hold, Jonas showed his other visitors the more accessible parts of the vessel. Half an hour passed before the trader reappeared, hot and dirty. "Never saw such a mess as there is down there," he said. "Take a gang of men a month to sort it out in any kind of shape."

"And well worth the sorting, I should think," Tyson replied.

"Hard to say. There was some fairly good lumber put aboard, but Lord knows what it might be worth now! You staying in town, Jonas?"

"I expected to be here on board," said Jonas. "But if there has to be a shipkeeper I'll go home this afternoon."

"In that case, drop into my place after lunch, will you? Around two?"

Jonas called at the trader's office at the hour appointed. He had little doubt as to why Knudson wanted to see him. He wished to make an offer for the cargo, or the ship, or both together. Knudson came to the point at once.

"Glad your boys got her in, Jonas," he said. "But they took an awful chance of losing everything."

Jonas smiled. "Guess you're not so glad as you make out, Tom. You made the boys kind of mad, trying to take the ship right out of their hands the way you did."

"It was for their own good; but I won't say it was nothing but kindness of heart." He leaned back in his chair. "Now that they've got her in, what do you expect to do with her?"

"We got to wait till they settle the law about it:

that's what Mr. Tyson and the harbor master say."

"So you do, and that'll take time. I've been reading up the law. Suppose they award you the ship and everything in her, your troubles will just be starting. I've been going over her manifest. It'll take months and months to sell all that lumber, and a lot of it's spoiled most likely. You'll have to keep books and run a regular store; and you'd have to collect for what you sold. That's the hardest job of all."

He paused to let Jonas ponder this information. The latter was in a position to realize, better than the speaker, perhaps, the truth of the last remark.

"You see, Jonas, how it would be? Now then, I'm willing to take all the worry and fret off your hands if you say the word. I got a good business head. You know that."

"I know you're mighty tight with credit."

"Couldn't stay in business if I wasn't. There's no telling how long it'll take the local market to absorb all that lumber. A year, that's sure; maybe longer. Suppose I make your boys an offer for their rights. Would it interest you?"

"It might," said Jonas. "Depends on what the offer was."

"Good. Have them sign over their rights to me, ship and cargo, and I'll give them four hundred thousand francs — cash down."

Jonas's astonishment was so great that the expression on his face remained completely wooden. Knudson's words conveyed no real meaning to him beyond a vague sense of limitless wealth. Had the trader said two hundred thousand, or six, the impression would have been the same. He made no reply — none would come. Knudson waited for the full significance of the offer to sink in.

"That's a big offer, Jonas. Take my advice and tell the boys to accept. I'm taking a long chance. No telling what the teredos may have done to the lumber by this time. I might clean up, of course, but I might finish in the hole. Anyway, that's what I'll give. Go home and think it over, but let me know by tomorrow."

Jonas drove home in such a daze that he would have passed his own place had he not been halted by a shout from Fana and Tamara, who were crossing the road from the beach.

"Don't you know your own house?" Tamara asked.

"Guess I'm kind of up in the air today, Tamara," Jonas replied, as he backed the truck and turned into the driveway. The family were gathered in the shade of a great mango tree that stood at the right of the house, where Nat, Chester, and Ru were still telling the tale of their adventures. Emily Taio and Paki were both present.

"You didn't bring no gas home?" Nat asked.

Jonas shook his head. "I been talking to the consul. They ain't sure yet about the law. We can't take nothing off the ship."

"We can't?" said Chester. "Why not?"

"Looks like everything's got to go through some kind of a court. They may have to sell it at auction."

"How long'll that take?"

"Might be a year."

"A year! What's the good of our finding the old tub, then?"

"Now you boys just wait a minute." Jonas glanced from face to face with a triumphant smile. He paused, dramatically.

"What's up, Jonas?"

"I been talking to Knudson . . ."

"I knew it!" Effie exclaimed. "Some of us ought to have stayed in town with him. We might have known he'd let Tom Knudson get around him!"

"*We* found it, Jonas, don't forget that," said Nat. "If it's worth a cent, that ship and cargo is worth seventy-five thousand francs."

"You think so?" said Jonas. "Fine head you got for business! How'd you boys like to sell your rights for four hundred thousand francs?"

A pause of stupefaction followed the announcement. "F-f-f-four hundred thousand?" said Chester.

"Spot cash. That's Knudson's offer."

"He's kidding you, Jonas," Fana said, incredulously.

"No he ain't. He wants us to come in first thing to-morrow. We can get our money right then."

Emily Taio shook her head. "Go easy, Jonas. If Tom Knudson's offering you that much, he's not doing it with his eyes shut."

"*Parau mau,*" said Paki. "He's half Tuamota. Knows what he's about, Knudson does."

"Take it!" Fana burst out. "Who wants to wait a year?"

"Sure! T-t-take it right off, Jonas! He might change his mind."

"We better go in now," said Nat.

"We'll do no such thing," Jonas replied, firmly. "Don't want to make it look like we was too anxious. Tomorrow morning's time enough, and that's when he said to come."

"You Tuttles!" said Emily. "I'd do a lot of thinking before I'd accept any offer Knudson makes. He's not doing this to help you out."

"My goodness, Emily!" Effie put in. "What do we care? Four hundred thousand francs! We couldn't spend that in all the rest of our lives!"

"Maybe I didn't need looking after as much as you thought, Effie," said Jonas. "Mama, what do you say?"

"They're all safe home," his mother replied. "I don't care what you decide about the money. Except for one thing: you must pay Dr. Blondin the first thing you do."

"He ain't here," Jonas replied. "We got plenty of time to do all that."

"But didn't you tell me that Monsieur Dorme was looking after his business while he's away? You must see him, Jonas."

"I would have this morning, but he's sick. He's got inflammatory rheumatism. They had to take him to the hospital."

"But you will see him, just as soon as you can?"

"*Aué*, Grandma," said Chester. "You d-d-d-don't need to worry about that. Four hundred thousand francs! We could pay the Doc t-t-t-twenty times over and still have a lot left."

At nine o'clock the following morning, Jonas and his four sons, in the Tuttle truck, drew up at the door of Knudson's trading establishment. He was waiting for them in his office. Island custom, which requires that matters of importance be led up to gradually, was all but dispensed with on this occasion. After the briefest of conversations on indifferent matters, Knudson turned to the head of Tuttle-ma. "Well, Jonas?" he said.

"I talked it over with the boys," Jonas replied. "We'll take the offer."

Knudson nodded. "You done just right, if you ask me. This'll save you a long wait and a lot of bother. I ain't saying I won't make something out of the deal. Wish me luck, anyhow!"

"We don't grudge it to you, Tom. Four hundred thousand francs is enough for us. Make out the papers and we'll sign 'em right off."

"I've done it already," said Knudson. He opened a drawer of his desk and drew out a document which he handed to Jonas. "Read that over. Get a lawyer if you want to. I meant to ask Dorme to come in, but he's sick in hospital."

"So I heard," said Jonas. The deed was brief and simple, stating that, in return for the sum of four hundred thousand francs, receipt of which was hereby acknowledged, the Messrs. Tuttle, of Vaipopo, conveyed to T. Knudson, merchant and shipowner, all of their rights in the derelict *Charlotte* and her cargo. Jonas read the document aloud to the boys.

"That's plain enough," he said. "We don't need no lawyer. You pay us and the boys'll sign."

"Give you a check right now," said Knudson. "How'll I make it out?"

"To Jonas," said Nat. "He runs things, home."

When the boys had affixed their signatures before two witnesses called in from the store, Knudson shook hands warmly, all round. Jonas took up the check, staring at it doubtfully. "What do we do with this, Tom?" he asked. He had expected to be paid in bales and bundles of currency which would probably fill several copra bags.

"Take it over to the bank. They'll give you cash if you want it, but if I was you I'd deposit it and open an account. Get a checkbook like mine; then you can draw what you need. You're a rich man now, Jonas. Hope you take care of it."

"That's just what I'm going to do." Jonas turned to Nat. "You boys wait for me out in front. I'll be along in a minute." He waited until his sons had closed the door behind them. "There's a lot of things I want to get, Tom, mostly out of my mail-order catalogue."

The trader smiled. "Going to furnish up the house again?"

"The first thing," said Jonas, happily. "Always meant to do it, soon's I could get twisted round; but I don't want the rest of 'em to know till the things come."

"That's all right with me. Want me to send the order for you? I'll have to charge you 5 per cent commission."

"It don't matter about that. I'd like to get the order in so's it can go north on the next steamer."

"That'll be day after tomorrow. All right. Make out your order and I'll see that it goes through. You'll have to pay 20 per cent of the value of the goods in advance, and the balance when the shipment arrives."

This matter settled, Jonas joined the boys in front of the store. They walked to the bank, only a block distant. Jonas halted at the gate leading to the well-kept gardens surrounding the establishment.

"There's one thing we ought to decide now," he said. "It's about Paki. We owe him a lot. Don't know what would have happened if he hadn't been on hand to get the *Zimba's* engine going when he did."

The boys were in hearty agreement with this. "Make it fifty thousand," said Chester. "That ain't a bit too much."

"Just what I was thinking," their father replied. "Paki won't have no good of it. He'll put it in his safe, like as not. But it ain't our business to tell him what to do with his own money."

"What about our shares?" Fana asked.

"I don't want no checkbook," said Nat. "Who wants to be writing all the time? I'll take fifty thousand to start with."

"In cash?" said Fana. "You're crazy, wanting to carry all that money around with you. It'll be easier writing checks, like Knudson says."

"Fana's right," said Jonas. "You don't run no risk losing your money that way."

But Nat held to his purpose of taking cash. The other boys decided with their father to have check-books. Jonas then led the way into the bank. It was the first time that any of them had entered the place. They removed their hats at the door, and walked on tiptoe, as though entering a church. After a puzzled glance along the many windows, Jonas stepped up to one with the word CAISSIER above it, on a glittering brass plate. Taking Knudson's check from his pocket, he passed it under the grille and stood regarding the ceiling with an air of careless interest.

They emerged half an hour later, Nat with a cloth currency bag filled with bills in denominations of five, twenty, and one hundred francs. Jonas had, in the inside pocket of his coat, two parcels of bills, one of them Paki's reward, and the other the exact amount of the debt owing to Dr. Blondin. All were plentifully supplied with checkbooks save Nat, who wanted none, and Ru, who, being under twenty-one, was not permitted to have an account.

"It's too bad, Ru," Jonas said. "You call on me for whatever you want."

"There's only one thing I want for all of us," said Ru. "A new launch, with an engine like the *Hina's*. We better order that the first thing."

"The *Hina!*" Nat snorted. "We don't want no little tub like that."

"First thing I'm going to do is buy b-b-back my accordion," said Chester. "We can stop at Emily's on the way home."

"Now wait," their father said. "We got to plan things out. Ru's right: the new launch is the first thing. You boys go out to Ellacott's shipyard right now and talk things over with him. We won't decide about an engine till we have Paki along with us, but we can get things started. . . ."

He broke off as a boy drew up on a bicycle and handed Jonas a receipted bill. It was from a tinsmith, for soldering the *Zimba's* gasoline tank two years before. Jonas scanned it carefully, as if he suspected some irregularity in the account.

"That's right, son," he remarked at last. "Eighty-one francs, fifty. Here's a hundred. Keep the change for yourself."

The boy's eyes widened. "*Maururu*, Jonas!" he said. Then, vaulting onto his bicycle, he pedaled away at top speed.

"You boys go right along to Ellacott's," Jonas said. "I'll be up there soon's I can."

"Where you going now?" Chester asked.

"To the park by the post office. I know what's going to happen. Anybody wants to know where I am you can tell 'em."

Having provided himself with his first necessity, a fountain pen, Jonas proceeded to the park and seated himself in a shady spot. Tahiti's news service, known as the "Coconut Radio," had been working with even more than its usual efficiency. By the time Jonas reached his destination, not a merchant in town but knew that Tuttle-ma had received and accepted from Tom Knudson a huge cash offer for their rights in the derelict. Errand boys from various mercantile establishments began to arrive, on foot and on bicycles, carrying receipted bills, all for small amounts, but some of them dating back to purchases made half-a-dozen years before. For the next hour and more these messengers arrived. Bland but grave, Jonas accepted the bills, scrutinized them carefully, then, with his checkbook resting on his broad knee, he canceled these ancient obligations with a few strokes of his smooth-flowing pen, his heart growing lighter with each delivered check.

It was a busy day in town for Jonas and his sons. Ellacott, the boatbuilder, had a model for a new launch which pleased them so well that the building of it was decided upon at once. But, owing to other commitments, the work could not be started for another three months. The launch would be five feet longer and eighteen inches beamier than the *Hina,* equipped with a six-cylinder eighty-horsepower engine which would drive her at fifteen knots, three above the *Hina's* best speed. So eager were the boys to have this engine ordered by the next steamer that a car was sent to Vaipopo to fetch Paki, who spent the rest of the afternoon in a careful examination of the specifications of the machine, agreeing at last that the Tuttles could not do better than to buy it. The order was therefore made and 20 per cent of the purchase price paid by Jonas as a guarantee. A new Renault truck, to come from France, was also ordered and the same advance payment made upon it. The ease and the speed with which these long-cherished dreams were made realities so bewildered Jonas that he could scarcely believe in them; but there, moored to the buoy in Papeete harbor, lay the *Charlotte,* visible proof that he was no longer living in a world of make-believe.

The evening was well advanced when he returned home. He had hired the Lincoln for an indefinite period, at a monthly rental of three thousand francs, gas and oil not included. He meant to purchase a car later, but there was plenty of time for that. The boys had gone on before him two hours earlier, Nat and Fana in their own hired cars filled with friends and Ru driving the old truck, which they had loaded with food and wine.

When Jonas turned in at home the dining shed was filled with people, young folk mostly, who had gathered to join in the Tuttle festivities. Chester had his accordion once more, and the strains of the "Poet and Peasant" filled the air.

"That's what I like to hear, Tutu: plenty of music and fun."

"There ain't no place on Tahiti where people have such good times as they do at your house," the chauffeur replied, as he brought the car to a halt. "Coming over?"

"Not tonight. I got a lot of things to do yet. Go ahead and enjoy yourself. Some of the boys'll fix you up about sleeping."

"Needn't bother about that. I'll sleep in the car."

Jonas found his mother in her little sewing room off the back veranda.

"You've had your supper?" she asked.

"Yes, in town. It's been a great day, Mama. Ain't they enjoying themselves, out there?"

His mother smiled. "We had a hard time getting the children off to bed. Listen . . . that's Effie's laugh."

"You don't need to tell me. Paki's staying in town tonight. We gave him fifty thousand francs and he's going to buy some land with it. There's four Papeete lots, three of them with houses on 'em, he's been wanting to buy for a long time, he said. With what he's saved and what we gave him, he's got enough to do it. He's going to stay in town till he's got it all settled."

"I wish the boys had a little more of Paki's good sense," Mama Ruau replied. "They came home with the truck and two cars filled with nothing but food. I can't help being worried. Have we really enough money to buy so much?"

"Enough! Mama, you make me laugh! Don't you know we got four hundred thousand francs?"

The old lady shook her head. "I just can't imagine how much that is. . . . There's something I wish you'd do, Jonas. You know what a good old man Miro is, and what a hard time he's had, all these years. He's wanted so long to buy that little land he lives on . . ."

Jonas's face beamed. "I've done it, Mama! I knew how you felt about that — same as I do. It's one of the first things I thought of. Miro's got his land and ten thousand francs besides. I fixed it all up this afternoon. And I paid all the little bills there was. We don't owe nobody a cent."

"Jonas! You've paid Dr. Blondin's debt?"

With a smile of triumph Jonas drew from his pocket a thin bundle of bank notes, pinned together. "There it is, Mama, every penny. But the doctor's away and Lawyer Dorme's in the hospital, so there wasn't anybody I could pay it to. Had to bring it home."

"There, that's all I care about," his mother replied, squeezing his hand. "Take it right upstairs and put it in your chest."

There was no one in the house except Mama Ruau and the sleeping children. Having bid his mother good-night, Jonas searched for his mail-order catalogue, which he found in the front room. With this under his arm he tiptoed up the front stairway. In the privacy of his own room, the door closed behind him, he lighted the lamp, which he set on the lid of his clothes chest. Making himself comfortable on a mat, with two thick kapok pillows between his broad back and the wall, he laid beside him the block of writing paper he had brought home and opened his mail-order catalogue on his knees. Slowly he turned the pages of the section devoted to furniture.

For years Jonas had dreamed of furnishing the Tuttle mansion in a really imposing style, something even to surpass its original splendor. Had he always possessed the necessary funds, he would have been the kind of customer dreamed of by the presidents of mail-order houses. He knew the catalogue as an old-fashioned parson knows his Bible.

After an anticipatory survey he began to study minutely an illustration of an enormous overstuffed davenport and easy chair to match. "Over six hundred springs for luxurious seating comfort," he read; "a comfort miracle of living-room groups. Two pieces as shown, $119.95." It would be just the thing for the big room downstairs, but they would need more than two pieces. Squinting to read the fine print, he jotted down the order number, and then wrote: "Four sets — $479.80."

There were two spacious apartments on either side

of the hallway below, intended originally as drawing room and reception room. Their names had long since been forgotten, but Jonas realized that they had been designed as places of social gathering. He now proceeded to furnish them lavishly, one in overstuffed, the other in Glamorous Old Mission style. There were occasional chairs, easy chairs, tables, *tabourets,* davenports, and strange wooden odds-and-ends of which only the compilers of mail-order catalogues know the names. Absorbed and deeply happy, Jonas closed his eyes and saw just how the rooms would look with fine red-bordered Manihiki mats on the floor, and all this furniture grouped invitingly here and there. He thought of the bare walls and the oil paintings in his grandfather's bedchamber. "Funny they don't sell no pictures," he thought. He would have to search elsewhere for them. Knudson might be able to tell him where they could be bought.

The lower floor furnished, Jonas turned his attention to the upper chambers. This bedroom set would be just the thing for Nat and Hio. When making out his dream orders, Jonas had always been a careful buyer, and he now scrutinized every specification of the bed, dresser, vanity, chest, bench, and "nite-stand" which gleamed so richly in the full-page illustration. "Matched walnut, inlaid maple, and zebrawood," he read; "genuine veneers." He didn't know what veneer meant, but genuine had a rich, reassuring sound. Pretty reasonable, too, at $77.95 for the group. He'd order two of them, now that Fana was going to build his house. And this superb set in *kelobra,* butt-walnut, and Oriental wood — just

the thing for Mama's room! One by one Jonas furnished
the upper chambers until he came to his own. He
glanced about him, frowning slightly in his abstraction.
A bed? His mat on the floor was cooler on hot nights.
Chairs, tables? What would he use them for? No, his
own room was better without so much in it. Deserting
the furniture section, he was progressing toward the
hog fence when a streamlined lady's bicycle caught his
eye. What a gift for Maitu! And if anybody in the family deserved a reward, she did. She'd be the envy of the
whole district. Jonas could hear Maitu's gasp of astonishment and delight. Better say nothing about it, though;
keep that for a little surprise. Here were harmonicas —
a whole page of them. "Hohner's finest Chromatic, professional model. Greater range than the melody keys of
a piano accordion." And it came in a plush-lined, wal-
nut-finished case. Jonas put down order number and
price. Nothing he could buy for Tupa would please him
as much as that.

The column of orders lengthened as the hours passed:
tools, china, cutlery, pots and pans, glassware. In his
increasing happy absorption, he had forgotten the workaday world around him; forgotten even the *Charlotte*
and the fact that, for once, he really had the means to
pay for all these things. He turned to the tires, and
after a careful study of the different qualities, he ordered a dozen casings with inner tubes, to fit the truck.
Then realization came: "Huh! No need for them tires.
Cross 'em off. We'll be getting the new Renault from
France. No fooling about this order; it's real!" A wave
of warm happiness swept over him.

Coming to the end of his task, he began the long process of addition, frowning in his concentration and moistening his pencil frequently. After going over the figures three times he was convinced that he had the total correct: $3681.70.

"A lot of money," he muttered; "a whole lot! But look what we're getting for it! Emily's right — nothing like putting your money into something solid."

CHAPTER XIV

Two months had passed since the Tuttle boys, with Jonas in the lead, had walked into the Papeete bank to deposit their four hundred thousand francs. Many a checkbook had been emptied since that day, but fresh ones could be had for the asking. Fana's somewhat belated marriage to Tamara was celebrated with a five-day feast, memorable even in the annals of Vaipopo. Jonas built a special house for the festivities, sixty feet long and forty wide, with a roof of plaited palm fronds on posts of *purau* wood. Tupa was provided with three assistant cooks, but without the aid of numerous volunteers the four of them could never have dressed food in the quantities or at the speed demanded by so many unrivaled appetites. The family's hired cars shuttled back and forth between Vaipopo and Papeete all day long, departing with as many joy-riders as space allowed, and returning with cargoes of cheeses, hams, tinned food, kegs of salt beef and pork, smoked salmon, blocks of ice, and numberless demijohns of wine and cases of Pilsener. In their intervals of leisure, which were few, the chauffeurs were sent out to purchase mounds of breadfruit, taro, yams, sweet potatoes, and the fowls and hogs required for Jonas-ma's basic victualing.

All day long the feasting house was the scene of merrymaking enhanced rather than halted by frequent enormous meals. In the evening, four gasoline lamps, suspended from the rafters of the pavilion, threw upon the assembly a radiance brighter than the light of day, and this, together with the music furnished by a superb orchestra, attracted guests from miles around. Dancing and singing would continue until a late hour, when the company would spread their mats to sleep on the veranda or under the trees. In addition to the amusements at home, round-the-island excursions were made by various members of the family, with picnics on the way. Ropati, with fifteen thousand francs given him by Jonas, made one of these tours, taking half a dozen old cronies with him. He returned four days later, broke and happy, declaring that he had gathered during this time enough happy memories to last him for the rest of his life. The children were not forgotten. They, with friends from various districts, had their picnics and excursions as well, with added evenings of pleasure spent at the motion-picture theaters of Papeete and Taravao. So it went, each day happier than the one preceding, for in their capacity for enjoyment and their ability to prolong it almost to infinity, there are no people to compare with those of Tahiti.

But weeks of continuous good times began to pall at last. The better sort of guests, whose leisure was not completely unlimited, had now taken their departure, declaring that they had never before enjoyed such hospitality. A score of visitors of another sort remained — professional guests who made a vocation of being on hand wherever the festive spirit prevailed and wine and food were free. In spite of their wealth, Jonas and the boys were more than willing to enjoy a period of rest and a return to their everyday occupations. In fact, the only members of the family whose zest for amusement seemed unlimited were Effie and Ropati.

But how rid themselves of these indefatigable hangers-on who now seemed to consider themselves members of the family? Jonas was considering this matter one day after lunch as he lay on his mat in his room. He had not enjoyed the meal and racket from the feasting house had ruined his attempted siesta. All the Tuttles, save Effie and Ropati, had excused themselves after the meal was over and gone elsewhere; but this expedient, already tried a number of times, had no effect upon the guests. There they were, making as much noise as three times their number had two weeks ago. They couldn't play like his boys: this music wasn't worth listening to. With an exasperated sigh, Jonas rose from his mat. No use trying to sleep.

Something would have to be done. The steamer from San Francisco was due on the following day, bringing, as Jonas knew, the furniture, fencing, kitchenware, and other things he had ordered. He had kept this matter a secret from the family, and he wished them to be alone when he came home from town with this great surprise. And it was high time that he had leisure to give his attention to the more solid benefits their wealth had brought them. The 500-gallon tank for gasoline was already in place, set on cement posts near the boat shed, ready for the fuel supply for the new launch. Ellacott, the boatbuilder, had informed him that the engine for the launch would come on the next Messageries steamer from France; within two weeks after its arrival he would be ready to begin work on the launch itself. The same steamer from France would bring the new truck. There were numberless things to be done which couldn't be done while they had a house filled with guests who didn't have sense enough to realize that the party was over.

Maitu met him at the foot of the stairs with a letter in her hand.

"I'm awful sorry, Jonas," she said. "This came, it must have been a month ago. It was when we was so busy getting ready for Fana's wedding. I put it on a shelf and forgot all about it."

Jonas glanced at the envelope, which was covered with drawings and scribblings in pencil. "It don't matter, Maitu," he said, as he thrust it into his pocket. "Guess it ain't nothing but a bill. I'll pay it next time I go in town."

"I found some of the children writing on it," Maitu added, apologetically.

"Where's Tupa?"

"Down at the beach. Said he wanted a little quiet."

"Don't blame him. Like a little myself."

Jonas walked on to the beach, where he found most of the family gathered in the shade, watching André and Mara, who were giving the new gasoline tank a coat of paint. He seated himself in the midst of them.

"Glad to see something's getting done," he said. "Looks pretty nice, don't it?"

"Had enough of it up there?" Paki asked, with a nod of his head toward the house.

A burst of distant music floated to their ears over the treetops.

"It's your fault, Paki, as much as anybody's," said Hio. "Why don't you tell Effie to stay away from 'em? She and Ropati are the ones that keep it going. Enough's enough, it seems to me."

"None of my business," said Paki. "I wouldn't have let 'em come in the first place. Jonas is head of the family, ain't he? He brought 'em here. He can get rid of 'em."

"You ought to, Jonas," Tamara said. "I want Fana to get started on our house. We can't do anything with all that crowd around."

"They're a lot of s-s-s-spongers," Chester sputtered, indignantly.

"Say the word, Jonas," said Nat. "I'll kick 'em out. Who do they think they are, anyway? Tuttles?"

Jonas shook his head. "Mama'd be gladder than any of us to see them go, but she wouldn't want us to tell 'em. It wouldn't be right."

Tupa gave a snort of impatience. "Make me sick, Jonas! What of it, right or not, polite or not? Drinking two demijohns of wine a day. Know what butter's costing you? Twelve francs a tin, and there's some eats it with a spoon, I've seen 'em. Twelve loaves of bread, morning and night, for them alone. I ain't counting us."

"I know, but . . ."

"I'm wore out, cooking for 'em. Leave it to me? I'll get rid of 'em — starve 'em out. Give 'em bucket-of-water soup, nothing else. 'Sorry we're running short on things. They ain't no more wine, neither.' That'll fix 'em."

"Let him do it," Fana urged. "They won't never go if you don't."

"Go ahead, Tupa," said Chester. "We'll have to starve with 'em for a few days, but that won't matter. What do you say, Jonas?"

Their father was silent for some little time. "Guess we'll have to," he said. "It seems awful mean. The Tuttles ain't never done nothing like that before. But there don't seem to be no other way."

"We let our cars go today," Nat informed his father.

"Good idea. What do we want with 'em? I only kept the Lincoln on account of Effie. Seems like she never gets tired, riding."

Chester smiled in spite of himself. "Ain't she a wonder? Up there dancing right now! You can't wear Effie out."

Tupa's plan, put into effect the same evening, worked magically. Two days later the last of the guests who had enjoyed Tuttle hospitality for so many weeks took their leave, and the family resumed the old routine with a relish heightened by so long a departure from it. Meanwhile, the steamer from San Francisco had come and gone, bringing the furniture Jonas had ordered, and he waited with an impatience he could scarcely conceal until word came from Knudson that the shipment had been cleared through the customs and was now at his disposal.

Knudson's note had arrived too late for anything to

be done on that day, but the following morning, as soon as he had finished his coffee, Jonas prepared to go to town. The womenfolk were mystified at his behavior. He had dropped a few mysterious hints, but nothing which gave them a clue as to the nature of the surprise in store for them. Effie, who knew that she was concerned in it, was the most curious.

"I'm coming with you, Jonas," she said, when her brother was ready to leave.

"You won't do nothing of the sort," said Jonas. "You can wait as well as the rest of 'em. I won't be gone more'n a couple of hours."

"But what is it you're up to? Why can't you tell us now?" said Hio.

Jonas's reply was a smile and a wave of the hand as he climbed into the Lincoln.

He settled back to enjoy this last ride to town in his hired car. The boys were right, he thought. They'd had fun enough; let the cars go, now. How long had it been since he'd gone to town behind Nellie, in the surrey? Six weeks, anyway. The Lincoln was nice smooth riding, no doubt of that, but you couldn't beat going along slow and easy like you did in the surrey.

Now let's see: what did he have to do first? There were a few bills to pay . . . of a sudden he remembered the letter Maitu had given him a couple of days before. He had it in his pocket with the other bills. Might as well see what it was.

He examined the envelope, which some of his grandchildren had scribbled over on both sides; then, despite the scratchings, he observed on one corner: "Henri Dorme. Avocat." Jonas gave a little start of surprise and opened the envelope quickly. The letter bore a date over a month old. It was brief and to the point, congratulating him on the good fortune that had come to the family, and requesting him, with just a touch of sternness, to deposit the amount of his debt immediately to Dr. Blondin's credit at the bank.

Jonas felt guilty and apologetic as he read the letter. What would the lawyer think of him for such neglect? Dorme was still in the hospital; at least he had been there only a few days before. And Dr. Blondin had not yet returned from Mangareva. He'd been so busy with one thing and another he'd scarcely thought about his debt, planning to pay it the very day of the doctor's arrival at home. It had not occurred to him to deposit the money at the bank. He'd try and see Monsieur Dorme at once, today. No, he wouldn't do that. Getting the furniture home would give him all he could attend to today. But the first thing tomorrow, he'd carry the money to the lawyer in person, and explain about the lost letter. The eighteen thousand, four hundred and forty francs were safe in his camphorwood chest, at home. He would tell Monsieur Dorme how he had put this money aside on the evening of the very day that Knudson had paid them for the *Charlotte*.

Arriving in town, Jonas got down at the garage and there gave up his car, paying by check the last month's bill. Tutu, his chauffeur this long while, well deserved a liberal reward. Jonas would have written him a check for a thousand francs, as a tip, but found that his check-

book was empty. He had nearly eight hundred francs
in bills in his pocketbook, and the driver was more than
pleased with that sum.

"*Maururu*, Jonas!" he said, warmly. "I ought to be
the one to pay you. Never had such a good time as these
two months, working for you."

"Glad you have, Tutu. Glad you have. Shouldn't
wonder but I'll still be wanting you every now and
again. Effie will, anyway."

Knudson was waiting for him at his office.

"Everything's all ready, Jonas," he said. He took up
the bill already made out. "The duty was a straight 35
per cent. Freight was $420. You've paid 20 per cent of
the cost of your goods. That leaves a balance of
$4633.15, freight and duty included. It comes to
138,990 francs."

"That's a lot of money," said Jonas.

"You bought a lot of stuff," Knudson replied. "It'll
take all three of my big stake trucks to cart it home
for you. Want it to go out today?"

"That's just what I do want, Tom. I ain't told none
of 'em about it. It's a surprise for Mama."

"Good. Give me a check for the balance and I'll have
my men take it right along."

Jonas then remembered that he had nothing but an
empty checkbook. Knudson demurred at delivering the
shipment without payment, but upon Jonas's promise
to settle the full amount on the following day, he agreed
to let one truckload go out at once.

Jonas's promised two hours' absence dragged on to
three, and it was not until the children were coming

home from school that shrill cries from them and the loud honking of a motor horn announced his return. Knudson's largest truck, loaded to capacity and something more with huge packing cases, turned in at the drive, to be met in front of the house by a crowd that comprised nearly the entire clan.

"Jonas! What in the world . . . !" his mother exclaimed.

"Furniture, Mama," he replied, a triumphant smile on his face. "There's two more truckloads coming tomorrow. We're going to fix the house up just like it used to be!"

The unloading began amidst a chorus of excited comments. It was then lunchtime, but the meal was partaken of hastily, and by some not at all. Jonas stood by while the enormous cases were carried to the front veranda for opening. "Effie," he said, "I got a whole set of new things for you, a lot better'n the ones you lost at the cockfight. They'll be coming out tomorrow. This load's mostly things for the big living room."

"*Au-é!*" Effie cried. "Ain't that a brother for you? Sewing machine and all?"

"Sewing machine and all," Jonas replied, rewarded a dozen times over at seeing his sister's delight.

She threw her arms around him, kissing him on both cheeks. "Paki wouldn't never have done it," she said.

"Won't have 'em long," Paki replied. "You're a fool, Jonas. She'll lose 'em like the ones I bought, first chance she gets. What's the good of all this?"

But no one paid any attention to Paki, except to urge him on to the work of opening the cases. He was the one for that job, with his nail-puller. The work began on case No. 27, containing one of the davenports for the living room. Paki took great care to pull the nails without injuring the boards of the cases, making sarcastic comments the while at his brother-in-law's extravagance.

"What you going to do with these cases, Jonas?" he asked, presently.

"Nothing," said Jonas. "Tupa can have 'em for firewood."

"Just like you — burn up money. Give 'em to me?"

"Sure, if you want 'em."

"Enough good boards here to start another house on the land I bought in town. All I'll have to buy is tin for the roof."

"Ain't that like him?" Effie asked. "He's just like a Chinaman: builds houses out of old packing cases!"

"Laugh," said Paki. "I don't care. Good lumber. Wait and see. Build a house out of this and what's to come. Rent it for a hundred francs a month."

"Sure," said Fana, derisively. "I wouldn't even buy the roofing if I was you. Get some old gasoline tins and flatten 'em out."

"I might at that," Paki said. "Give it a couple of coats of red lead. Last about as long as corrugated iron."

The top and one side of the case were off at last, every board intact. All gathered around eagerly, as the davenport was lifted out and the excelsior and wrapping paper removed.

"Oh, Jonas!" Mama Ruau exclaimed. "It's lovely!"

"*Aué te nehénehé é!*" Cries of wonder and delight from all the womenfolk greeted the sight as the davenport was carried into the living room. The few battered odds and ends of furniture that the room contained were quickly removed to the back veranda so as not to shame these superb pieces which were to replace them. Hio fetched a new broom to remove all traces of excelsior.

"Not a scratch on it," André remarked. "Them people know how to pack things."

"Try it, Jonas," said Hio.

After a doubtful glance at his trousers, Jonas dusted them carefully and sank down on the davenport. The catalogue's description, "A miracle of seating comfort," had been an understatement; no words could be adequate for such luxury as this. Jonas leaned back, an expression of pure felicity on his face. "Hand me that bit of paper, Fana," he said. "I want to try stretching out." The paper was placed at one end of the davenport, and with his bare feet resting on it Jonas lay back with his hands behind his head.

All the afternoon the family labored until the complete furnishings for the downstairs living room had been removed from their cases and carried inside to be grouped invitingly, in accordance with the catalogue illustrations. When all was done the clan trooped in to inspect. The children could not resist such tempting invitations for bouncing, but they were soon brought to order and shooed out of the room. Something appeared to be wrong. Tamara was the first to notice this. "Don't it look kind of funny?" she asked.

"Funny?" said Jonas. "Ain't it all right? I don't see nothing funny about it."

"I'm not talking about the things. It's the room, Jonas. You ought to have fixed the house up, first."

Hio was the next to comment. "It does make the room look kind of dingy, the things are so new and all."

"What do you think, Mama?" Jonas asked.

Mama Ruau had kept her own counsel until that moment, but now she was forced to speak. "They're beautiful, Jonas — everything," she said. "But I'm afraid the girls are right. They're too good for the house, the way it is now."

Jonas scratched his head. Of a sudden, the incongruousness of the splendid furniture in the dilapidated interior of a room that had endured without renewal more than half a century of Tuttle wear and tear seemed to strike all of them. Tamara sat down on one of the davenports and burst out laughing; then Hio did. The mirth was contagious, and others joined in, even Jonas himself.

"Guess I'm about half crazy," he said. "I never thought about the house. Don't know's I'd have thought about it now if Tamara hadn't spoke."

"I could have told you how it'd look," said Paki.

"Why didn't you, then?" said Effie.

"None of my business. Didn't ask me."

"Nothing's your business except to squeeze every penny you get hold of," Effie replied.

"*Aué*, Jonas," Tamara said, still laughing. "Now you'll have to build a new house to fit the furniture!"

"He won't have to do any such thing," said Effie. "All we need . . ."

She broke off, observing that Nana and some of the other children had stolen into the other end of the room and were bouncing again on one of the davenports with its six hundred springs. She drove them before her, then returned to the others. "I see what you can do, Jonas," she resumed. "Don't bring the rest of the things yet. And we'll move these out on the verandas and cover 'em up well. The walls will have to be plastered some, then you can tint them nice like they are in Knudson's store, and paint all the woodwork. 'Twon't take a month to fix the house up as nice as anybody could want it."

"What about the roof?" said Hio. "That'll have to be fixed too. We can't be moving these heavy things around every time it rains."

"Jonas and his furniture!" said Nat. "What do you want it for? Lot of bother all for nothing. 'Twon't seem like home any more with all this stuff."

"You're no better than a bush Kanaka, Nat," his wife replied. "We want it if you don't."

"You didn't get no beds, did you, Jonas?" Chester asked.

His father nodded in a half-apologetic manner, but he made a sudden resolve not to be bulldozed by the boys, nor would he give way to his own misgivings.

"And you boys are going to sleep in 'em," he said. "We all are. We're going to fix the house up just like it used to be and live the way we ought to."

This announcement started an argument that continued throughout supper, the women supporting Jonas against the other male members of the family. In the midst of it an electric torch flashed on the drive and the district postman dismounted from his bicycle.

"Jonas!" he called.

"Come in, Roro! You eat yet? Sit down and have a glass of wine anyhow."

"Got a letter for you," the postman announced. "I'm kind of late this evening; had to ride clear down to Tarahoi."

Jonas took the letter absent-mindedly and tucked it under his plate.

"Your folks all well?" he asked.

"My wife's got the grippe. Seems to be a lot of it going round these days."

"We been lucky so far," said Jonas.

"You Tuttles don't never get sick. Your friends is lucky, too," the postman added, warmly. "I put that five thousand francs you gave me in the *Caisse Agricole*. My oldest girl's got a good chance to win a scholarship; maybe she'll be going to France next year. We'll have something to buy warm clothes for her and all that."

"You got a fine daughter, Roro. Smartest girl in the district."

The postman took leave of them presently, and Maitu began to herd the children off to their sleeping places. Mama Ruau rose to go to her room. She stopped a moment beside her son. "You didn't tell me about Roro," she said.

"I forgot, Mama. Don't he seem pleased?"

"You couldn't have helped anyone who deserved it

more. You're a good man, Jonas. I might have known you would."

"There's another Ch-ch-Charlotte, Jonas," Chester announced with a grin. "I just heard about it today."

"Another!" Jonas exclaimed. "Whose family?"

"Don't know. Somebody in Papeari. They'll be telling us soon enough."

"We won't do nothing for this one," Jonas replied. "Enough's enough."

An infant born on the day the Tuttle boys brought in the derelict had been named Charlotte in honor of the event, and Jonas, learning of it, had presented the parents with a check for five thousand francs. Another Charlotte arrived shortly after, followed by a male infant whose parents, not to be forgotten, had named him Charlot. All these had received the same handsome present from the Tuttles, but they now agreed that it was time to call a halt.

"What's the letter Roro brought?" Fana asked. "Might be from them, whoever they are, telling us about it."

Jonas took the letter from under his plate, pulled the lamp closer, and scrutinized the envelope. "No, this was written on a typewriter," he said. "Read it, Chester. I ain't got my glasses."

Chester opened the letter, glanced through it, read it again, and then stared at his father, hissing and sputtering, unable to make an intelligible sound. Helpless, he passed the letter to Nat, whose manner of reading was that he had learned in school: a slow deliberate pronunciation of every syllable. He now read, aloud: " 'We beg to no-ti-fy you that your joint ac-count is overdrawn to the sum of eight hun-dred and fifty-one francs. Kind-ly de-po-sit this sum at your ear-li-est con-ven-ience.'

"What's that mean?" he asked.

"You p-p-p-poor idiot! C-c-can't you s-s-see what it means? Money's gone. We're busted again."

"It ain't so!" Jonas exclaimed. "It can't be so! We spent four hundred thousand francs in two months? I don't believe it!"

"M-m-more," said Chester. "Eight hundred and fifty-one f-f-francs more!"

"There goes my house," said Fana.

Nat burst into a loud laugh. "You fellows with your checkbooks! Banks don't make no mistakes. I'll bet it's gone, all right. Well, what of it? We had a good time."

"What of it!" their father exclaimed. "I ain't paid for the furniture yet! And the truck's coming on the next French boat, and the engine for the new launch! How we going to pay for them?"

Silence followed. Nat looked glum; he had forgotten about the new launch. "We'll have to do without 'em," he remarked. "We ain't no worse off than we was before."

"But we ordered 'em," said Jonas. "We got to pay for 'em."

"No we don't," said Chester. "We paid 20 per cent advance. Wait and see. We make 'em a present of that. They'll be glad enough to take 'em off our hands."

"I don't believe we spent all that money. Fana, you and Chester go and get your used checkbooks. We'll see about this."

"The *used* ones?" said Fana. "Didn't save mine."

"Where's yours, Chester?"

"Must be around somewhere," Chester replied vaguely.

Then Jonas lost his temper. His eyes blazed with anger, and, for the first time in years, he gave his three older sons a dressing-down which they received in awe-struck silence. "You're nothing but a pack of loafers!" he concluded. "Ru's got more sense in his little finger than the three of you in all your worthless bodies! . . . And I'm as bad as any of you," he added, wretchedly. "Shouldn't wonder if I was the worst one of the lot."

"We ain't none of us as bad as you make out," Fana ventured to say, humbly. "The only trouble with us is we don't know how to hang on to money."

"Knudson's the man for that," said Chester. "But I wouldn't trade you for a f-f-father, Jonas, for a whole *Ch-ch-Charlotte-ful* of Knudsons!"

"*Parau mau!*" said Nat. "Forget it, Jonas. It won't worry me a bit to see all that furniture going back."

"Won't be so sorry, myself, to tell the truth. But I don't know what your grandma will think. And Effie. I got it for them more'n anybody else."

"I'll bet they don't want it any more than we do," said Chester. "Think of all the work taking care of it."

Jonas rose with an air of resolution. "I'm going to tell 'em now and get it over with," he said.

The brothers exchanged glances when their father had gone.

"Good old Jonas," said Nat. "What a blast!"

"Guess we deserved it," said Fana. "I never thought

about keeping my empty checkbooks." He took a mouth organ from his pocket and began playing softly, his brothers listening absent-mindedly.

"What's that, Fana?" Chester asked, of a sudden.

"What's what?"

"That tune?"

"Nothing, far as I know. I was just playing."

"Wait a minute! This is the way it went."

He hummed a bar or two, Fana listening with an air of mild surprise.

"It *is* pretty," he said, "and I wasn't even thinking!"

"Pretty? Sure it is! We can make something out of that. Maitu!" he called. "Bring my accordion."

CHAPTER XV

ANDRÉ, one of the unmarried members of the clan, with whom Jonas shared his room, had long been asleep when the head of the family came in. Jonas lighted the lamp and set it on his camphorwood chest. He stood for a moment looking down at André, snoring away so peacefully. Well, why shouldn't he sleep? He could — all of 'em could. What did *they* have to worry about? "And he ain't fixed that board yet, on the front veranda," Jonas muttered to himself. "For all the times I've told him and Pico and Mara . . ." He welcomed this diversion from his thoughts, this relief from self-accusations, but it could not serve him for long.

Four hundred thousand francs, and all of it gone! How? What had they done with it? They couldn't have spent that much!

Jonas seated himself on the chest, his hands resting on his broad knees, staring at the floor between his feet. But they must have. Nat was right: banks don't make mistakes; they keep track of everything. They know down to five centimes how much money their depositors have got left.

He rose to fetch a pasteboard box from a shelf in the corner. He'd put all his own used checkbooks there. "See what *I* spent, anyway," he muttered.

With a pencil and a piece of paper he began to note down the amounts: —

```
 5,000 frs.
   842  "
10,000  "
12,789  "
 3,900  "
22,080  "
```

Slowly, doggedly, he worked through the stubs, muttering with vexation, out of patience with himself to find that, sometimes, he had neglected to fill out the stubs. "I'm no better'n the boys — that's the plain truth."

Nevertheless, he went on with the task, and when he had painfully added the long columns of figures, checking each of them over three times, he found that the total was a staggering one. "There ain't no doubt about it," he thought. "With all the boys has spent added on . . ."

He undressed, put on his waistcloth, blew out the light, and stretched out on his mat.

Well, it was gone; that's all there was to it. Despite his astonishment and dismay, Jonas was aware of a sense of relief, deep down in his heart. He had Dr. Blondin's money safe. Thank the Lord he'd had sense enough to get that the first thing and put it away! He was out of debt, anyway, and all the other little bills was paid; they didn't owe nobody a cent, except the eight hundred and fifty-one francs overdraft at the bank, and they could scrape up that much amongst them. He had nearly enough, himself, to pay it. . . . All that furniture. He'd been foolish to get it; wouldn't never have thought of getting it if it hadn't been for that catalogue. What if Knudson wouldn't take it back? What if he said they had to pay for all of it, and the new truck that was coming from France? "Tom, I can't, that's all. And you got the 20 per cent I paid in advance, on the furniture and the truck, both. You get that for nothing, and there's plenty people that'll want the things. You know that as much as I do." "Ain't saying I don't, Jonas. Well, all right. I'll take it back."

The night was windless and sultry. Jonas turned his pillow to the cool side, and composed himself for sleep. "I ain't as sorry as I ought to be, maybe," he thought. "It's too bad, though, we can't have the new launch. Well, the old *Zimba* ain't wore out yet. Now we're out of debt, shouldn't wonder if we can make enough fishing to have a new launch, anyway, before the year's out."

Considering this possibility, which seemed far from unreasonable, Jonas's reflections became pleasanter and vaguer, and melted gradually into the refreshment of sleep.

Early coffee the following morning was the usual pleasant, haphazard meal, the various members of the family partaking of it as they chanced to be ready, from daybreak until the sun was an hour high. Nat and Fana, who were going fishing off the reef, were the first to come in. When Jonas, after his bath in the river, entered the dining shed he found Hio there, with Chester, and a moment later Effie came to sit with them.

"Had your coffee, Effie?" Hio asked.

"Yes, but I can do with another cup. Well, Jonas, here we are again right back where we was before."

"They all know about it?" Jonas asked, glumly.

Effie nodded. "Ain't we a family? I thought four hundred thousand francs was a lot of money, but I see it ain't so much after all."

She laughed lightheartedly, Hio joining in. Jonas regarded them with an air of mild astonishment. "I'm awful sorry about the furniture," he said.

"I should think you would be!" Effie laughed again. "Oh, Jonas! You're a good one! Buy me a new *armoire*, and a fine new bed, and a sewing machine and all, and away they go, before I even have a chance to see 'em."

"Didn't I tell you, Jonas?" Chester said. "Effie d-d-don't care no more about the things than the rest of us."

"Course I don't," his aunt replied. "Maybe it would have been nice to have 'em, but it'll be a lot more comfortable without 'em."

"That's what I think," said Hio. "We'd have been worked to death taking care of it all. I've got Maitu over there now to keep the children away. They'd have the springs bounced out of everything in no time."

"Guess maybe it *is* better, all round, the way things has worked out," Jonas said. "If I was sure Mama didn't mind . . ."

"She don't, no more'n I do," his sister replied. "She said to me this morning, 'Effie, I'm kind of glad down in my heart. But don't tell Jonas.' So don't let on I did. All she wants is for you to get Dr. Blondin's money paid."

"I'm going to, right this morning," Jonas sighed heavily. "Don't see how I can get everything done there is to do. I'll have to see the bank, and Knudson, and Ellacott to tell him we can't take the engine . . . I don't fancy it none, telling Knudson. If he wanted to make trouble . . ."

"Let me see him, Jonas," said Chester.

His father's face brightened. "Would you, Chester?"

"Sure. Make trouble? After all he's got out of us from the *Charlotte?* And now he'll have the furniture and the new truck and what we paid on 'em beside. I can see him making trouble!"

Jonas felt deeply relieved. He lacked sixty francs of having enough to pay the overdraft at the bank, but Chester and Ru together made up the balance. The two boys set off for town in the truck, to arrange matters with Knudson and Ellacott. Jonas wasn't ready; furthermore, he wanted to make his own journey in the surrey. One of the men was sent to hitch up Nellie while Jonas went to his room to change from his *pareu* to his best pair of white duck trousers and a neatly laundered pongee shirt. His thoughts became more and more cheerful as he dressed. They'd had a wonderful time with their money, and so had all their friends. And what was money for if it wasn't to give pleasure? Couldn't nobody say the Tuttles was mean. They'd shared their good luck, and given most everybody on the island good times to remember for the rest of their lives.

He was all ready, fastening his belt, when Effie appeared at the door.

"I've started the men to putting the things back in the crates," she said.

"Tell 'em to be awful careful, Effie. I want 'em to wrap up the chairs and all in that burlap just like they was, so's they won't get scratched."

"They are. Hio and I'll see to things. You don't need to worry."

"I don't want none of 'em but Paki to nail up the crates."

"He's here, helping."

"Got something to say, ain't he?" Jonas asked, as he opened the lid of his clothes chest and began feeling around in it.

"Wouldn't be Paki if he didn't have. He wants all of 'em to know what fools the Tuttles are."

"Guess he ain't so far off at that," her brother replied, as he continued his search. His face assumed a puzzled expression as he fished in one corner of the chest after another.

"What is it you're looking for?" Effie asked.

"Dr. Blondin's money. Thought I put it down in this corner. Give me a hand, Effie. Guess I'll have to get all this stuff out."

His sister knelt down beside him, and together they lifted out successive layers of shirts, coats, trousers, towels, and waistcloths. Jonas's expression became increasingly anxious as they approached the bottom. When at last everything had been removed he continued to peer incredulously into the empty chest. " 'Tain't here!" he said, blankly.

"Now don't worry," said Effie. "If you put it here,

it's here somewhere. Most likely it's slipped in between some of the clothes. . . . Here's Mama," she added, as the old lady looked in from the doorway. "Jonas can't find Dr. Blondin's money," she explained, as their mother came in.

"Jonas! You haven't lost it!"

"Of course he hasn't. Mama, you help me. Jonas is no good at finding anything."

The elder woman knelt down beside her daughter while Jonas looked on, numbly. Every garment was unfolded and searched, even to the pockets of the coats, shirts, and trousers. At last Effie sat back, one arm braced on the floor. "Well, it ain't here — that's all there is to it."

"It *must* be here!" Jonas declared.

"You're sure, Jonas, that you put it in your chest?" his mother inquired.

"I *know* I did! Don't you remember that night when I came home with it and showed it to you? It was the very day Knudson paid us. I came upstairs right afterward . . ."

"That's what you *think*, Jonas, but I'll bet it's not what you *did*," Effie replied.

"I'm telling you I *know* I put it here! It was the same night I was making out the order for the furniture, right in this room."

"Try and remember what you did that night, after you left Mama's room."

"I don't have to try," Jonas replied, with some heat. "I came straight up here; and I didn't go nowhere else."

"Then why isn't it here?" his mother asked.

Another careful search was made of everything the chest had contained. They looked, then, beneath the chest, behind the cracked mirror on the wall, shook out the bedding, lifted the mats. The room was so clean, so bare of furnishings, that a pin could not have remained hidden for long.

When they had made yet another search of the clothing, Mama Ruau seated herself on the chest, trying to keep back the tears that filled her eyes.

"What will the doctor think?" she asked, miserably. "With all the money we've had . . . And now it's gone, and he's still unpaid!"

Effie, who had left the room for a moment, returned. "I've told the others," she announced. "We'll find it, if it's in the house. Whatever you think, you couldn't have put it in your chest."

"What did you do the next day, Jonas?"

"I remember what he did," said Effie. "Wasn't that the day you was measuring the land in the valley, the part you was going to fence?"

"Yes . . . Guess it was," her brother replied, wretchedly.

"And you still had the money in your pocket, if I know anything about it. You lost it somewhere in the valley."

Jonas shook his head, stubbornly.

"But you might have," Effie insisted. "Go right off now and look. The children are home today. Take them with you. We'll search the house while you're gone."

With his two assistants, André and Pico, Paki proceeded with the task of repacking the furniture, but

the united efforts of the rest of the family were devoted to the search. The house was ransacked from top
to bottom; then the dining shed and kitchen, and the
pavilion where the great wedding celebration had taken
place. All the land around the house and on the beach
side of the road was gone over, foot by foot; not even
an empty matchbox could have eluded so many pairs
of sharp eyes. Jonas and the children returned at lunchtime; the others could see from afar that his search had
been as fruitless as their own.

Chester and Ru arrived from town while the family
were still at table, Jonas at his end, not even pretend-
ing to eat.

"All fixed up, Jonas," Chester announced, cheerily.
"Ellacott didn't make no trouble at all. Said he had
a buyer for the engine, if we didn't want it. Old Knudson raised hell. Going to sue us and all that. Couldn't
fool me. I told him something, the fat hog! He's got
the *Charlotte's* lumber sold already. I heard in town
he's made as much again out of it as he give us, and
he's got the gas and the ship besides."

"He'll take the furniture back?" Hio asked.

"Sure he will, and glad of the chance. Send his truck
out for it tomorrow."

The boys ate heartily. Presently Ru looked up from
his plate. "What's wrong with everybody? What you
all so glum about?"

Paki, who was having the meal with the family, gave
his favorite nephew what was meant to be a smile. "Ask
Jonas," he said.

"He's lost Dr. Blondin's money," Tamara explained.

"Good Lord! Ain't you paid that yet?" Chester said, giving his father a blank stare. "He's back."

"The doctor is?" Mama Ruau asked.

Chester nodded. "Came on the *Denise* day before yesterday; so we heard."

"You must go right in to see him, Jonas — today," his mother said. "What he'll say I don't know, but you must tell him."

"Fetch Nellie round, one of you," Jonas replied.

The little horse, after her long rest, trotted briskly down toward town. Jonas held the reins slackly in one hand, heeding nothing, scarcely aware of the greetings of the neighbors he passed. When approaching Emily Taio's place, he drew Nellie down to a walk. Maybe, if he was to tell Emily . . . Yes, she might . . . if he told the whole truth about the mortgage and all. There was nobody else to lend him the money. The bank wouldn't, that was sure. It would be all he could do, for shame, to go in to pay the overdraft. Knudson . . . he gave a shiver of repugnance at the mere thought of humbling himself yet further before the trader. Even if he was sure that Knudson would loan him the money, he couldn't do it. But Emily . . . Yes, he'd have to ask her. There wasn't anybody else.

He looked ahead anxiously as he approached the Taio place, relieved to see that Emily was at the roadside pruning the scarlet bougainvillea that arched her gateway. He drew in at the side of the road.

"*Ia ora na*, Jonas!" she called cheerily. She laid her pruning shears on top of the stepladder and descended

carefully. "Glad to see you driving Nellie once more."
She shook her head. "Think of all the money you've
thrown away on cars!"

"Come and sit down a minute, Emily. Want to talk
to you."

She climbed into the seat beside him. "Boys didn't
stop here this morning?" he asked.

"No. I saw them go by, but they didn't stop." She
gave him a sharp glance. "What is it, Jonas?"

"Emily . . ." He hesitated, then, gathering up his
resolution, he managed to blurt it out. "We've spent all
our money."

"Jonas Tuttle! All of four hundred thousand francs?
I don't believe it!"

"It's so. Even more. Got a letter from the bank last
night. We even overdrew what we had. Eight hundred francs. I'm going in now to pay it."

Emily heard him through. She knew, vaguely, of the
borrowings from Dr. Blondin. Jonas now told her the
extent of them. Of the mortgage taken on Vaipopo, and
how the arrival of the Rarotonga relatives and the cost
of suitable entertainment had prevented the clearing of
the debt at the time of the vanilla auctions. All the
following circumstances since the receipt of Knudson's
four hundred thousand francs were fully explained.
"And now," he concluded, "they'll take Vaipopo away,
certain, if I can't raise what I owe the doctor."

"But Paki'll let you have it, surely?" Emily said.

Jonas shook his head. "He might, if he had it. But I
ain't asked him. He's spent all he had saved, and what
we give him, for that land he bought in town."

"Jonas, Jonas, Jonas! Does your mother know —
about the mortgage, I mean?"

"No. And how I'm ever going to tell her . . ."

"I wouldn't; not till you find you must. I don't believe Dr. Blondin will sell you out."

"It ain't in his hands now, like I told you. Dorme's
the one, and he's a hard man. He'll put it through. And
why shouldn't he? What excuse have I got?"

A long pause followed. Emily realized to the full
what their valley meant to the Tuttles, how harsh life
without Vaipopo would be for them. For one member of the clan, at least, she felt sincere pity: Mama
Ruau.

"You Tuttles!" she said, at last. "You're the biggest
pack of fools in all the islands! And I'm just fool enough
to be sorry for you, Jonas. If I had the money I'd
make you a present of it — honest I would."

"You ain't got it?" Jonas asked, falteringly.

She shook her head. "I just bought fifteen head of
heifers. Haven't got a thousand francs left, in cash."

Jonas closed his eyes for a moment, then gave her
an appealing glance. "You couldn't . . . ?"

"Borrow money to loan to you? No, Jonas. I've never
owed a penny in all my life. I'm not going to start now,
not even to save your land."

He reached town at three o'clock and left Nellie
hitched at the market place; then he went to the bank.
He was fully aware of the glances and whisperings of
the bank's employees while he was settling the business
of the overdraft. Everyone in the place knew. Never-

theless, thinking of the ordeal still ahead of him, he made a sudden resolve and asked to see the bank manager. The result was what he knew it would be — nothing but humiliation. The manager had been polite enough, but he wouldn't even consider taking a second mortgage on Vaipopo. The coolness of his manner was, Jonas knew, only a foretaste of what was to come when he would meet Monsieur Dorme.

In desperation, he considered the possibility of seeing Dr. Blondin first, but although he twice succeeded in getting as far as the corner of the block where the doctor lived, his feet would carry him no farther. After all the delays, postponements, explanations, excuses — no, he couldn't. Not again.

At eight o'clock that evening, Maître Dorme lay on a sofa on his veranda, reading by the light of a student lamp. He had returned from the hospital only the week before. By nature a spare man, his long and severe illness had left little of him save bones, covered with parchment-like skin. Arrears of business had piled up during his absence. Immersed at this moment in the study of a complex legal document, he had no eyes for a bulky figure, moving softly and halting irresolutely from time to time, in the shadows on the opposite side of the street.

Jonas's mental state was that of a man with an abscessed tooth, pacing the corridor outside his dentist's office, afraid to go in, yet knowing that he must. There was still time to retreat. Maybe it would be better to put off seeing him till morning. Clasping and unclasping his hands, Jonas stood in the deep shadow gazing

toward the bony figure reclining in the circle of yellow
light; he seemed held to the spot with a kind of fatal
magnetism. Of a sudden, not knowing how it had happened, he found himself mounting the steps to the attorney's veranda. He knocked softly on one of the
veranda posts.

"Yes? Come in!"

Maître Dorme turned his head to regard his visitor,
then, with a wince of pain, lifted himself slightly on
the sofa.

"Good evening, Monsieur Dorme."

"Oh . . . It's you, Jonas. Come at last, have you?
Take that chair."

"You better now?"

The lawyer nodded. He removed his reading glasses
and laid them with his papers on the table. With an
effort he propped himself up on the sofa. "You've taken
your time in replying to my letter," he said. "However, it doesn't greatly matter. Dr. Blondin's only just
returned."

"It got lost, Monsieur Dorme. They only found it at
the house a couple of days ago."

"I see." The lawyer smiled faintly. "Well, Jonas,
how does it feel to be rich? I've not yet seen Dr. Blondin.
But I know he'll be as happy as I am about your good
fortune."

Jonas made no reply.

"You don't seem as pleased over it as you might be."

"It's gone, Monsieur Dorme."

The attorney stared at him. "Gone? What do you
mean? What's gone?"

"The money. We ain't got none of it left."

"Four hundred thousand francs? Gone? In . . . in two months? You're joking!"

Jonas shook his head, mournfully. "It's so," he said. "I wanted to see Dr. Blondin this afternoon; then I decided I'd better come to you first. I thought that, maybe if . . ."

"Listen to me, Jonas!" The expression on the attorney's worn face became stern and hard. "The money you owe to Dr. Blondin is going to be paid here and now — to me. That's final. This matter is in my hands. You'll borrow none of it back, I promise you!"

"But . . . but I ain't got it, Monsieur Dorme. That's what I come to tell you. That's gone, too."

The lawyer's voice became as cold as ice. "You're telling me that, out of a fortune of four hundred thousand francs, you have not even saved the money you owe to Dr. Blondin?"

"I did!" Jonas exclaimed. "I put it aside the first thing! The very day we got the money from Knudson! That's what I want to explain!"

Torn between shame and his eagerness to make all clear, Jonas now spoke in eloquent, persuasive, apologetic words. The lawyer listened in stony silence, regarding him with a gaze hostile and curious, as though attempting to see into the workings of a mind so different from his own.

"That's how it was, Monsieur Dorme," Jonas concluded. "And if . . ."

"*Bien!* And I'll tell you how it's going to be now," said Dorme. "The law is going to take its course just as soon as I can have the papers put through the government *bureau*."

"If you could give me a little time . . ."

"Not a day! Not an hour! Make your preparations, for out you're going!"

Jonas stooped to take up his hat. He turned it round and round in his hands.

"You're going to sell us out?"

"Of course."

"When'll the auction be?"

"In about three weeks, I should think."

"And we'll have to move out before then?"

"Certainly, unless you can manage to raise and bring to me every centime that you owe Dr. Blondin."

A long silence followed these words. Jonas rose. "Well, I'll be getting along," he said. "I don't blame you none, Monsieur Dorme."

"Blame me? I should think not! You've spent, or squandered, in two months' time, a sum greater than I've saved in all my life. You've no one but yourself to blame, Jonas Tuttle!"

CHAPTER XVI

WHEN Jonas first announced the result of his interview with Maître Dorme, it was as though he had said nothing at all, insofar as most of the family were concerned. They could not conceive of being dispersed as a clan, of living elsewhere than at Vaipopo, and Jonas's humbler dependents went about their tasks as though no such danger were impending, convinced that some new and miraculous dispensation of Providence in their favor was, somehow, bound to come. Paki had tried to convince these foolish ones of the full extent of their imbecility, but they knew Paki's nature; he was always foreseeing calamity for Tuttle-ma, predicting the day when the family would be thrown out of Vaipopo. Therefore they gave no heed to him until one afternoon when he returned from Papeete with half a dozen handbills which he distributed amongst them in silence, with an air of bitter triumph. These were bills from the government *bureau* announcing that, at 10 A.M. on the 23rd of July, the valley of Vaipopo, comprising a twelve-room dwelling house, various outbuildings, and 18 hectares of land, would be sold at public auction, bids to start at 12,000 francs.

For a week thereafter, the family went about the task of existence with an expression of shocked incredulity common to all faces. Mama Ruau, however, after one day of grief spent in solitude in the bed-chamber of old Nathaniel Tuttle, set about, with quiet fortitude, the task of preparing for departure. No words of reproach passed her lips nor, indeed, did she lock them in her heart. There was not room in her generous nature for feelings of anger or contempt or bitterness. Her grief was less for herself than for her children, grandchildren, and great-grandchildren, never more to be gathered under the roof of the old house. Her gentleness and forbearance were as marked now as they had always been, and Jonas's heart was wrung with anguish and self-reproach, realizing as he did that he, the head of the family, was the cause of all their misfortunes. He wandered about the homestead for several days, heeding nothing, speaking to no one, seeking only to escape from the sorrowful and reproachful glances which he imagined were turned upon him wherever he went.

One afternoon, having ransacked for the twentieth time the old camphorwood chest in his room, he went into the depths of Vaipopo Valley for a final search along its boundaries; for, surely, clear as his recollection was of having placed the money in the chest, he might have been mistaken. Perhaps the packet of bills had been in his pocket on the day when he stepped off those portions of land which required fencing. It might be lying at this moment trodden into the damp black soil somewhere along the borders of the valley.

He went over the ground again, leaving no foot of it unscanned, and, as before, without success. Returning, hopeless and sick at heart, he seated himself on a grassy spot by the river and gave himself up to bitter, self-accusing thoughts. The money would never be found. And what a trifling sum it was compared with what had been theirs only a few short weeks ago! How, how, in the name of common sense, had they managed to throw away so vast a fortune in so brief a time? The boys had done their share, more than their share, perhaps, but whose fault was that if not his own? His mother had warned him, Emily had warned him, Paki had warned him, even Knudson had given him the best of counsel as to what he should do with his money. Instead of heeding them he had been a greater fool than any of his sons, writing checks without number as though his funds at the Banque de l'Indo-Chine came from an inexhaustible supply. And now the combined family could not have raised twenty francs amongst them; except for a three-hundred-franc loan from Paki, they would not have been able to buy gasoline for the *Zimba* and the necessary journeys to town by the truck.

Jonas had no reproaches for Dr. Blondin. It might be true that, if the doctor had been acting for himself, he would not have proceeded to the extreme measure of turning them out of their home. That was, unquestionably, the doing of Dorme, the lawyer. But who could blame the doctor for having allowed himself to be persuaded? He had been kindness itself to the Tuttle family, and how had they repaid him? By throwing away a fortune that would have paid their debt more than twenty times over.

And yet, the amount of the debt *had* been put aside for the express purpose of paying it; there was a grain of comfort for Jonas in that thought. It was not as though he had entirely neglected his obligation, whatever Monsieur Dorme might believe. The lawyer had not accused him in so many words of lying, but Jonas could tell from his manner that he had not credited the story of the lost money. He winced at the thought that Dr. Blondin himself must have doubted his word. Jonas had not seen the doctor since his return from Mangareva, but the fact that he had maintained a complete silence, had sent him no message, and was letting the law take its course, showed clearly enough how he felt.

And now what was to be done? Always, at this point in his melancholy reflections, this question presented itself as though written in huge letters upon an otherwise blank wall blocking the way of the family to any conceivable future. And nothing but the wall could be seen as he peered toward that uncertain tomorrow.

It was midafternoon. Jonas rose wearily and took the path down the valley. He had sent Fana into town that morning in the truck, with two pigs to be sold for necessary immediate expenses. Nat, Chester, and Ru had gone out with the *Zimba* to fish for the family needs. Jonas went round the house and on to the beach, where most of the family were gathered, watching Paki and two helpers, Pico and André, who were demolishing his dwelling, preparatory to carrying the materials to Papeete where the house was to be reërected upon the land Paki had bought there. The furniture had been moved into the thatched cookhouse; the roof of the dwelling was already off, and Paki and his helpers, on

scaffoldings, were now engaged in taking down the walls
of tongue-and-groove.

As he joined the spectators lounging in the shade,
Jonas was surprised and shocked to find that some of
them were chatting almost as cheerily as though life
were going on as usual. Seeing Paki's house come down
was a diversion, and they were making the most of it.
But his mother was not present, and Paki worked in
dour silence, paying no heed to the remarks and suggestions shouted to him from time to time. Effie motioned her brother to a place beside her on the grass.

"Been looking again?" she asked. "Give it up, Jonas.
It's gone. There's no use thinking about it any more."

"Don't listen to Effie," Tamara said. "Keep right on
searching, Jonas. You know what Taio Vahiné told me.
I believe every word of it."

Effie gave a scornful sniff. "And what did *she* say?
That a man had lost it and a woman would find it. Not
much to go on in that. I don't believe Taio Vahiné
knows any more about it than I do."

"She's been right hundreds of times," Hio replied.
"What about Naia, Mauri's daughter, at Vaihiva, the
one that married the young Englishman who went blind?
Taio Vahiné told Mauri everything that would happen
long before it did happen."

"She's right sometimes; I'll admit that," Effie replied; "and that's all we hear about. We never know
the times she's wrong."

Jonas gave small heed to this women's talk; and yet
he had believed enough in the words of the old sooth-

sayer to search and search again, in every conceivable place where he might have lost the money. But now he wanted to hear no more about it. He turned to his new daughter-in-law.

"I suppose you'll be going back to your mother's house now, Tamara?" he said, mournfully.

The girl shook her head. "No. Now that we're married, Fana's got to take care of me." Of a sudden she burst out laughing. "Look! There's our house," nodding toward the cement foundation posts placed there so long ago. "*Aué*, Jonas! You Tuttles certainly take your time getting things done."

The Tuttles had the precious gift of laughter at their own expense, and the sight of Fana's proposed house which he had started when he first courted Tamara, three years before, struck them all at once in its true and ridiculous light. Ropati in his wheelchair chuckled with mirth, and Hio laughed till the tears came. Even Jonas was able to smile with a kind of mournful appreciation of the situation. There were Fana's cement foundation posts, waiting for the house which never materialized. Placed on top of them were a dozen sheets of corrugated iron to shelter a meager supply of lumber consisting of a small pile of two-by-fours, and some sixteen-foot lengths of tongue-and-groove. And this, for all his hopeful plans, for all the money that had passed through his hands since the *Charlotte* was found, was as far as he had progressed toward homemaking.

"Take our time?" Effie asked, in reply to Tamara's last comment. "Look at our gasoline tank. It's all finished and ready. And the men didn't work a week on it."

On the beach, thirty yards from the boat shed, was the superb new 500-gallon tank set on cement posts and provided with a tap at the bottom for drawing off the gasoline. It was the only material possession the Tuttles had to show from the sale of the *Charlotte*. But it was bone-dry. Near it, on the ground, was a five-gallon tin from which the boys had replenished the *Zimba's* tank before going out fishing that afternoon. Hio got to her feet, walked to the tin, and kicked it. "It's empty, too," she said. This situation, so typical of the Tuttle fortunes, provided further matter for mirth, and, in the midst of it, their sore hearts were forgotten.

"I ain't going to forget how to laugh," said Effie; "no matter what happens."

"It's well enough for you to say that," Hio replied. "You and Paki still have a house, and a piece of land to put it on. What about the rest of us?"

"You needn't worry," said Effie. "As soon as we get our house put up in town, we'll take as many of you as we can crowd in till things get settled."

Paki, who had overheard this offer, turned on the scaffolding to scowl down at his wife.

"We won't do no such thing," he replied. "Ru's coming with us and nobody else. That's all we got room for."

Effie was about to struggle to her feet for a hot rejoinder but Jonas seized her arm and kept her where she was.

"Paki's right," he said. "It's not his place to take care

of the Tuttles. You leave things to me. I'm making my plans."

Jonas had not even the ghost of a plan in mind as he said this, but the merriment of a moment before had, somehow, eased his heart, and the future, for no reason at all, looked less dark than it had an hour earlier. Tamara, who was seated beside him, leaned over and put her cheek against his arm.

"I don't care where we go, Jonas," she said, "so long as I and the children go with you. The only reason I haven't come before is because I was so put out with Fana for never getting on with our house. And it's been my own loss. *Éaha nei!* I'd rather starve with the Tuttles than feast with anybody else."

Jonas patted her hand. "There's none of us going to starve, Tamara. We've always managed before, and I guess we can keep on doing it."

Paki, who had halted in his work to listen to these remarks, gave a skeptical grunt. "So you think, Jonas," he said. "You had a hard enough time when you owned the valley. How you'll get on now you've lost it is more'n I know."

"*Mamu!*" said Ropati, who, for all the distant relationship, was a loyal Tuttle. "We ain't asking you for no help. What I say is I don't begrudge a franc of the money I spent, and I ain't got nothing to show for it no more than the rest. But there's nobody on the island ever had a more wonderful time than us Tuttles has had these few weeks. And what's better than that?"

"There! That's just what I think," said Tamara, "and I'm only half a Tuttle."

Effie gave her an affectionate glance. "You ain't got much of your mother in you, Tamara. She wouldn't understand that at all; but it's true just the same."

The *Zimba* was now sighted heading for the passage, and a quarter of an hour later she reached the boat shed. The boys had caught three twenty-pound tuna, and though all were sick of fish, they pretended, with Jonas, that there was nothing they craved more than fresh broiled tuna steak. Fana returned from town just as supper was ready and the family were thronging into the dining shed.

"Got six hundred and twenty francs for the hogs," he announced.

This was a comforting announcement to Jonas. The past ten days had been lean ones indeed and six hundred francs once more looked like a small fortune to him. Fana handed over the bills. He had spent the extra twenty francs for tobacco, a legitimate purchase, and Jonas was pleased to see that, instead of buying ready-made cigarettes, he had invested the money in fine-cut native tobacco and some books of papers which would serve their needs for a much longer time. Even Fana was beginning to realize the need for economy.

Supper was eaten in silence. With the coming of night, the sadness of their situation returned to all. Only two weeks remained before the auction when Vaipopo would pass into the hands of strangers. Leaving the others, Jonas walked slowly down the driveway to the road. The full moon, rising above the mountains, flooded the valley with mellow light, lending to the old house that held so many happy memories an august and timeless beauty. It belonged where it was. It seemed to Jonas as enduring as the mountains behind it, and he had lost it, lost it, lost it through his own inconceivable folly! And if he loved this dear place, what of his mother? How many of those trees, breadfruit, mango, lime, avocado, casting their shadows on the grass, had she planted and tended with her own hands? It had been her home ever since her marriage nearly sixty years before, and so deep was her sense of belonging here that she could rarely be persuaded to leave, even for a day. Not in years had his mother gone to Papeete; her farthest excursions had been of a few hours only: to church, and to visit old friends of her own generation in Vaipopo village. What must be her desolation of heart at the prospect of being torn from this place, of spending away from it the few years that remained to her?

Jonas looked up to his mother's room. A light was burning there, and he could see her shadow on the bare walls as she moved here and there still busy with her preparations for leave-taking. One grain of comfort remained to him as he thought of her: the burial ground at one side of the valley was not to be included in the sale. This plot, fifteen meters square, was reserved to the family; it had been expressly mentioned in the bill of sale.

Unable to endure longer the bitterness of these reflections, Jonas returned to the house. Hio and Tamara had gone upstairs to put their children to bed, but the others were gathered below, for such comfort as numbers could bring. Jonas seated himself in silence on the steps. Presently they saw Paki coming up the path, dragging his grotesque little shadow after him. It was not often that Paki joined the family of an evening, and the boys could surmise the reason for his coming now. The silence was not broken on his account.

"Ain't heard no music up here these few nights," he said. "What's happened, Jonas? Boys busted their instruments?"

There was no reply.

"You got two weeks yet," Paki went on. "Don't see why you quit playing just because you're going to be kicked off your land. What's land amount to? Good times is the main thing, so I've always heard."

Paki had gained, through long experience, a nice sense of how far he might go in exasperating the Tuttles in times of stress brought on by their own folly. He could not resist these opportunities, and the boys seemed to take a gloomy satisfaction in being baited by him, provided he didn't carry matters too far. On this occasion, having added a few more biting comments which no one replied to, he returned to the beach.

"There's one good thing about leaving," said Fana. "We won't have that pest around all the time. You ain't really going to live with him, are you, Ru?"

"Not me," said Ru. "Paki's all right, but not in the same house."

Old Tupa now put in a word. "But where we all going to?" he asked. "Seems like we ought to be getting things fixed up pretty soon. We ain't got any too much time. Whoever buys the land will want us to get off it soon's we can."

"You don't need to worry," said Nat. "You and Maitu will be taken care of. We're all going to stick together, that's sure."

"How much is it we owe Doc Blondin?" André asked.

They waited for Jonas to reply, but he was wrapped in his own sad reflections and was giving no heed to the conversation.

"It's around eighteen thousand francs," said Fana.

"The valley will sell for a lot more'n that. Who gets all the money that's left over, after Blondin's paid?"

"You're the du-du-dumbest member of the family," said Chester. "We do, of course. Don't you know nothing about auctions?"

"And a lot of good it will do us," Nat went on, gloomily. "We'll never get Vaipopo again. There's too many people wants this valley. Whoever gets it would never sell it back, even if we had the money to buy it."

"Then I don't see where we're going to," Tupa repeated. "It's all right to talk about sticking together, but there ain't no way we can."

"I was talking to old Le Brunnec the other day," Nat remarked. "You know that sail loft he owns down near the Papeete waterfront? He wants to rent it — a hundred francs a month."

"What's that you say?" It was Jonas who spoke.

"That old sail loft," Nat repeated. "It's been empty three or four years. Le Brunnec was telling me he wanted to rent it."

"And you ain't said a word about it till just now!" Jonas replied.

"What of it?" said Nat. "We ain't sailmakers."

"When I been racking my brains trying to think how we could manage," Jonas went on, in a tone of voice meant to convey to the others some conception of Nat's vast stupidity. "We're going to live there — that's what of it."

"In town?" Ru asked, incredulously.

"Why not?" their father replied. "I ain't going to have us scattered, no matter what happens. That old loft's got floor space bigger'n our house."

"It wouldn't be such a b-b-bad place at that," said Chester, his interest suddenly aroused. "There'd be room enough for the lot of us, th-th-th-that's sure."

"And how'd we live when we got there?" Nat asked.

In ten seconds Jonas had thrown off apathy and discouragement. He saw light ahead, and the immediate solution of all their problems. Le Brunnec's sail loft had been empty for years. Why had he never thought of it?

"Like we always have, for the most part," he replied. "We still got the *Zimba*, and think of the gas we'll save, fishing from Papeete instead of way out here! When you come in at night you'll be right at market. Ropati'll have more work than he can take care of mending nets on both sides of town. André and Pico will have plenty of jobs stevedoring when the mail boats and cargo boats come in. We'll earn more money than we ever could here. We won't need the Ford for ourselves any more. I'll start up a little trucking business with it, out through the districts."

Energy and enthusiasm now radiated from Jonas,

stirring the hopes and kindling the spirits of the others. The prospects for this new life grew brighter as they discussed them. They talked until a late hour; then Jonas went to his mother's room, where she was seated by a clothes chest, with a lamp on the floor beside her. He poured out to her his hopes and plans. "And we'll all be together, Mama," he added. "That's the main thing. There's room in that sail loft for a family twice as big as ours, and when we get it fixed up, I shouldn't wonder if we'll like it better than we ever did out here."

The old woman took his hand in both of hers, trying to smile as he finished. "That *is* the main thing," she replied. "It doesn't matter where we go if we can still be together, under the same roof."

CHAPTER XVII

The following week was a busy one for the Tuttles. No time was lost in getting ahead with plans for moving. Since they had to go, all wished to leave as soon as possible, and while every member of the family knew what the others thought and felt, there was no shedding of tears or wringing of hands, even on the part of the women.

Le Brunnec's sail loft was even larger than Jonas had supposed. Upon measurement, it proved to be seventy-two feet long and forty-eight wide, with five windows on either side and huge double doors at the end facing the waterfront, with a view to the westward across the lagoon where schooners, cutters, launches, and other craft were moored along the sea wall, and the island of Moorea, with its changing lights and colors, in the distance. It was decided to make this end of the loft the family living room; there was to be a corridor entering it midway, and on either side the quarters of the various members of the clan. Jonas marked off the space with a view to the needs of all. Then they set to work at the task of converting the loft into a home.

The materials were at hand. Le Brunnec had stored there a quantity of old canvas, the sails of vessels long since wrecked or condemned. As it was of no value, he made Jonas a present of it, and both women and men proceeded to cut and sew it into sections to be used as partitions for the various chambers. And now, at last, Fana's small hoard of lumber, bought so long ago for the house he had never built, was put to service. This was his contribution to the family needs, and it sufficed for the framework upon which the canvas was to be tacked. The two-by-fours were used for uprights and crossbeams, and the boards of tongue-and-groove were sawn into two-inch strips for battens. When the work was done, there remained but one sixteen-foot board; as Jonas said, Fana's lumber seemed destined for this particular use. The canvas walls for the various chambers were eight feet high, and over all stretched the steep-slanting roof of the loft itself, with its age-blackened beams and rafters and rusty roof of corrugated iron with splinters of sunlight coming through the holes. The loft would not be wholly dry when it rained, and Jonas was already marking off, in his mind's eye, the places where tins would be set to catch the trickles that came through. At the rear of the building was a yard of the same dimensions and twenty feet wide. A wooden fence divided it into three sections, two of which were used by Chinese families who owned the bakery, restaurant, and store which occupied the lower floor of the building. The third belonged to the Tuttles, and here they erected a shed for the kitchen. The framework was made of *burau* poles brought from Vaipopo, and the shed was made just large enough to be covered with Fana's sixteen sheets of corrugated iron.

During these alterations, more and more of the family and their scanty furniture were brought to town in repeated journeys of the truck. The best room of all, at one corner of the building, with a view toward the mountains and another to seaward, had been prepared for Mama Ruau, and by the end of the week all of old Nathaniel Tuttle's furniture, except his portrait, had been installed there and arranged in the same order as at Vaipopo. It had been carted in, piece by piece, and hoisted into the new home by block and tackle through the double doors at the end of the building. Mama Ruau was still at Vaipopo; she wished to remain there until the last moment. All the family were now in the new quarters excepting herself, Tupa, and his daughter, Maitu, whom Jonas was to fetch on the following morning.

It had been a costly week. The six hundred francs received from the sale of the two hogs melted away rapidly; there had been many small purchases to make beside the cost of the food bought from the Chinese restaurant below. But the *Zimba* was now in town, moored in the basin reserved for the market fishermen. Now that the new home was in order, the boys were to resume fishing at once.

Cleanliness was a necessity to the Tuttles. They could put up with anything in the way of shelter, but all were enemies of grime and dirt. While the men had been at work on the alterations, the women had given the old loft such a cleaning as it had never had in all its sixty years. On the evening when the final tasks had been completed, Le Brunnec, the owner of the building, came to inspect his property. He gave a low whistle as Jonas met him at the head of the staircase.

"I wouldn't have known the place, Jonas," he remarked, wonderingly. "The man that drives the rubbish wagon told me he's carried six full loads of dirt and trash away from here since yesterday. I didn't believe him, but I do now."

"We like things clean," Jonas replied.

The Frenchman nodded. "Don't need to tell me that." He smiled. "Ought to boost the rent up on you, now that you got things fixed up so nice. Make a good hotel, wouldn't it?"

"I guess it would at that," Jonas replied. "Takes a kind of hotel to hold us Tuttles."

"How many rooms you got out of it?"

"Twelve, beside this living room."

"Funny I never thought of it," Le Brunnec added, musingly. "Be a good enough lodging house for seamen, and banana tourists, the kind of people can't afford to pay much for rooms. If I charged 'em five francs, that'd be sixty francs a day if they were all taken — call it forty, clear profit."

Jonas gave him an anxious look. "I hope you won't be thinking of that now, Mr. Le Brunnec, just when I've got my family about settled?"

His landlord laid a hand on his arm. "No, Jonas," he said, heartily. "This place is yours as long as you want it. I said the rent would be one hundred francs a month, and that's what it will be. It's yourself that's made it worth more, but that don't count while you're my tenant. Is your mother here?"

"I'm bringing her tomorrow."

"Don't believe I've seen your mother in all of ten years."

"It's been about that long since she was in town," Jonas replied.

"I'd like to bring my mother over to see her when she comes," Le Brunnec added. "You know what great friends they were in the old days?"

Jonas nodded. "There's nobody on the island Mama thinks more of than Mrs. Le Brunnec. That's one thing she's looking forward to, coming to Papeete, seeing her more often."

"It will be fine for both of them." Le Brunnec held out his hand. "Good night to you, Jonas. And don't worry over what I said about the hotel. This place is yours if you want to stay — as long as the white ants let it stand."

When his visitor had gone, Jonas seated himself in his deck chair in front of the great open window, and looked out over the lagoon, which was like a nether sky at this evening hour, when the first stars were beginning to appear. Supper was over and most of the family were gathered in the yard below. Chester was playing his accordion, but Jonas could tell by the manner of his playing and the half-hearted voices that joined in the singing that the rest of the family were feeling as melancholy as himself. The chorus sounded like a lament, a dirge. Not in that fashion did they sing at Vaipopo. Well, perhaps later, when they were used to this change in life, they would get some of their old gaiety back again.

Framed by the open window, and black against the fading western light, Jonas could see the *Charlotte* moored to the buoy in mid-harbor, tattered bits of canvas hanging from the foresail yard. The cargo was out of her now. Knudson had the lumber and gasoline stored in his warehouse, and both were selling at top prices. Jonas had heard that the ship itself, just as she lay, would bring one hundred thousand francs. He put his face in his hands, groaning inwardly at thought of his colossal folly. Why couldn't he have been a Knudson, with a head for business? More than likely Knudson would get Vaipopo as well. Of all possible purchasers, Jonas could think of no one whom he would rather not see there. He would cut down every tree that could not earn money for him. A rain cloud from over the mountains moved slowly seaward, releasing its cool burden when directly above the town. The old sail loft resounded like a drum thumped gently by innumerable fingers, and presently a tiny trickle of water descended directly upon Jonas's head. Rising with a sigh, he went along the canvas corridor to the window at the rear, which gave a view into the yard.

"Nana!" he called.

"Yes, Jonas?"

"Get the tins and basins."

Jonas had meant to go to Vaipopo the first thing next morning, to fetch Mama Ruau, but when morning came he delayed his departure from hour to hour, making little excuses to gain more time. For one thing, he wanted to get the boys off fishing; as Ru had some repairs to make on the engine, the morning was nearly gone before they were ready. Eight gallons of gas were put into the tank, and having paid for this, Jonas had only three francs left. He stood in the shade of the customs shed looking after the *Zimba* as she passed behind the *Charlotte* at her moorings, crossed the harbor, and headed out to sea. The boys would have to be lucky today; otherwise, there would be no supper for anyone. There was no Vaipopo Valley to fall back on now, with its fresh-water shrimps, its breadfruit and coconuts and taro beds.

Jonas returned slowly to the truck, cranked the engine, and sat motionless for some time, staring blankly before him. Was it a dream, some horrible nightmare that he would presently wake from to find himself still at home, with life going on in the old happy way? He roused himself at last. Mustn't sit idle, like this, using up gas for nothing.

By force of habit, he followed the back streets until he was through the town; he had reason enough now for wishing to avoid greetings from his Papeete friends and acquaintances. They knew, of course, that he was losing Vaipopo and had been more than kind during these trying days. No one spoke of the matter, but Jonas had no heart for greetings of any sort.

The last journey. He kept the gas full on all the way, staring straight ahead as he drove. When he turned into the old place the radiator was steaming violently; under usual conditions he would have replenished the water three or four times on the way. However, he had gotten through all right. He would try to remember on the way back.

The midday stillness was unbroken as he walked toward the house. He blessed the consideration of their friends and neighbors. They knew he was coming to-day, and for the last time, and their houses looked as deserted as the Tuttle place itself. They were keeping out of sight to spare his mother and himself the pain of farewells.

Jonas halted at the top of the steps. The old house had been swept and scrubbed from top to bottom. He walked through the hallway, glancing into empty rooms with mournful approval. The new owners would find no rubbish left for them to clear away. The house and the grounds around it were immaculate; not a fallen leaf had been left to litter the dooryard.

Tears started into his eyes and he let them fall un-checked. Was it possible that he was seeing his old home for the last time? It must be so: he would never come again. He would never suffer the needless misery of a return when the place was in the hands of strangers. Strangers, whoever they might be, however well he knew them, for Vaipopo could never truly belong to any family but the Tuttles.

He looked into the little room opening on the east veranda, a sunny cheerful place where his mother had loved to sit at her sewing with the busy family life going on around her. Stepping in, he closed the door be-hind him and seated himself on the floor with his back against it. Putting his head in his hands, he wept with a despair that would have wrung the hearts of his sons, had they seen him. Laughter came as easily as breathing to Jonas, but never in his life before had he given way in this manner to grief.

He composed himself at last and stepped out once more on the veranda. Heaped up against the wall were a number of bundles, odds and ends of things done up in *pareu* cloth, and boxes filled with miscellaneous articles, ready to be taken into town. Tupa and his daughter were nowhere to be seen.

Jonas mounted the back stairway, treading softly in his bare feet. Upon reaching the upper corridor he halted.

"Mama!" he called.

His voice echoed through the bare hallway. He knocked gently on the door of his mother's room, and, receiving no response, looked in. She was not there. Knowing where he would find her, he descended by the front staircase and took the path leading to the family burying ground.

This was a beautiful place that seemed to have a peace of its own, held there by the thick border of hibiscus bushes which enclosed and hid it from view. The lawn was shaded by four frangipani trees, filled with blossom, that had been planted by old Nathaniel Tuttle when he had first laid out the little plot. Flower-bordered paths surrounded the graves, kept white and immaculate from year to year with freshly strewn coral sand, and now all were banked with flowers Mama Ruau had placed there.

She glanced up, hearing her son's step, and then went

quietly on with her work, which was nearly finished. She had been sprinkling the flowers to insure their freshness as long as possible, and they glistened with coolness and moisture in the dappled light and shade which fell upon them. When her task was completed, Mama Ruau set her sprinkling can in a little arbor where she kept her tools, and turned to her son.

She gave him a wan smile as she brushed her black gown.

"I'm ready now, Jonas," she said, quietly.

"This little place will always be ours, Mama," he said, in a trembling voice. "Don't forget that. We'll all sleep here together, at the end."

"I know, dear. You've seen Tupa and Maitu? They're ready, I think."

"And I'll bring you out whenever you want to come, to look after things."

His mother shook her head. "I wouldn't want you to. I'm not coming any more. I know how you feel: just as I do. We'll let some of the others take care of the graves after this. Let's go now. There's nothing more to be done."

When they returned to the house they found Maitu placing the boxes and bundles in the truck which Jonas had backed up close to the front steps.

"I'll help you, Maitu," he said. "Leave the heavy things for me. Where's Tupa?"

The girl nodded inland and went on silently with her work. She got into the truck and took the boxes Jonas handed to her, storing them neatly in the forward end of it. As she got down again she glanced at Jonas, then, covering her face with her hands, she burst into tears. Jonas put his arm around her shoulders, trying to comfort her.

"There, there, Maitu. It's going to be all right. Wait till you see what a fine new home we've got. And there's two nice rooms for you and your father, where you can look right down on the street and see everything that's going on."

"I don't want to see it, Jonas. I don't care how nice it is," the girl sobbed. "It'll never be home."

"We'll make it home, Maitu," Mama Ruau said, gently. "It won't matter so much where we are, as long as we're all together."

Jonas felt his own self-possession giving way once more. With his arm around her shoulders he led Maitu to where his mother was sitting and there the girl sobbed out her grief, her face hidden in Mama Ruau's lap.

Jonas turned from them and walked to the end of the veranda to recover his composure. He then walked slowly back over the ancient planking worn smooth and polished by the bare feet of four generations of Tuttles. As he approached the others, one board tipped up from its place, and Jonas took his weight from it just in time to prevent a fall.

"I don't know how many times I've asked André to nail a piece of joist under that board," he said, sorrowfully. "Pico, too."

Maitu raised her tear-stained face.

"I t-t-told 'em again what you s-s-said, Jonas," she replied, in a quivering voice. "André promised he'd fix it before he left. He must have forgot."

"We're not going till it *is* fixed," Jonas replied. "Ain't there a can of nails in one of them boxes?"

While Maitu was searching for the nails, Jonas went to the shed which had been used as a workshop and to house the truck. He returned with a small piece of two-by-four. Maitu had found some nails, but the tools had already been taken into town and Jonas was forced to use a stone *penu,* a taro masher, as a hammer. Removing the loose board, he managed, with difficulty, to nail the piece of two-by-four to the beam underneath; then the plank was replaced and nailed to this. Jonas tried it out with his weight, stepping on it carefully, and found that it held.

"Wouldn't want to leave a place like that for somebody to break their leg on," he said.

This commonplace incident seemed, somehow, to relieve the soreness of their hearts. Maitu dried her eyes on the hem of her dress.

"We've got some more things to do," she said. "They're out by the cookhouse."

Jonas followed her there just as Tupa appeared on the path from up the valley with two heavy bunches of taro roots fastened at the ends of a carrying pole. Jonas now saw that Tupa had been collecting everything edible or salable that might be carried off before Vaipopo was abandoned: green drinking coconuts, several hundredweight of taro, baskets of limes and papayas and a dozen bunches of bananas. In addition to this were three bags of copra. There was enough food heaped up by the cookhouse to have filled the truck twice over. Jonas regarded it all with mournful gravity.

"I wouldn't have done it, Tupa," he said. "I don't think we got the right to take all this."

"No right!" said Tupa, with a snort. "The place ain't sold yet. I don't want to leave nothing for *them*."

"I know it ain't, but . . ."

"I didn't leave one ripe nut on the ground," Tupa added with an air of bitter triumph, "and I'd have climbed all the palms if there'd been time. We got better than three hundred kilos in them three bags. That's four hundred francs' worth of copra *they* won't get!"

Jonas paused to reflect. Tupa was right: Vaipopo belonged to them for another five days, until the sale at auction. They were justified in taking with them the food and copra.

"We can't take it all in one load," he said.

"What's it matter?" said Tupa. "You can send one of the boys back for the rest if you don't want to come yourself. Look, Jonas."

The old cook rummaged in a box standing on the old dining table, and brought forth a cloth bag containing about four pounds of sugar. He untied the string so that Jonas could see the contents.

"Didn't know we had it," he said. "And I found a tin of butter, ain't been opened, that was left over from parties when Fana and Tamara got married."

The loading of the truck was completed in silence. It was decided to leave the taro, the coconuts, the bags of copra, and most of the bananas until some of the boys could be sent for them the next day. For all that, the truck was well filled when Jonas helped his mother into the front seat. There was just room enough, behind, for Tupa, who sat on a box with the portrait of old Nathaniel Tuttle held upright before him, the bottom of the heavy gilt frame protected from rubbing on the floor of the truck by several thicknesses of copra bags. Jonas's grandfather seemed to be regarding the now completely gutted house with the old expression of grim watchfulness, as though the very spirit of the founder of the family had returned to animate his likeness, and could not yet believe that all his well-laid plans, and the years of patient labor spent in fulfilling them, had gone for nothing.

Jonas cranked the engine again and again without result, then paused to regain his breath before resuming the labor.

"It don't want to go no more than we do," Tupa remarked to the midday silence.

After repeated efforts the engine started. Jonas took his seat at the wheel and they waited for Maitu, who had gone for a last look round to see whether any small articles had been left behind. She appeared in the front doorway with Jonas's dog-eared mail-order catalogue in her hand.

"I nearly forgot this," she said, "and I'd put it aside, special, so I wouldn't."

"I don't want it no more," Jonas replied, glumly.

"You don't want your *catalogue?*" Maitu exclaimed, incredulously.

"No. Go off yonder and burn it where the ashes won't show. Can't leave rubbish lying around."

The girl still gazed blankly at him as he felt in his pockets and offered her his box of matches.

His mother now spoke. "No, Jonas; you mustn't burn it. You know how much you've always enjoyed looking at your catalogue."

"Not any more. I ain't going to take it."

"Then bring it for the children. Please, for my sake. They love to look at the pictures."

Little as he wished to obey, Jonas could not refuse a request from his mother. Maitu climbed on the wheel of the truck and laid the catalogue in a dishpan full of tableware above Tupa's head. She then took her seat beside Mama Ruau.

"Well, guess we're ready, ain't we?"

There was no reply. The truck started with such a jerk that the dishpan, insecurely placed, slid from its position, spilling the contents along the roadway before Jonas could bring the car to a halt. Maitu climbed down to collect the articles: tin forks, a saltshaker, a frying pan, some battered vegetable dishes of enamelware, and the catalogue. Jonas gazed somberly before him while they waited.

"*Aué, Jonas! Aué! Aué! A hio! Teié! Teié!*"

Jonas turned his head slowly at this outburst, and at the same moment there was another resounding clatter as Maitu dropped the dishpan and came running toward him, clutching the catalogue in one hand and something else in the other.

"*Teié!*" she cried again. "*Aué, tatou é!*"

"What is it?" he asked, wonderingly, staring at the tattered catalogue she was waving before him.

"*Te moni!*" she cried. "*Ta taoté moni!*" Then, realizing that she was offering the wrong thing, she thrust into his hand a packet of five-hundred-franc bills.

"It was in the catalogue," she exclaimed, breathlessly. "It's the doctor's money you lost! It must be, Jonas, there's such a lot of it!"

Jonas stared at the packet for a few seconds with an air of unbelief, of complete bewilderment. Then, somehow, he tumbled out of the car and folded Maitu in a huge embrace, waving the bills behind her back as he did so.

"Mama! Tupa!" he cried. "Maitu's found it! Dr. Blondin's money!" Half out of his senses with joy and relief, he ran around the car showing the bills first to his mother, then to the old cook, who peered out from behind the portrait of Jonas's grandfather with skeptical amazement. "Then we ain't going?" he asked.

For answer Jonas seized the portrait from Tupa's hands and ran with it to a near-by tree, where he set it gently down, leaning it against the trunk.

"We don't have to," he exclaimed. "*Aué, Mama 'ti é!* Hurry! *Haere mai!*" Taking his mother under the arms, he lifted her clear of the truck and ran with her to the house, where he set her down on the steps. "Here's your home again, Mama! You won't never have to leave it now!" Without giving her time to reply he ran back to the truck. "Hurry, Tupa! I ain't got no time to back up. Unload everything right here! You can carry it in while I'm going to town!"

"You ain't counted it yet," Tupa said. Jonas was still clutching the bills in one hand.

"No — wait!" Putting one foot up on a hubcap, Jonas wet his thumb and with trembling hands fingered through the notes still fastened together with a pin at one end. His mother returned from the veranda while he was thus engaged.

"It's all there," he announced, jubilantly. "Thirty-six five-hundreds, four one-hundreds, and two twenties. Eighteen thousand, four hundred and forty francs!"

"Oh, Jonas! Thank God! Thank God!" his mother exclaimed. He hugged her close.

"What a fool I am, Mama!" he said, tears trickling down his cheeks and laughing at the same time.

"And you wanted me to burn it up," said Maitu.

Releasing his mother, he gave Maitu another hug that almost crushed her.

"But how did it get there?" his mother asked.

"I remember, now," Jonas replied. "It was that night when I was writing out the order for the fence. I must have left it in the catalogue then; and I was so sure I'd put it in my chest, upstairs!"

"And the catalogue's been on the shelf in my sewing room ever since, until today," his mother added.

"Don't I know it?" said Jonas. "There never was such a fool as me! . . . Hurry, Tupa! Get everything out! I'm going right into town to take it to Dr. Blondin."

"I'm going with you, Jonas," his mother said, quietly.

"You'd better," Tupa said. "He'll lose it again if you don't."

"No I won't! I'll hold it in my hand all the way."

His mother took the money gently from his hand and thrust it in the bosom of her black gown.

"I'm going too. I won't feel safe or happy until I see it in Dr. Blondin's hands."

"You'll see it there just as quick as we can get to town," her son replied. He climbed quickly in beside her and glanced back. "Everything out?"

"Wait!" said Tupa. He came round to the front of the car and peered down the radiator pipe. "You ain't got no water." Taking the dishpan, he went to the river to fill it. Maitu made a funnel of her hands as the water poured in. The radiator cap, long since lost, had been replaced by a wooden plug. But this too was missing.

"I must have blew it out, coming home," Jonas remarked. "I wasn't paying no attention."

Tupa made a serviceable substitute of a fragment of tightly wrapped banana leaf.

"Now you and Maitu get right busy while we're gone," Jonas said, as the old cook was putting in the plug. "We're all going to have supper here tonight, every last one of us. No matter how late it is."

"How you going to bring 'em?" Tupa asked. "You can't carry more'n a dozen in the truck."

"I don't know, but they're coming. I'll find some way. Maitu, you take Grandfather's picture in first thing you do."

Mama Ruau clung to her son's arm as the truck whirled out of the driveway and headed for town. For all the years they had owned the Ford, this was her first ride in it. She disliked motorcars and made her excursions in Vaipopo either on foot or in the surrey. They rattled through Tarahoi at thirty miles an hour, and

Jonas gave a quick glance at Emily Taio's house as they passed. He saw no one about the place.

"They're keeping out of sight, Mama, like the other neighbors. They think we're going for good. Won't they be surprised when they see us all coming back tonight? We can stop then and tell 'em. I can't hardly believe it! It just don't seem possible!"

"Jonas, please go slower! You're nearly bouncing me out of the seat."

"Sure. I keep forgetting it, I'm in such a hurry to get there."

As they passed through the district of Faaa, Tupa's banana-leaf plug blew out in a cloud of steam. Bringing the truck to a halt near a mountain stream, Jonas borrowed a tin and replenished the water. Then, having made another leaf plug, they went on. By keeping his mind on his driving he now managed to go more slowly, so that his mother was able to enjoy the latter part of the ride. She looked about her with keen interest, noting the changes that had taken place during the ten years since she had last gone to town. "It's like a different island, this part," she said. "I wouldn't hardly have known Faaa."

Jonas gave her an affectionate glance. "You're such a stay-at-home you'll forget what Tahiti's like, all but Vaipopo," he replied.

"That's enough for me. Home's best."

"*Parau mau, Mama! Parau mau!*" Jonas replied, fervently. "I wouldn't care if I never saw Papeete again, after this time. . . . I was just thinking how we're all going to get home tonight," he added, a moment later.

"The boys can bring some in the *Zimba*, when they get in from sea. And Emily's truck's pretty sure to be in town. I'll ask Moa to bring as many as he can."

Presently they rounded the hairpin turn by the wireless station and saw the curve of the Papeete waterfront in the distance. Jonas coasted the truck down the little hill and they entered the long shaded road leading to the town. As they were approaching the cemetery the engine suddenly stopped, but the truck had enough momentum to carry them another fifty yards and Jonas steered it to the side of the road, taking advantage of every slight declivity to get them on as far as possible.

"What is it, Jonas?" his mother asked.

He shook his head as he unscrewed the cap of the gas tank and peered in; then he thrust in the measuring stick.

"No more gas," he said, impatiently. "Might have known this would happen just when we're in such a hurry!" He scratched his head. "You wait here, Mama; it's a nice shady place. It ain't more'n half a mile to Doc Blondin's office. I'll be back just as quick as I can."

His mother climbed down and shook out her black dress. "I'm going too!" she replied, firmly.

"I don't like to have you walking to town this first time you've come in so many years."

"It don't matter, Jonas. What's half a mile? And I've not seen Dr. Blondin in a long time."

For all her seventy-six years, Mama Ruau was an active little body and the walk was anything but a hardship for her. She searched for pins in her bodice and fastened up her skirts so they wouldn't drag. They went at a good pace along the dusty road, checkered with the lengthening shadows of midafternoon. They had not gone more than two hundred yards when a young native approaching on a bicycle halted at sight of them. He was the boy-of-all-work at Dr. Blondin's place, who cared for the garden, ran errands, and the like.

"You've saved me a ride, Jonas," he said. "I was just coming out to your place. Here's a letter the doctor wanted me to give you right away."

Jonas glanced gravely at the letter handed him, then thrust it into his hip pocket, unread.

"He's home?" he asked.

The boy nodded.

"Tell him I'll be along there in about ten minutes. . . . And you can tell him I've found it," he added.

"Found what?"

"That's all you need to say. He'll know what I mean. Go right along, now, and tell him that before you do anything else."

CHAPTER XVIII

JONAS betrayed none of his inner excitement as, with his mother holding his arm, he walked up the graveled path to Dr. Blondin's veranda. He was the head of Tuttle-ma coming, just in the nick of time, to reclaim his home. Though he well knew that the doctor had been justified in taking action to recover his debt, he felt, deep in his heart, that his old friend and benefactor had been needlessly harsh in going to the extreme measure of foreclosing on them. However, Jonas had so keen a sense of his own blameworthiness that the doctor's seemed light in comparison, and as the latter came forward to greet him he gripped his friend's hand in the old friendly way.

"Well, well, Mama!" Blondin exclaimed. "This *is* a surprise! It couldn't have happened better, Jonas. You've read my letter?"

Jonas shook his head. "I ain't had time. Mama and me wanted to get along here soon as we could."

"I didn't quite understand the message you sent by the boy."

"Didn't he tell you right? We've got it, Doctor! The money! The eighteen thousand, four hundred and forty francs! Mama . . ."

His mother was already drawing forth the packet of bills, which she placed in the doctor's hand, closing his fingers over it gently.

"You'll never know, Doctor, what a happy day this is for us. They'll stop the sale now, won't they? The money's all there — every penny."

The doctor was conscious of a vexing moisture in his eyes.

"There would have been no sale in any case. That's what I wrote to tell Jonas. I stopped the proceedings. I want you to forgive me, Mama."

"Forgive you? For what? It's us *you* must forgive. After all you've done . . ."

"I lost patience, that's the truth of the matter. I felt that . . ."

"You needn't go on, Doctor," Jonas said. "Who wouldn't? There's nobody but me to blame for the whole thing. But it wasn't as though I didn't intend to pay you. And if Monsieur Dorme hadn't been sick you'd have had the money long before now. But I put it away at home, so careful . . ."

"Careful? Oh, Jonas *rahi!*" his mother exclaimed, reproachfully. "Do you know where he did put it, Doctor? In an old mail-order catalogue. And he was so sure he had it in his clothes chest! We only found it by accident."

The old lady was proceeding to relate the circumstances when Jonas interrupted her.

"Now, Mama, there's no need going into all that. The doctor don't care how we found it just so we did."

"But I *do* care. I want to hear all about it," Blondin said.

"Then I'll explain it in a minute or two. Mama's

so anxious to tell the rest of the family. She wants to
get right over to Le Brunnec's sail loft quick as she can."

"That's right, Doctor, I do," the old lady added,
with a happy smile. "I grudge every minute they don't
know."

"You ain't forgot where it is?" Jonas asked.

"The sail loft? Of course I haven't. 'Twon't take me
five minutes to get there."

"I'll be right over. Tell some of 'em to find Moa
Taio and see if he can help us getting home."

When Mama Ruau had gone, the doctor pushed forward an armchair for Jonas, who lowered himself
into it in the old familiar way, putting his hat on the
floor beside him.

"Now, Jonas, I want you to read my letter."

Jonas drew the letter from his pocket and laid it on
the table. "I don't need to," he said. "You told me
what's in it. That's enough." He gave the doctor a
steady glance. "But there's one thing I'd like to know.
When I told Monsieur Dorme I'd lost your money,
he thought I was lying. He didn't say so, but I could
see it. Did you think so, too?"

Dr. Blondin nodded. "I did, Jonas. I'm ashamed to
say it, but I did. Could you blame me?"

"Not the least bit," Jonas admitted, heartily, and
immediately the cloud he had felt over the old relationship melted away. "I'd have believed it in your place.
But I'll say this, Doctor: I've borrowed money from
you, and I ain't paid it back when I meant to and
when I should have. But I never lied to you in all the
years we've known each other."

"You must remember, Jonas, that I'd not seen you. I'd have known the truth if *I'd* been the one you told. But you didn't come . . ."

"I couldn't, Doctor. I was so ashamed and worried, I just couldn't."

They were on the old footing once more, and Blondin listened with inward delight to Jonas's story of the lost money and how it had been found. Then he told Jonas how, on the evening before, he had walked past Le Brunnec's sail loft, feeling as wretched in spirit as he knew that the Tuttles themselves must feel.

"But it was on your mother's account more than yours, Jonas. I'll admit that. I was as angry with you as ever, or nearly so. I knew that you had received four hundred thousand francs from Knudson. I was angry, in the first place, because you'd let him do you in so badly. The *Charlotte's* cargo is worth twice what he gave you for it, and he has the vessel beside. Even so, four hundred thousand francs is no small sum, and with all that, you'd not been able to pay your debt to me. How in heaven's name have you been able to get rid of such a fortune in two months' time?"

"I wish I knew, Doctor. I've asked myself the same question more than once. My boys are awful spenders, that's the plain truth. But I can't put it all off on them. I'm just about as bad as they are. Seems like we just can't hold on to money, whether it's forty francs or four hundred thousand. It goes, that's all I know about it. . . . You'll probably think I'm crazy," he added, after a pause; "but when I found we hadn't none of it left, I was kind of relieved. That was before I knew I'd lost your money. I thought I had that safe in my clothes chest."

"And now, what, Jonas?"

"We're going right back home, just as quick as we can get there. I don't want none of 'em in that old loft tonight."

"What were you doing out by the cemetery? My boy said he met you there."

Jonas hesitated, raised his eyelids, and let them fall again. "It was that old truck," he explained. "Thought I had plenty of gas to get in town with, but it had to give out, of course."

"Have you money to buy more?"

With an effort, Jonas worked his huge hand into his trousers pocket and drew it forth with his fingers closed. For a moment he gazed at his fist as though hopeful that what he felt inside it might be golden guineas or louis d'or: but when he opened it, what he discovered there was a small handful of brass and nickel coins. The amount was three francs fifty. Without comment Jonas returned the money to his pocket.

There was a moment of awkward silence, but Jonas didn't permit it to be prolonged. He groped for the hat at the side of his chair.

"I'll have to be going, Doctor. They'll be waiting for me at the sail loft."

He heaved himself out of his chair and held out his hand, but instead of taking it, Dr. Blondin laid his own hand on Jonas's arm.

"Jonas, I want you to do me a favor. I feel more than guilty to think I've put you to all the expense and

trouble of moving to town. As a matter of fact, I
didn't know till yesterday morning that you had
moved." He unpinned the packet of bank notes Mama
Ruau had given him and stripped off one thousand
francs. "Take this . . . for my sake, Jonas? Now wait!
I want you to have a fair start when you get settled at
home again. This will be a small help to you."

Jonas shook his head, resolutely. "I couldn't, Doctor.
Not after all you've done."

"It isn't a loan," Dr. Blondin insisted. "It's . . . it's
what I feel I owe your mother, yourself, all of you, for
the trouble I've caused. Please, Jonas!"

Jonas looked at the money wistfully, but shook his
head once more.

"No, it wouldn't be right . . . not so much as that.
But . . ."

"Well, Jonas?"

"I ain't going to start borrowing again, Doctor. Not
after I get twisted round. But . . . if you'll let me use
it these few days? Not a thousand, though. If you want
me to, I'll take that four hundred and forty that was
over, but put it right down in your book."

"I'll do it, Jonas, and there's the money with all my
heart."

"Gas is still eight francs," Jonas said. "That'll buy us
fifty-five gallons. It'll give us a wonderful start, Doctor. And I wouldn't be a bit surprised if I could come
in here in a couple of hours and pay it right back. The
boys is out fishing with the *Zimba* this afternoon.
They'll be in by seven or eight o'clock, and like as not
they'll have the launch loaded. Tuna was bringing thirty

francs at the market this morning, and if they only caught a dozen . . ."

"All right, Jonas, I won't keep you any longer. I know how anxious you are to get started home."

Jonas clasped his hand warmly, his face beaming.

"We're going to have supper there tonight, that's sure," he said. "Even if we have to call it breakfast."

#39 7176